BETWEEN GIRLFRIENDS

ELIZABETH DEAN

KENSINGTON BOOKS
http://www.kensingtonbooks.com

KENSINGTON BOOKS are published by

Kensington Publishing Corp.
850 Third Avenue
New York, NY 10022

All Kensington titles, imprints and distributed lines are available at special quantity discounts for bulk purchases for sales promotion, premiums, fund-raising, educational or institutional use.

Special book excerpts or customized printings can also be created to fit specific needs. For details, write or phone the office of the Kensington Special Sales Manager: Kensington Publishing Corp., 850 Third Avenue, New York, NY 10022, Attn. Special Sales Department. Phone: 1-800-221-2647.

Kensington and the K logo Reg. U.S. Pat. & TM Off.

Library of Congress Card Catalogue Number: 2003100381
ISBN: 0-7582-0364-0

First Printing: July 2003
10 9 8 7 6 5 4 3 2 1

Printed in the United States of America

Books by Elizabeth Dean

IT'S IN HER KISS

BETWEEN GIRLFRIENDS

Published by Kensington Publishing Corporation

BETWEEN GIRLFRIENDS

To Judy, my long-time friend, my life, and love confidante.

And to John Scognamiglio, my editor at Kensington Books, whose enthusiastic determination has challenged me, guided me, and inspired me. You da man, John!

Introduction

My name is Gracy Maynard, and until about a year ago I was just another struggling writer in the big city.

No, not that big city. And, truth be told, I don't really live *in* the big city of Boston. I rent the top floor of a precariously listing-to-the-left triple-decker in Somerville (or Slumerville, as many of the residents call it), just outside of Boston. Somerville is also a city, although it's not as big as Boston. But it still has buildings—lots of them—the blare of police sirens twenty-four, seven, and noise. Nonstop noise. Cities have always enthralled me, but my preference is to keep a safe distance from them. My bank account, however, has suppressed this preference—or at least has put it on hold. Call me a village girl at heart. I want the wide open spaces. Neighbors nestled somewhere off in the distance. A narrow, winding country road—with small farm stands along it—leading to my home. Wildlife traipsing through my backyard. Fame and fortune. I realize the last two are not components of a neighborhood, but rather how I'd qualify to live in a lovely country home. (*Writer Gracy Maynard, whose fame and fortune has driven her to seek quieter solace outside the city of Boston, has consented to give* Town and Country *a tour of her lavish country estate.*)

Yes, I know I'm a village girl at heart (as opposed to a Village Person, because I can't sing and I don't have a mustache), because whenever I venture out into any big city, I feel overwhelmed.

There's way too much sensory stimulation for me. As a writer, I try to take everything in. Which means that a big city can make me go a bit nuts.

> *The streets were quiet—too quiet. I lifted the collar of my overcoat, shivered, and held my position tight against the concrete wall, hoping the shadows would hide me. Despite the icy rain and the unsettling big-city stillness, I kept watch outside the darkened apartment building, knowing that eventually she would exit, drawn to the streets like a mosquito to blood, ready to—*

Sorry for that aside. But if you're going to get to know me, you're going to have to go inside the mind of a writer from time to time. I'm like most of those people who have been blessed (or cursed) with an artistic bent; I have a mind that never shuts off. I'm always thinking. Always creating. Always imagining.

Sometimes that works to my detriment. I can drive myself crazy thinking about all the novels I dream of writing. *Someday,* I'll tell myself. Someday, I'll write a book. Someday, when I get some money in the bank from freelancing, I'll be able to work full time on something of my own creation. I'll get an agent. She'll make a big sale. In the six-figures. And that will be the beginning . . .

See, that kind of thinking isn't good because I've lived from check to check for over a decade, and I don't see that changing in the near future.

But sometimes, all that thinking and creating and imagining works to my benefit. Like the time I was dating a very controlling woman. I kind of knew from the get-go that she and I would never last. But I hadn't dated for a while—since about World War II—and I figured, what the heck.

She was an accountant who lived in a small Cape and kept her home so immaculately clean and free of clutter that Felix Unger would've asked her to marry him. It made me nervous.

So did making love with her. She was definitely the aggressor and had her own way of doing things. I think she thought that what she was doing was exactly what I wanted, but it was really taking me nowhere. When I tried to suggest something I might like, she told me to just relax and continued on her pre-set path.

So I lay there beneath her. I stared at the ceiling. I took in deep breaths and rubbed her back. I moaned from time to time.

And I started thinking. Started imagining. Started letting my mind go.

And I ended up having an incredible fantasy.

I'm in a gynecologist's office, sitting on the examining table, with nothing on but a paper gown. The gynecologist walks into the room.

"I hope you don't mind," she says as she sits down on the wheeled stool in front of me. "But several med students are here today, and I thought I'd take them through an examination on you. If that's all right with you, of course."

Before I can answer, the door opens and several beautiful women dressed in lab coats walk in.

"These are the residents," the doctor tells me. "Do you mind if they each take a turn examining you?"

Hell no, I think, and lay back. The women gather around me. Each takes a turn massaging my breasts and nipples. I willingly spread my legs in the stirrups. No one has to tell me to slide down. Fingers are inserted inside me.

It's clearly the best trip to a gynecologist I've ever experienced.

After a very short time, I come. I come because of where my mind took me. The neatnik accountant who doesn't give a crap about what I want in bed thinks I come so hard that I nearly scream because of what she's done to me. But she's no competition for my mind.

Every time I was in bed with the number-cruncher after that, I fantasized. Then, after we broke up, I continued to have great orgasms.

I guess you could say that I really didn't miss her.

Anyway. Back to the city. There are far too many people to

look at in a city, too many window displays to take in, too much hustle and bustle, too many smells—both enticing aromas and nose-wrinkling odors. A short ride on the subway usually overdoses me on stimulation, making me yearn to retreat into a long nap or a lingering bath when I return to the relative peace of my apartment. With the view I have from a sagging wooden back deck, which would collapse if my cat were to join me out there, I can see the Boston skyline. It's there, but I'm not there. If you know what I mean.

So. I'll begin again. My name is Gracy Maynard, and until about a year ago I was just another struggling writer living outside the city of Boston. (Or as former mayor Kevin White used to call it, with his funny way of speaking, the shitty of Boston.)

Tell anyone you're a writer—that you work for yourself, set your own hours, and answer to no one but yourself—and watch as their eyes glaze over. They get that look on their faces that conveys exactly what they're thinking: *I wish I could work for myself.*

Up until a year ago, that's where I preferred that the conversation would end. I learned that if I paused for too long, I'd be inundated with questions that were, more often than not, offensive. Because people think that if you work at home, you don't have a real job. That you don't have to take a shower more than once a week. That you can work in your pajamas. That you're rich.

So I learned to head off the barrage of questions and jump right in and ask what they did for a living. That way, I wouldn't be asked the inevitable: *What have you written?*

Because, until a year ago, I hadn't really written anything of importance, anything I was proud of, anything that would call recognition to my name on the printed page. As a struggling freelance writer, I've had to go wherever someone has been waving the promise of money for words I can string together. (*Writing isn't rocket science, best-selling author Gracy Maynard tells the* San Francisco Chronicle. *Writing is a process of stringing together words, words that you breathe life into, that you give meaning to, in your own unique way, which will guide readers to feel an emo-*

tional connection.) You learn to accept the label "freelance writer" because that implies some semblance of success, of actually being able to make money, more so than the label "unpublished writer" does.

So you write taglines and descriptions of catalog products, for instance. *(World-famous writer Gracy Maynard, burnt out after completing the fifteenth in a series of* New York Times *best-selling novels and an international book tour, takes time away from the loves and labors of her heroine, Constance Pennifort, to knock off some quick copy. See story, page 12.)*

One freelance job I had was for a company that produced collectibles. I was hired to write the catalog copy for two dozen Christmas tree balls, each adorned with its own jingle-bell scene. The job was assigned in August, so to get into the spirit I dug out my seasonal music and sat in front of my computer in a tank top and shorts as sweat soaked me and Barbra Streisand, Anne Murray, Kenny Rogers, and the Beach Boys trilled Christmas carols. My fingers raced over the keyboard like a one-horse sleigh gliding over packed snow because the company was paying me twenty-five dollars per tagline.

A Norman Rockwell Christmas comes alive with this seasonal scene from a New England town, filled with joyous celebration.

As the children sleep nestled in their warm beds, Santa Claus delivers gifts of joy and merriment.

And so on. That job really messed with my mind. I found myself dating checks December and, whenever I ventured out of my apartment, it would take me a few disorienting minutes, seeing the undecorated homes and streets and the dry, steaming pavement, to realize that I was still locked in the dog days of summer. By the time I had reached the twentieth Christmas ball, I was ready to embark on a whole new seasonal outlook.

Frightened by a loud noise, the herd of reindeer thundered through the sleepy town, stomping to pieces the exquisite nativity scene that had been set up on the town common.

As Santa Claus makes his way down the chimney, he readies his machete in his murderous plan to take out all the good citizens of Whoville.

Hey, the job paid the bills.

I penned several high school teaching packages to accompany great classics like *To Kill a Mockingbird*, *The Diary of Anne Frank*, and *Catcher in the Rye*, which I retitled *Catch Her By and By* as an inside joke to myself, but which I never shared with anyone because when you work for yourself, most everything you think or say out loud is an inside joke. Try to share your maniacal mind wanderings with anyone in the outside world, and you're often rewarded with a smile laced with pity. *Poor Gracy*, you imagine them thinking. *That working at home thing is just not the best thing for her.*

For years I lived from paycheck to paycheck. I wrote copy someone else hired me to write. And then, in those terrible lulls between assignments, when I thought that I would never, *ever* get another call from a client and I would lose my apartment and possessions and end up pushing a shopping cart up and down the city streets, sleeping under bridges at night with my rail-thin cat, I started fantasizing about all of the great American novels I wanted to pen—the ones that would bring me fame and fortune—but for which I had yet to conceive a plot, characters, time, place, setting, or even genre. I'd break out into a cold sweat knowing that if I didn't truly embrace the title of freelance writer, I'd have to finally go out into the real world and do that nine-to-five gig everyone else was doing. So I'd brew pots of coffee and send out my resume and make phone call after phone call, never giving up until I had a new assignment.

Which meant that I could then go another month without buying an alarm clock, a subway pass, or a decent pair of shoes.

Lest anyone think that working for yourself is the way to

go, let this serve as a warning: It ain't all it's cracked up to be. Unless, of course, you can make a killing doing what you're doing—and love it. But that didn't happen for me until after I had forced myself out of my pajamas and into an outfit that I considered acceptable attire for a New Year's Eve party. It was either that or sit at home and drink cheap wine while I tallied up how much money I had made that year and asked myself, for the hundredth time, *What was I thinking, working for myself?*

My cousin had passed along the party invitation to me from her boyfriend's sister's partner. Which is not quite six degrees of separation, but it was enough to assure me that I would be going to a party where I knew no one. I didn't even know my cousin's boyfriend's sister's partner. I did the weighing-out thing in my mind: go crazy figuring out my finances, or be a wallflower at a party, go crazy, be a wallflower, crazy, wallflower. When you work at home, you kind of lose your ability to be socially adept. I was good at holding a glass of wine, but I knew that making conversation at the same time would be a stretch.

I love my cousin dearly, and she loves me. But she had had just about enough of my working at home and being without a partner.

"Gracy, it's just not healthy," she had told me.

"Eating eggs and bacon every morning isn't healthy," I had countered. "I can be healthy without a partner."

I considered telling her how my sexual fantasies were far more exciting and stimulating than anyone I had ever gone to bed with. I decided to keep that to myself. Because once you tell a straight woman that a vibrator is much better than a man, and they then discover that for themselves, they never forgive you for ruining their sexual experiences with a man. After all, no straight woman wants to have a battery-operated boyfriend for the rest of her life. As stimulating as B.O.B.s can be, they don't mow the lawn on Saturday afternoons or fix the damn toaster after you've nagged them for months. Those things are what makes a heterosexual relationship strong.

But I knew what my cousin was telling me. Because when you're without a partner, especially in the lesbian community, the words *single* and *alone* are the kiss of social death. No one wants you at any gathering because you have the potential to disrupt "established" couples, and more often than not the women your friends choose to fix you up with are so far off the mark of what you're both looking for that it's humiliating. Such fix-ups are painfully laughable, because you both know that even if you were the last two lesbians left on Earth, you would each opt to be single.

To you, however, the words *single* and *alone* make you feel as if others perceive you as unloved (or unlovable). You're the stray dog in the farthest cage from the front entrance in the animal shelter—the pathetic, ugly mongrel that never gets to go home with anyone.

> *Jessica had never felt such a stab in her heart than when she finally heard the door slam. Because that meant the bags had been packed and the relationship was over. What would she do with herself? How could she survive? Blind and glued to a wheelchair since the tragedy, she feared she would not be able to survive a single day on the deserted estate.*

Single. Alone. Unloved. All terms of endearment linked to anyone who is, as some would call it, "between lovers"; or, as others would call it with a sly grin, "between ex-lovers." Like many lesbians who have been single for a while, I've set my love standards consistently low to find a partner and have been rewarded accordingly—by the jobless, the bank-account challenged, the liquor-lovers, the self-absorbed, the perpetual students, the women who were way too young for me, and the women who were way too immature for their age.

But my cousin was bound and determined not to see "the most sane lesbian" she'd ever known spend her days in solitude writing at home and her nights snuggled in front of a television watching videos with a cat named Hemingway. Since my cousin prided herself as being gay-conscious because she knew two lesbians—me, and her boyfriend's sister (well, three if you count her boyfriend's sister's partner, whom she really didn't know but knew of)—she figured that the numbers were so low in the lesbian community that anyone who was a lesbian would be thrilled at meeting another lesbian.

"It's not like lesbians are a species or members of some club," I had told her. "We don't flock together all the time. And even when we do, it's not always amicable."

"Gracy," she had countered, "it's high time that you got off your duff and made an effort at being social and then maybe, just maybe, you could finally meet someone nice."

"We can all hope," I replied. "But remember," I had added, "I've never met anyone nice."

You see, I haven't been burned by my past lovers. No. I've been scorched, torched, roasted, basted, broiled, boiled, and fricasseed. Being burned isn't as bad. At least you can heal. But being scorched, torched, and so on is not like getting back on the horse after it has thrown you. Being scorched, torched, and so on means you should give up riding altogether. Which is what I've done. For years.

And so to say that I was less than thrilled to receive an invitation to a party where I wouldn't know a single soul is an understatement. "But hey, they're all lesbians," my cousin had argued, as if that would make me feel much more at ease than attending a New Year's Eve party for, say, African-American acupuncturists. But getting drunk on cheap wine while I reviewed my meager earnings for the year was something I relished even less. So I donned my gay apparel—black boots, a clean pair of jeans (which I pressed after I had figured out where I had stored my ironing board and iron), a baby blue sweater, and a leather jacket. I doused myself with patchouli, and headed out into the night.

And so this is where it all began. At a New Year's Eve party in a house full of strangers, I met Parker Lowell, Blair Brown, and Lindsey Tompkins and subsequently came up with the idea to write an article about the lives and loves of lesbians. I sent the article out to a dozen newspapers, with ideas for more to follow and, much to my surprise, the *Boston Globe* thought it was great. So great that the newspaper hired me to write the column on a weekly basis, an agent eventually marketed the column nationally, a publisher negotiated a deal to compile the columns into a series of books, and I became a well-known syndicated columnist for the lesbian community.

But now I'm really getting ahead of myself. So I'll take you back to that New Year's Eve party.

1

It's Not My Party (So I'll Criticize It If I Want To)

World-famous author Gracy Maynard decided that this year she would take time off from her hectic, international book tour to stand alone at the most boring party in the world, tucked into a corner of a room, a pathetic wallflower with whom no one was interested in engaging in a lively conversation—

I broke off my spiraling-downward-into-the-depths-of-depression-on-New-Year's-Eve thoughts by taking a sip of some liquid I had ladled out of a container in the crowded kitchen shortly after I had entered the house. I had slopped the drink into a cup, smiled at women who clearly had no interest in returning my smile, let alone a halfhearted nod, then squeezed my way out of the tight gathering of estrogen and into a corner of the living room. There I had pitched a tent, lit a campfire, and settled down for what I knew would be a long night.

I swallowed whatever was in my plastic tumbler, but still couldn't fathom what the concoction was. I sighed and glanced at my watch. A full two minutes had ticked by since I had last checked the time. The stroke of midnight was still as far away as Mars. I was bored, tense, edgy, lonely, and sad. I was going to have a stroke just trying to make it to the new year.

Just another typical New Year's Eve in my life, I thought, then gave myself a sound mental scolding. *Don't go there. Just finish your drink and exit, stage left. No one will miss you. After all, no one even knows that you're here.* I cursed my cousin, immediately regretted taking out my bad evening on her and removed the curse, then turned my attention back to the only entertainment I had found enjoyable.

Three women, who were standing about an arm's length away from the spot of the wallpaper I had claimed as my territory, had been chatting together for a while. From what I had been able to gather in observing them and listening in on their conversation (translation: eavesdropping), they knew no one at the party and had just met one another as well. A large woman—in height, width, and the design of her hairstyle—who was wearing a jewelry counter's worth of gold bracelets and rings and was femininely and fashionably attired, had introduced herself to the others as Parker Lowell. Standing next to her was an African-American woman, who was a shade above five feet tall and a little bit overweight, but who was really cute and had a beautiful, ear-to-ear smile. She had straightened dark brown hair that was held back from her face with a clip and was wearing a black and off-white herringbone wool skirt, an off-white sweater, and a string of pearls. I had heard her introduce herself to the others as Blair Brown.

Blair kept her head perpetually skewed to one side as she listened attentively to Parker and Lindsey Tompkins, a woman who stood stiffly in front of them sporting a tailored pin-striped gray pantsuit and black silk tie, an outfit which matched her short, salt-and-pepper wavy hair. I pegged her as a funeral director because I hadn't seen anything other than a furrowed brow and a tight, tense smile displayed on her face.

I took another sip of my drink, then tuned back into their conversation.

"Honey, this isn't a party. Not in the truest sense of the definition," Parker declared as she sipped her drink, then grimaced and secreted the plastic cup behind a flourishing Wandering Jew that was set on a table behind her. "I mean, plastic cups? And this drink that some butch in the kitchen informed me was a mocktail? What the hell is a mocktail? It sounds like some species of animal that men hunt down in the fall. 'Hey, Ed. I hear dem mocktails is running this year. We gonna bag us some?' "

Lindsey chuckled.

Parker flashed a smile at her. "Let's just call a spade a spade, shall we?" she asked, then picked at an invisible speck of lint from her deep purple silk shirt that was unbuttoned to reveal a generous line of cleavage from her enormous breasts. "This isn't a party, and this drink isn't even close to a cocktail. This is a gathering of women—and I use that term loosely as well—who are clearly entertainment-challenged. And this drink is—"

"Delicious, I think," Blair cut in with a bright smile, then raised her eyebrows and lowered her voice. She leaned in closer to the other two. "You see, I think there are no alcoholic beverages here because a couple of the women may be recovering alcoholics," she whispered with a concerned look on her face.

Parker leaned toward her and kept her voice low. "Oh? Really? There are *lesbian* alcoholics? What do they look like? I don't think I've ever seen one before."

Blair shrugged her shoulders. "Parker, they look just like you and me." She nodded her head knowingly. "But they have a problem with alcohol. Which makes them alcoholic. So they have to stop drinking. Alcohol, that is."

"Really!" Parker exclaimed. "So if they don't drink anymore, why aren't they called nonalcoholics? Like this damn drink."

Blair tipped her head to the other side, then shook her head. "That's a really good question. I don't know the answer to that."

"Cut it out, Parker," Lindsey hissed with a scowl, then looked at Blair. "She's teasing you."

Blair glanced at Parker, then smiled and blinked her big brown eyes. "Oh. Well, that's okay. People do that to me all the time. They tell me I'm naive." She took a sip of her drink, then another. "It's really not so bad. It's, well, refreshing."

Parker let out a loud snort. "Refreshing? My guess is that it's

Diet Sprite and cranberry juice, which some butch poured into a spaghetti pot shortly before we arrived." She crinkled her nose and sniffed. "Refreshing would be a martini in a chilled glass. Refreshing would be a Manhattan or a gin and tonic, or even a simple rum and Coke. Refreshing would be any drink but this."

"It's a holiday punch, I think," Lindsey clarified as she pulled out a pair of glasses from the breast pocket of her jacket, brought her drink up in front of her eyes, and closely regarded it with an intensely serious look. "It *is* a bit festive-looking."

"Just because it's red doesn't mean it even qualifies to be called punch," Parker argued, then shook both of her arms so the dozens of bracelets embracing them jingled like sleigh bells on a Clydesdale. "And just because it's served in a pot and there's a ladle—"

"I think you're being way too critical, Parker," Blair cut in. "I for one think it's important for lesbians to address the issues that confront them. The difficulties each one of us faces in—"

"Knowing that we'll never be able to hold a candle to gay men when it comes to throwing a party?" Parker broke in. "Honey, Martha Stewart was born into this world solely to give gay men a reason to get up in the morning. Several theories are being kicked around that she's really a gay man in drag. Perhaps that's why straight people simply can't wrap their brain cells around her ideas. Only gay men can see her visions."

"So do you disagree with lesbians being PC?" Lindsey asked Parker as she picked up a paper plate from a table next to her. "I think I'm going to go ahead and try some of this," she said as she shoveled a plastic fork into a mound of pasta and scooped a healthy forkful into her mouth. "I mean," she continued as she chewed and then swallowed, "don't you agree that we need to be sensitive to the particular issues that each lesbian faces?"

"If PC stands for plastic china, then yes, I disagree with lesbians being PC," Parker answered. "I mean, have you ever been to a party thrown by gay men? Their subscriptions to *Martha Stewart* get used. They plan their parties for weeks. They're very much *events*. They lay out fancy table settings. There's delicious food. And alcohol. Lots of alcohol. Not the cheap stuff, either. And honey, there are the richest, most mouthwatering desserts you could ever imagine. But the most important part of their parties is what gay men do best. They always have a theme. When they're not fucking or playing out some high drama or trying on women's clothing—and don't they look great in it, by the way?—they're using all of their creative energy to come up with *a reason* to gather people together. A white party. A diva party. A favorite literary figure party. There's always some sort of theme that unifies everything. The theme of this, well, whatever it is," Parker said as she waved an arm in the air, then shook her head and dropped her arm on her lap, "is, I believe, chaos."

"This is a New Year's Eve party," Blair said. "That's the theme."

"Then where are the noisemakers?" Parker countered. "I mean, other than the loud dykes in the den? Where are the party hats and favors? The decorations? Is there any indication in this house that this is, in fact, a New Year's Eve party?" She ran a tongue over her teeth and then sucked air between them. "Party? Ha! I wouldn't use the word party to describe this, unless you put the word pity before it," she concluded as she balanced a large hip on the edge of an overstuffed chair and crossed her ample legs. Her slit skirt opened to reveal a large, muscled calf and a foot housed in a black heel.

"A party can be defined as a gathering of people," Lindsey said as she shoved her plate on a side table, wiped her face with a napkin, then tossed the wadded napkin onto the plate. She pulled up the sleeves on her blazer and tucked her short hair behind each ear. "People are gathered. Thus, it's a party. I think you're being way too critical."

"Me, too," Blair agreed. "But, I mean, I'm not trying to be critical of you in saying that."

"What do you think?"

I listened to the pause in the conversation and waited for the answer. When none was offered, I shot a quick glance in their direction and noticed all eyes were on me.

"Yes, you," Parker said as she nodded at me. "You're not the hostess, are you?"

I shook my head. "No. A reluctant guest. I really don't want to be here."

"Neither do we." Parker smiled, then waved an arm noisily in the air. "Come. Come join the joyless club. I'm Parker Lowell."

"Blair Brown," Blair introduced herself as I stepped next to Lindsey. Blair extended a hand to me, and then shook mine. "It's a pleasure to meet you."

"She's the polite one in the group," Parker said. "I think we'll call her Miss Manners."

"There's nothing wrong with manners," Blair sniffed.

"I'm Lindsey Tompkins," Lindsey said as she turned to me. "I'm an attorney in Boston. Here's my card."

I stared down at the embossed card she extended to me, then took it and slid it into a pocket.

"Lindsey is going to sue for defamation of the character of this, well, I don't know what it is," Parker said as she looked around the room. "An excuse for me to get out of the house, I guess. Since Bob and Tom broke up this summer, there's no New Year's Eve party at the boys' house. Which is usually where I go."

"Gracy Maynard," I said as I nodded at the group. "So, do you all know each other?"

Heads shook.

"I guess we're the outcasts from the party." Blair frowned.

"Honey, we *are* the party," Parker pointed out.

"I was invited here through friends of friends, who haven't shown up yet," Blair continued. "I don't know a soul here. So I just stuck myself in this corner of the room and gave myself a time limit for how much longer I was going to stay."

"And I came over and asked Blair what time it was," Lindsey cut in. "I've been meaning to pick up my watch from the repair shop, but I never seem to get out of work in time. I don't know a soul here either. One of my coworkers told me about it. I think one of the women here is her ex. She advised that I get out of the office and do something social. I kind of, well, work hard. And for some reason tonight they closed the building where I work."

"It's New Year's Eve, honey," Parker said. "Although you wouldn't know it from this party."

Lindsey shrugged her shoulders. "I had a ton of work to do tonight. Briefs. Cases to review. Some dictation, too. Seems like I have to work double-time to earn my keep, compared to the men in the firm. I mean, if I'm going to make partner some day . . . anyway, I won't bore you with job-talk. I heard that the party was potluck, so I thought, *Looks like a free home-cooked meal for me*. I don't think I've used the stove once in my apartment. I usually order out. I eat out of containers in front of the television when I'm home. Or at my desk at work. You know, the food here isn't that bad."

"I haven't tried it," I told her. "I'm not really hungry, I guess. Or maybe I'm just a little nervous." I met Parker's eyes. "And so your story is . . . ?"

"Well." Parker shifted her weight and recrossed her legs. "I joined this little group because these women were the only ones in this house who were not wearing jeans and a flannel shirt. The kitchen brigade looks like they're putting on a fashion show for Woolrich, Dockers, and Levis." She glanced down at my jeans. "At least you ironed yours, honey. And that jacket is to die for. I love a girl in leather."

"She's not a girl," Blair corrected her. "I teach girls in my school."

"I hope you teach them how to dress well," Parker countered. "You dress nicely, Blair. You dress like a girl."

"Woman," Blair corrected her.

"The paralegals and secretaries in the office hate being called girls," Lindsey said. "And yet the men keep doing it."

"The point I'm trying to make," Blair continued, "is that a girl is a young female. The people here are women. And I think they would object strenuously to being called girls."

"Of course they would," Parker snorted. "That's because most of them would be shocked if you told them they were women. 'You gotta be shittin' me!' they'd probably exclaim."

"I think they know they're women," Lindsey said. "They're just not girly-girls. They're more butchy. Dykey."

"Don't we call that 'soft butch' nowadays?" I asked.

"They looked like hardasses to me." Parker chuckled. "Did you see the Arnold muscles on the one who was wearing—"

"Maybe we should call them tomboys," Lindsey suggested.

"No!" Blair protested. "And you shouldn't call them girls, either. How would you like it if I called you a girl, Parker?"

"I'd love it," Parker replied. "Because I *am* a girl. And so are you, Blair. And you, Lindsey. And you, Gracy. Girl, girl, girl, girl."

"Wasn't that the name of an Elvis Presley movie?" I asked with a grin.

"I remember that one!" Lindsey smiled. "I once dressed up as Elvis for an office Halloween party."

"It's just not politically correct," Blair told Parker.

"To dress up as Elvis?" Lindsey asked her. "Gay men dress up as women all the time. Why can't I dress up as a man?"

"I'm not talking about you, Lindsey," Blair said, then let out an exasperated sigh. "All I'm saying is that it's not politically correct to say *girl* when you mean woman."

"Well, tough titties, Blair," Parker said as she placed her hands beneath her breasts and jiggled them. "I'm the most un-PC lesbian you'll ever meet. I'm here, I'm queer, but I have a lot of problems with most things here and queer. Like this sorry excuse for a party, for instance. Potluck! Can you believe it? Only in the lesbian community do women invite other women over to their homes with the request to bring food. Don't lesbians shop? Is no one in the lesbian community capable of cooking for a group? And there's no alcohol served because of"—Parker raised both hands in the air and then shot two fingers from each hand up and down—"alcohol issues. Issues. God, I love that term. It seems like everyone in the lesbian community has some sort of issue. Even if it's not an issue, they make it an issue. And there's no smoking. Sure, I know it's dangerous to your health, but how else can you drink? And there's not one woman here wearing a skirt besides you and me, Blair. Here's my opinion. Take it for what it is. Girls cook. Girls entertain. Girls get drunk.

Girls smoke. Girls wear skirts. Girls wear makeup. Honey, while most of these dykes here are out camping in the wilderness—which to me is a very scary place to be and why the hell anyone thinks that's fun is beyond me—I'm enjoying a makeover at Filene's counter. Or trying on clothes at Lord & Taylor. I enjoy being a girl. And I like girls who are girls."

"I shop at Lord & Taylor," Lindsey said, then opened her palms in front of her. "This suit."

"Love it!" Parker smiled. "Very snappy. But why not a skirt? Lesbians do have legs, you know. Or perhaps you're not into shaving."

"I think you're getting too personal, Parker," Blair said.

Parker raised an arm over her head and nodded at her bare underarm. "See? Shaved. Not braided. I don't have shaving issues." She lowered her arm. "And here's another thing that drives me nuts. I spell woman w-o-m-a-n. Not w-i-m-m-i-n or w-o-m-y-n. I love being a woman, and I love to be with women who love being women. There, Blair. I've said women several times. Are you happy?"

"I'll tell you what I don't like about these parties," Lindsey said as she pushed her hands into the pockets of her tailored pants. "Everyone here is a couple. Every party you go to in the lesbian community, it's couples, couples, couples."

"Except for us," Blair pointed out.

"Who wants to be in a couple?" Parker asked. "There's way too much to choose from out there. Who wants to get tied down? Except in bed, of course."

"I wouldn't mind being tied down," Blair said.

Parker beamed a broad smile at her. "I didn't think you were the type."

"Not for that—for what you're thinking," Blair quickly added. "But for being in a relationship. A lasting, true love. Forever and ever."

"I bet you read a lot of fairy tales when you were growing up," Parker said.

"There's nothing wrong with wanting a happily ever after," Blair answered as she played with the string of pearls around her neck. "I've liked being in relationships. Waking up with the same person every morning. Talking about the day you've had in the evening when you come home. Deciding what to do for the weekend or where to go for a vacation."

"I bet you just rope 'em in as fast as you can." Parker snickered, then turned to me. "I gather you're the shy, quiet type, Leather."

I shook my head. "Not really. I just, well, I'm not into the party scene. I used to go out all the time. With, you know, whoever I was with at the time and all of her friends. Now that I've been single for a while, I just can't seem to get too excited about trying to meet someone again. In a social situation like this. It's all too . . . too—"

"Painful?" Blair suggested.

"Problematic?" Lindsey offered up.

I paused to search for an answer.

"Honey, you're not going to find anyone with potential at this, well, at this," Parker said. "Unless you're into lumberjacks."

"So where do you meet women?" Lindsey asked. "I've done the bar scene. And I've dated friends of friends. It's not easy finding a soul mate. And I work too damn hard. I don't think I have time anymore to be on the search, let alone try to make something work. But I hate coming home to an empty apartment."

"Well, this is certainly not a very upbeat conversation," Blair pointed out.

"You want upbeat, go into the kitchen," Parker responded. "They may be making another batch of Hawaiian Punch. Woohoo!"

"Well," I said as I glanced down at my watch. "I think I'll head out."

"Don't go!" Blair begged as she reached for my arm. "Okay. I don't like to be critical or judgmental—"

"Except with me," Parker cut in.

"—but you guys are the most interesting people I've met in a long time," Blair continued. "I mean, you women can actually hold a conversation."

"But you've disagreed with everything I've said," Parker pointed out.

"That doesn't mean I don't think you're interesting," Blair answered. "You're a very different person from anyone I've ever met. Before I came over to this corner of the room, I tried talking to the people in the kitchen. But they're all—"

"Couples, talking about couple things they've done together," Lindsey finished. "When *we* went to Yosemite. When *we* played for the championship softball game. When *we* decided to add on to our house last fall. What happened the last time *we* went to the gynecologist because *we're* trying to have a baby."

"Exactly!" Blair exclaimed. "And I'm sorry, but I think that's rude. I mean, how can you meet new people or hear different points of view or—"

"Find out common interests or even things you don't know about," Lindsey added.

I nodded. "I did try to engage some of the kitchen people in conversation. And then I got this look from a few of them—you know, it's a look that's kind of off-putting, a look that tells you—"

"—to butt out, it's none of your damn business," Lindsey cut in and frowned.

"Well, not so much that," I answered. "But like, well, I think Margaret Cho said it best in her one-woman show, *I'm the One that I Want*. She talks about going on an Olivia cruise with hundreds of lesbians and experiencing firsthand the lesbian drama that plays out whenever a new face shows itself on the scene. Except on that cruise, just about everyone on the cruise was a new face. So she said that each lesbian started questioning her lover, asking, 'Are you interested in her? In her? In her? In her?'"

"That's exactly how I felt when I went into the kitchen!" Blair exclaimed. "Everyone's looking at me like 'Who is she?' and then I could sense the couples pulling closer together. Like I was going to steal one of them away."

Lindsey nodded. "The new lesbian sighting syndrome."

"Circle them wagons, Alma!" Parker cried out. "Thar be a new lezzie in town, and ah'm thinkin' she gonna be stirrin' things up for the rest a us. Ah'll go git ma gun."

"Which totally puts a lid on the possibility of making a new friend," I pointed out. "I mean, I'm not looking for a potential partner here tonight, although everyone in the kitchen probably thinks that I am. I just wanted to get out of the house and have a good time."

"I'm having a good time with you guys," Blair said. "I really am."

"That's because we're way too good for anyone in the kitchen," Parker sniffed. "We've got class. We've got brains. We've got wit and charm."

"And yet they all have what we want," Lindsey added.

"A battleship-gray Saab convertible with heated seats?" Parker asked Lindsey, then laughed. "Sorry. That's what *I* want. Listen, honey, having someone doesn't mean you *are* someone. And having someone doesn't necessarily guarantee happiness. When you're in a relationship, it just means you have someone to go to the movies with. All the time. It takes a long time to find a lifelong partnership with someone that lasts. You have to do a lot of work and go through some rocky times as well as some good ones. It's fucking hell. Which is probably why I'm not in a relationship because I don't have the patience that's needed to process or to go deep and get heavy. I just want to be in bed with a woman. As much as I can."

"And then after bed?" I asked.

"Well, then, we usually go the kitchen and make a snack together," Parker answered with a smile.

"I was thinking about trying to meet someone through the personal ads," Blair said.

"Uh-oh," Lindsey answered, then shook her head. "I tried that once. Not a good experience. You have to read the fine print—"

"Spoken like a true attorney," Parker interjected.

"What fine print?" Blair asked.

"What someone writes in an ad is usually very different

from who or what that person really is," Lindsey answered. "I tried that route myself. I responded to an ad that was written by a woman who said she was slightly overweight. We talked on the phone a few times, then we decided to get together. She was the size of a house. Another wrote that she wasn't into the bar scene. So where do you think she wanted to meet me?"

I grinned. "At a bar?"

"Affirmative." Lindsey chuckled.

"I used to read the personals all the time," I said. "I never responded to any of them, but I got to playing this game whenever I'd read them. I'd try to look beyond what was written to get to the heart of what was really meant. So if I read that someone liked long walks on the beach, I'd think to myself, 'Uh-oh. There's someone who can't relate to people.' Someone who would write that she liked fine wines—"

"Is a lush, honey." Parker chuckled.

"People usually write the opposite of what they really are because they'd like to think that that's how they are," Lindsey said. "Someone may say they're sane, grounded, spiritual, strong, centered, and so on, but more likely than not they're none of those things. That's just how they'd like to be. And they think if they attract someone like that, those things will rub off on them. I found looking through the personals all too frustrating."

"I took out an ad once," Parker said with a sly grin. "Here's what I wrote: 'I want to meet other lesbians for casual sex. All I want to do is come, come, come. So come with me. I want to suck you and fuck you. Must be feminine and sexy.'"

"Oh, my!" Blair exclaimed.

"That's pretty clear," I said.

"I thought so," Parker answered. "And I got responses. I decided that I was going to meet each and every one of these women. So I told them all to show up at a certain place at a certain time."

"At the same time?" Lindsey asked.

Parker nodded. "The designated meeting place was at a restaurant near a women's bookstore in Boston. I sat in my car in the parking lot and watched woman after woman walk into the place. And several men as well. There was not one sexy, feminine woman in the lot. So I figured, why bother going in? They're each going to think one of the others took out the ad, and maybe a few of them will decide to hook up. That's the last time I took out an ad."

"So where the hell do you meet single women?" Lindsey said. "Wait. Let me clarify that. Where the hell do you meet single *quality* women?"

"Define quality," I told her.

Lindsey thought for a moment. "Someone like me. I think I'm a quality person. I'm looking for someone who's professional. Kind. Respectful. Honest. With a brain. And with good looks and charm."

"You want the whole package," Blair pointed out.

"Exactly," Lindsey answered.

"This small group of women right here in front of me is looking pretty good," Parker said. "You all seem to have those qualities. As do I. So let's go to bed and make wild, passionate sex."

Blair stared at Parker.

"Oh, for God's sake, I'm joking, Blair," Parker clarified. "You're the first group of women I've met that I haven't wanted to take to bed. No offense. I'm not saying that you all aren't attractive. But I actually would like to talk more with each of you. For the first time in my life, I've met some nice-looking, put-together, quality lesbians and just want to talk with them. What an eye-opening experience!"

"I agree," Blair answered. "I mean, with wanting to continue talking with you guys."

"So," Parker began, and then looked at us. "What do you say?"

"What do you say to what?" Lindsey asked.

"To all of us meeting up again," Parker suggested. "For drinks. Or coffee. Or dinner. We can go out and talk and enjoy each other's company. No strings attached."

"Sounds good to me," Lindsey said.

"Me, too," Blair chimed in.

I nodded. "Me, three."

* * *

As I headed home that night, I thought about the conversation I had had with Parker, Lindsey, and Blair, and about Lindsey's question, Where does a single lesbian, with quality, meet another single lesbian who also has quality? When I reached my apartment building, I bounded up the stairs, threw my jacket on the floor, raced to my computer, then sat down in front of the blank screen.

After a few minutes, I began to type.

Single lesbian. Lonely. Looking for love.
Please send directions . . .

Where do single lesbians meet other single lesbians?

The hardest part in seeking a definitive answer to this question—or at least some suggestions—is that every single lesbian approaches meeting another single lesbian with a certain set of expectations in mind, a certain itinerary, a certain plan for an outcome. Some want to meet just to have sex. Some want to meet to begin a friendship that may possibly develop into what the personal ads identify as LTR—long-term relationship. Some want a companion to join them for hikes up mountains, days on the beach, and nights at the movies, but with no thought of sex or intimacy—kind of like a date without potential. And some truly want to meet someone to begin a committed, long-lasting relationship—something they haven't been able to find in the many social avenues available to single lesbians: the bars, the discussion and book groups, the parties, the sports teams.

How does a single lesbian approach such a search without feeling that she may once again be setting herself up for defeat? That she's once again pining all her hopes and dreams on another person in the attempt to create something that may start out with a whole lot of potential and then, for a multitude of reasons that most often begin with, "It's not you, it's me," end in heartbreak?

The single lesbian is one of the gay community's most perplexing dilemmas. Because there are a lot of single lesbians out there. There are far less than six degrees of separation that keep single lesbians apart. Each day we pass by them unknowingly or even interact with them as we go about our daily business. Sometimes we don't have to work hard to find a lifelong partner. But more often than not we have to go through a series of heartbreaks in the search for our true soul mate.

But how does this happen? Where does the single lesbian begin her search?

I wrote for hours that night without realizing that one year had ended and another had begun. As I composed the last paragraph and then reread my words, I realized that I was just seeing the tip of the iceberg in the lesbian community. There was so much more for women to talk about, so many other things that were important to lesbians, and so many other, as Parker called them, *issues,* that affected lesbians in their pursuit of love.

I began writing down other questions I wanted to have answered.

I stared at the list as I printed the article I had just written. It didn't matter that I didn't know the answers. Because I knew Parker, Lindsey, and Blair could help me—and other lesbians—to find those answers.

2

Ask, and Ye May Be Shot Down
(But Better to Be Shot Down
than Never Shot at All)

"So here's what I want to know," Parker said as she handed her menu to the waitress and rested her elbows on the table in the restaurant where we had decided to meet for dinner a few weeks after the New Year's Eve party. "Are you the dumper or the dumpee in your relationships?"

"I thought we were going to talk about how to meet single lesbians," Lindsey said as she opened her napkin, placed it on her lap, and reached for the bread basket.

"Dumpee," Parker concluded as she followed Lindsey's hand into the basket, grabbed two rolls, and began to slather butter on them.

"You are?" I asked Parker.

Parker took a large bite from a roll, then shook her head. "No, honey, *she* is," she answered, nodding in Lindsey's direction. "Whenever someone doesn't want to talk about her past relationships, nine times out of ten it's usually because she's the dumpee. Dumpers don't mind talking about relationships that have ended because they've chosen to end them. The dumpees never get that chance."

"Well, I'm a dumpee, I guess," Blair said as she covered the remaining rolls in the basket and placed the basket in the center of the table. "And I don't mind talking about it. Because I can see now why many of my relationships ended. I just wasn't who they were looking for."

"Is that what they told you?" Lindsey asked.

"Well, I guess for the most part, yes," Blair replied. "And then they said they just wanted to be friends. So I've tried to be that to them."

"Aren't you nice," Parker said. "I bet you send all your ex-lovers Christmas cards. I bet you take all their phone calls when they call you up any time of the day or night to complain about how their new lovers just don't understand them as well as you did."

"Of course I do," Blair answered. "That's what friends are for."

Parker shook her head. "Honey, they're walking all over you."

"No, they're not."

"As Janet Jackson once asked—well, I'm paraphrasing here to make my point—'What have they done for you lately?' " Parker challenged Blair.

"Well, um," Blair began, then stopped.

"My point exactly," Parker said as she lobbed a hunk of buttered bread into her mouth.

"The line I'm usually given at the end of a relationship is, 'You don't pay enough attention to me,' " Lindsey said. "It always seems to end up being my fault. But I have a life, you know? A career that's very important to me. I have things I've got to do. I have pressures on me to try to make it in a man's world. How much attention do women want? How much do they need? I mean, really! How can you balance a career with meeting all of their needs?"

"I've been both," I said as I broke off a piece of bread. "Neither is very comfortable." I looked at Parker. "I imagine you're the dumper."

Parker smiled. "You've got me pegged on that. But here's the thing. I don't use any of those stupid breakup lines. Like, 'It's just not working out. You're not the one for me. I can't stand the way you brush your teeth in the morning.' Or 'I've met someone else.' "

"Ugh. That's my least favorite line," Lindsey groaned.

"I don't use any of those lines because I'm always very clear, right from the beginning," Parker continued. "I tell whoever I'm with that I'm not looking for a relationship. That I don't want them to move in with me. That I don't want to talk on the phone every day about absolutely nothing. That I don't need someone to take care of me. And that I really, really don't want to take care of someone else."

"So if you're so clear right from the beginning, then how have you even been put in the position of being the dumper?" I asked.

Parker pushed the last chunk of a roll into her mouth and chewed. "I've discovered that you can be as clear as all that and still not be viewed as telling the truth," she mumbled, then dabbed her lips with her napkin and swallowed. "You take a woman to bed, and the next thing you know she's got a couple of changes of clothes and a toothbrush in your home. I tell you, you give a woman a good orgasm, and she thinks you've signed commitment papers."

"I don't go to bed with anyone unless I really like them," Blair said.

"Yet another surprise." Parker snorted.

"There's nothing wrong with that," Blair said defensively. "I think lesbians have it all wrong. They go to bed with one another way too quickly. It's bed, and then relationship. I like to take the time to truly get to know someone. And for them to know me. I think that's why so many of my ex's want to be friends with me. Because we were friends from the beginning."

"And they've found someone else to be their lover," Parker pointed out. "I think this getting-to-know-someone thing is highly overrated. What's to know? You like to have sex with girls. They like to have sex with girls. So why not have sex? What's more important is how you interact in bed. That's what makes or breaks a relationship."

"In my experience, good sex only lasts for months," I pointed out.

Parker nodded. "I agree. That's why I don't need to be with someone longer than that period of time."

"Haven't you ever wanted to settle down with someone?" Lindsey asked Parker. "For the long haul, so to speak?"

"I felt that way once," she answered. "Once was enough."

"What happened?" I asked.

Parker sat back in her chair and crossed her arms.

Lindsey looked at her. "What? You don't want to talk about it?"

"I find talking about past relationships very painful," Blair said. "If she doesn't want to talk about it, then—"

"No, she *should* talk about it," Lindsey disagreed. "Parker, you started this whole conversation with whether we were dumpers or dumpees. You wanted us to talk. You can't clam up on us now."

"Isn't that the point of us meeting up together?" I asked. "To talk?"

"Exactly," Blair said.

Parker let out a sigh. "Okay. Here's where we'll go with this conversation. We're each going to talk about the greatest love of our lives and what happened when you first met her." She turned to Lindsey. "See, that way we'll get to talk about how we meet single lesbians."

"Fair enough." Lindsey nodded.

Parker leaned forward. "Picture this. Greece. The early eighties. I was traveling there for the import-export business I run. I was—"

"Oh, my God!" Blair cut in. "Lowell! Are you Pier Lowell?"

Parker beamed a broad smile. "I am."

"You have a lot of stores in the city," Lindsey remarked. "Man, you must make a killing."

"It's been a good business," Parker agreed.

"I'll say," I said. "I know that I give you a lot of my earnings. So how did you get into that?"

"My father started the business," Parker began. "He died when I was in my teens and left the store to me because my mother was only concerned with the money the business made and not how to run it. I hired a manager to continue Pier Lowell while I went to business school, then I took it over after graduation. I expanded the business—but, hey, we're not talking about our professions today. So I'll get back to my trip to Greece."

"I've never been to Greece," Blair said. "I hear it's beautiful."

Parker nodded. "It is. And the women there are gorgeous. Dark hair. Tan skin. Beautiful smiles. Sensual accents. Ah, yes. Well, during the day I'd look at products and do my ordering for business, and then at night I'd hit the women's bars. And I swear to God to you, when I walked into a bar one night and saw Ana Maria leaning against the bar in that sexy white dress that showed off her dark skin and her long, dark hair, I thought I had never seen anyone so beautiful in my life. It was more than a physical attraction, though. It was as if my heart swelled in my chest. Every fiber in my body tingled."

"Oh!" Blair exclaimed, then smiled, leaned forward, and rested her chin in her hands. "This is a good story."

Parker smiled and held up her hands. "My palms started to sweat. That had never happened to me before. I mean, I had kissed women and done some light-hearted fooling around when I was young. But I was never young *and* in love. I got really nervous just looking at Ana Maria. But I couldn't seem to move toward her. Suddenly, I felt all shy and uncertain—as if you can believe that! I ordered a drink and then stood a short distance away from her. But I just couldn't keep myself from looking at her. I'd glance in her direction from time to time. The music was playing, and she was swaying her body a bit, in a really sensual way. I remember thinking to myself, *Why is this woman not surrounded by women right now?* The way I saw it, she was like an enticing light that could draw anyone she wanted to her. I wanted to get up the courage to ask her to dance, but all of my usual assertiveness had left me."

"But you obviously *did* get together with her," Lindsey said.

Parker nodded. "Then, one time when I had glanced over at her, I saw that she was looking at me. I glanced away quickly, then looked back again. And still she was looking at me. Staring at me. Then she smiled, and it was as if a fire had been lit inside me."

"This is so romantic," Blair cooed.

"This is so *wow*," I added.

"Wow is right," Parker agreed. "And then Ana Maria started walking toward me. I turned, and suddenly there she was, standing next to me."

"And then what happened?" Lindsey asked.

" 'Do you want to continue to watch me all night, or do you want to dance with me?' she asked," Parker answered. "I didn't say a word. I took a step toward her, and she slowly placed her hands on my hips. And without even moving to the dance floor, we started swaying our bodies together right in that spot."

"Would you ladies like another drink?" the waitress asked us.

"Not now," Lindsey snapped as she waved a hand impatiently at the waitress. "Go on, go on," she urged Parker as the waitress hesitated, then turned on her heels. "So you're dancing with her," Lindsey prompted Parker.

Parker nodded. "I'm dancing with her. One song. Two songs. Three songs. I have my arms around her and she has her arms around me. And I said something that I've never said to anyone since."

"What was that?" I asked.

"I told her, 'I think I'm falling in love with you.' "

"You've never said that to anyone else?" Blair asked.

Parker shook her head. "No one has ever moved me the way Ana Maria did."

"So then what happened?" Lindsey asked.

Parker peered into the bread basket and took out another roll. "I had four more days in Greece. We spent every day and night together. And then I had to go home. Those were the days when E-mail wasn't really an option for staying in touch, so I racked up incredible phone bills. I traveled to Greece as often as I could, and each time I saw her and spent time with her I fell deeper and deeper in love." Parker buttered the roll, then set it down on her bread plate.

"A year went by," she continued, "and to celebrate our anniversary I had two beautiful matching rings made for us. I was going to surprise her with them and ask her to come to America and live with me. I guess you could say that that's the closest I've ever come to asking anyone for a commitment. I made arrangements to fly to Greece, but I didn't tell her exactly when I'd be arriving. But she knew I was coming to see her and that we'd be celebrating our first anniversary together. I think my plane landed at one or two in the morning. I got a taxi to her place, and let myself in with the key she had given me. I walked up the stairs to her bedroom—"

"Why do I get the feeling I know how this is going to turn out?" Lindsey cut in as she ran a hand nervously through her hair.

Parker closed her eyes and nodded. Then she opened them. "She wasn't alone. I didn't wake her. I just stared at the tangle of legs and arms clutched in an embrace on top of the bedcovers. To this day, I'll never forget how Ana Maria looked as she lay underneath the other woman—her eyes closed, a peaceful look on her face, with her arms wrapped around the woman's back. And then I stepped quietly out of the bedroom, let myself out of the house, and took the next flight home."

"How sad!" Blair said, then wiped an eye with a finger.

"Those long-distance relationships never work out," Lindsey commented.

"What did you do with the rings?" I asked.

"Oh, I still have them," Parker answered. "Whenever I get the feeling I might fall for someone again, I take them out and look at them. They still exude the pain I felt all those years ago. And so I look at them and repeat two lines from the movie *Galaxy Quest*. 'Never give up. Never surrender.' " Parker smiled, then stuffed half the buttered roll in her mouth.

We stared at Parker as she chewed.

"What?" she finally asked us.

"Did Ana Maria ever know that you had shown up at her place?" I asked. "I mean, how did it *end*?"

Parker laughed. "Oh, yeah. There has to be closure, doesn't there? It's not enough that I discovered her in bed with another woman. That to me was a mighty clear indication she no longer loved me or wanted to be with me. But for some reason, lesbians need to discuss the obvious. They simply have to process endings from each and every angle, almost as much as straight men like to rehash football games. What's the point? There's no reason to discuss who won or lost a game and why; it just is what it is. Likewise, there should be no reason to discuss the ending of a relationship. It's over. Bye bye. Enough said."

"Closure is good," Blair countered. "It's always good to process an ending and bring it to some sort of conclusion. I think it helps the people involved to feel better about an ending."

"I don't think any ending I've ever been through has felt good, no matter how much closure has happened," Lindsey said. "And who really wants to hear—needs to hear—all the blow-by-blow details of what led a lover into the bed of another woman?"

"So it won't happen to you again?" I suggested. "I mean, isn't it a good thing to know what you might have done wrong in a relationship so you don't do it again?"

"I think so," Blair answered. "I'm always looking for ways to make myself a better person."

"Just because someone leaves you doesn't mean you aren't a good person," Lindsey said. "I'm tired of ex's making me feel that there's something wrong with me. Why can't there be something wrong with them for a change?"

"Okay, then, here's the conclusion," Parker cut in. "I went downstairs in her house. I had my hand on the doorknob and my bags in hand and was ready to let myself out. Believe it or not, I was fighting back tears."

"Of course you were," Blair said.

"Tears are good," I added.

"Tears are a pain in the ass," Parker disagreed. "What's the point? They ruin your appearance worse than a few days spent in the sun. And tears can never change anything. Crying is a waste of time. Anyway, I'm about to leave and then I remembered the key. So I put down my bags, took it off the key ring, and placed it on the table in the hallway. Ana Maria had a pad of paper there, where she'd write her shopping lists. I ripped off a clean piece of paper and wrote, 'You're such a fucking jerk.' I dropped the key on top of the paper, picked up my bags, and left."

"This is *so* sad," Blair sniffed. "Why can't everyone have happiness?"

"Did you ever hear from her again?" Lindsey asked.

"On my answering machine," Parker answered. "But I never picked up the phone when I heard her voice on the machine or returned her calls. After a week, she stopped calling. And life, as they say, went on." Parker paused. "So," she said as she looked around at us, "that's my how-I-met-the-love-of-my-life story. Anyone else?"

"Well, I don't think I can top that one," Lindsey answered. "I met my true love, or who I thought was my true love, when I was going to law school. We roomed together, studied together, and flipped out over our grades together. Things were going fine between us for a year. Or at least I thought they were. That's the first time I heard the break-up line, 'You don't pay enough attention to me.' As if I could. Law school is tough, and the first year is both crucial and excruciating. I went away for a summer internship program, and when I had returned to start my second year, she had moved out of our apartment and found someone else. Funny thing was, I ended up graduating with a law degree and passed the bar on the first try. She dropped out a month after the second year started and got a job as a manager in a coffee shop. She's out in Seattle now. I think she's a massage therapist. I guess both law and I weren't in her heart."

"I met my true love at school, too," Blair said. "When I was student teaching. I'm a grade school teacher now, but I met her at a junior high school. She was a teacher; had been for some time. She was much older than I was."

"So you had a schoolgirl crush on her?" Parker smiled.

Blair returned the smile. "I guess you could say that. But she was very uptight. We had to be very careful. Being in a school and all—you know how freaked out parents and administrators can get if a teacher is openly gay. And she had been teaching at that school for years and didn't want to do anything that would jeopardize her job. We kept everything very secretive. Where we met up with each other and when we met were carefully prearranged. And I had to be very careful not to show how I felt about her while I was at school, even though I was madly in love with her. She treated me, well, when we were at school she treated me like I didn't even exist. But I knew she loved me and I loved her. Very, very much."

"But something happened, right?" Lindsey asked.

Blair nodded. "If I stayed over at her house on a school night, I'd sometimes write her these gushy love notes and stick them in her lunch bag in the morning. One day I guess someone mixed up her bag for his. And, of course, read the note. And then, for some insane reason, decided to share the note with the principal."

"Uh-oh," Lindsey groaned.

Blair nodded. "And that was that. She wouldn't have anything to do with me. I transferred out of that school at the end of the year. It was quite sad. It broke my heart. And that's a situation . . . a situation where I never was able to get closure. To this day, I wonder if she ever thinks of me. Because she didn't say one word to me, wouldn't return my phone calls or answer my letters, after that."

I reached over to Blair and patted her on the back.

She looked at me, then shrugged her shoulders. "Oh, well. Sometimes I guess you just can't get closure. But she was my first time, you know? My first woman."

Lindsey nodded. "That's tough."

"And you?" Parker asked me.

"Where else but on a softball team?" I asked with a grin. "In high school. I was the pitcher, she was the catcher. We had been friends for years, since grammar school."

"I bet you had a ball." Parker chuckled.

I nodded. "I did. Until, of course, the next season, when she decided to make the short stop her new best friend—and girlfriend. The bad thing was, she broke my heart. Just like you said, Blair, she was my first girlfriend. The good thing was, the speed of my delivery increased so much that she had to wear a glove on her catching hand, under her catcher's mitt. That resounding smack I heard every time I pitched to her helped me to get over her. And we won the state championship in our senior year."

"Now see," Parker said as she turned to Lindsey, "we've

just talked about all the places you can meet single women. In a bar. At work. At school. On a softball team. You've met someone before, and you'll meet someone again. That's what happens in the lesbian community."

The waitress arrived with our plates of food, and we watched as she served us.

"Let me ask you something, honey," Parker began as the woman set down the last plate. "Are you gay?"

The waitress peered at us over her glasses for a few seconds. "No," she finally answered.

"Okay. Just asking."

"Do you want anything else?"

"I think we're set," Blair told the waitress, then widened her eyes at Parker as the waitress left. "You can't just come out with a question like that to a perfect stranger!"

"I wasn't coming out." Parker grinned as she reached for the salt shaker.

"You know what I mean."

Parker shrugged her shoulders. "It doesn't hurt to ask. How else are you going to find out if a woman is, or isn't?"

"I think you should be in a situation where it's pretty much a given," Lindsey answered as she picked up her fork. "Like a bar."

"Honey, that woman is probably feeling pretty good about herself right now, thinking that four women were just hitting on her," Parker said as she doused her chef's salad with Russian dressing. "Anyway, you don't always meet someone in a bar. We've already established that. Each of you could meet your next lover in any number of places. I've hooked up with a nurse who was taking care of my uncle who had cancer, an airline stewardess on one of my European business flights, a customer in one of my stores, and yes, even a waitress. You never know when some woman is going to come into your life. So to speak. So you always have to keep your eyes open. And you can't be afraid to ask. I've certainly been lucky in that regard, and you guys can, too."

"Well, there is this court judge I kind of have a crush on," Lindsey admitted as her face reddened.

"So who's to say she's not gay?" Parker asked.

"She isn't wearing a wedding ring," Lindsey went on. "A couple of times I've walked out of court with her at the end of the day." Lindsey placed her fork on her plate and then sat back. "Now that I think of it, whenever she's the presiding judge on my cases I always seem to be scheduled as the last hearing of the day."

"Well, that should tell you something," Parker said.

"Huh," Lindsey grunted, then picked up her fork.

"Why don't you ask her out for coffee the next time you leave court with her?" Blair suggested.

"That's a good idea," I agreed.

"Tell her that you want to disrobe her." Parker chuckled. "You can ask her, 'So tell me. What do judges wear under their robes?' "

I smiled. "Maybe she's wearing a softball uniform."

"You never know if someone's playing on your team unless you check it out," Parker nodded. "That's the problem with most gay women. They wait for someone else to make the first move. I tell you, there are probably a whole lot of missed opportunities because of that. They see an attractive woman and rather than find out if she's interested, they keep waiting. Gay men just go for it. They make passes all the time."

"I don't think I'd know how to make a pass," Blair said. "I'm more, well, I'm more a waiter, I guess. I like to be asked out."

"Me, too." I nodded. "Until I get some sort of reciprocal interest expressed, I don't do a thing."

"Well, then, that'll be your assignment for the next time we get together," Parker announced. "Each of you should make a pass at a woman."

"A pass?" Blair asked.

"Ask them out on a date," Parker clarified.

"Oh, I don't know," Lindsey answered. "I took myself out of the dating pool several months ago. I don't think I have time to date anyone."

"Who's talking about time?" Parker asked. "It's just a date, not a lifelong commitment. See, that's where lesbians have it all wrong. You see someone once, and you think you're going to be walking down the aisle the next time you get together."

"I haven't been on a date in years," I added. "I don't think I'd know what to do."

"There's someone I like at work," Blair said. "But I don't know if she is. Gay, I mean. She might not be. But she always says hello to me in the morning. But perhaps that's because our classrooms are right across the hall. We can't help but see each other every day. But then there was this one time that she said she had run out of glue and she asked to borrow mine. And I told her I would get it for her. I brought it to her classroom some time later and put it on her desk—she wasn't there—but I noticed that she had a desk drawer open. I looked down, and there were *two* bottles of glue there. And they were full!"

"Well, there you go!" Parker said triumphantly. "She was probably just looking for an excuse to talk to you."

"Maybe," Blair responded. "But maybe she had just forgotten that she had two bottles of glue."

"I don't know if I can do this assignment," I said. "I work at home—I'm a freelance writer. I do all my business through phone calls, E-mails, or FedEx."

"Then get the hell out of the house," Parker advised. "You have to do the assignment. Everyone does."

"Except for you," Lindsey countered. "You already know how to pick someone up. I think your assignment should be that you wait for someone to ask you out."

Parker raised her eyebrows. "Me? Play the waiting game? Oh, I don't think so."

"I think so," I countered. "No, I *know* so. If you want each of us to do something we're not used to, then you have to do the same."

"I agree," Blair said. "We ask. You have to wait. It's only fair."

Lindsey nodded.

"Okay, okay," Parker gave in. "But does that mean I can't have sex with anyone until the next time we get together?"

"Not unless *she* asks *you* to bed," I answered.

"Me and my big mouth," Parker muttered, then waved her hand for the waitress. "Let's see what's on the dessert menu. I guess I'm going to have to get my oral gratification from somewhere else."

The Lesbian Dating Game: Who Asks Whom?

Why is it that lesbians can't be aggressive?

I don't mean on the softball field or on the basketball court. Nor do I mean in their professions or in setting limits with friends or family members.

I mean in getting up the courage to ask another woman out.

It took me ten years before I asked out a friend whom I was attracted to. It wasn't as if I were alone in my feelings; she had discussed her attraction to me on numerous occasions. But each time either one of us had brought up the topic, one or both of us had been involved with someone else.

I remember waking up one morning after months of being single—and after I had found out that she was also single— and thinking to myself, Okay. I'm going to ask her out. I *called her, we got together for dinner a few days later, and after dinner we took a walk.*

"So I've been thinking," I began.

"Yes?" she asked.

"Well, you know how when we first met you said you were interested in me, but you were in a relationship? And how I told you I was interested in you, but I was in a relationship as well?"

"Yes."

"And remember how we agreed that we weren't going to act on our attraction to each other as long as we were unavailable?"

"Yes."

"So," I began, then took a deep breath. "You're single now. I'm single now. And I've been thinking, maybe we should go out. You know, on a date. What do you think?"

"Yes," she answered.

And then I never heard from her again.

After a ten-year buildup and after assurances that, indeed, there was a reciprocal attraction, I had finally asked her out. And been given an affirmative response.

Followed by a rejection? Indecision? Fear? Second thoughts?

A yes *had turned into . . . well . . . nothing.*

What's up with that?

I know of other lesbians who tell me that there was clearly an attraction being expressed to them, but when they popped the dating question, they were told, "No, where did you ever get that idea?"

"Well, gee," they tell me they want to say to the woman, "perhaps from the more-than-a-friend kiss that you give me every time we say good-bye?"

What's up with that?

And I know of still other lesbians who have worked up the courage to ask someone out for coffee or dinner or whatever and are thinking in their minds when they're with this person that they're out on a date, only to discover that in the other woman's mind, it wasn't a date after all.

What's up with that?

I think the problem with women trying to ask out other women is that it's impossible to figure out what women want. There are no clear signals. There's no directness. Even when a hot, wet kiss is planted on your lips and you're thinking, "She wants to date me," you may later discover that what the woman wanted was simply to plant a single hot, wet kiss on you. Nothing more.

What the heck is up with that?

When a gay man asks another gay man out, the unspoken (or even spoken) sentiment is, "You want to have sex with me." When a straight man asks a woman out, the intention is also usually sex (although the woman often thinks, "He likes me. Maybe I'll marry him and bear his children.").

But how the hell does one lesbian say to another lesbian, "I want to date you?" Why is it that we can be assertive in coming out to friends, family, and colleagues, in going to bed with a woman, in renting a U-Haul and relocating our stuffed an-

imals to another location, and in making a commitment—
hell, even going through a commitment ceremony—but we
can't seem to work up the courage to ask a woman out on a
date?

I mean, is that too much to ask?

3

Dive into the Dating Pool
(Let's Get Soaking Wet!)

"I'm so confused," Lindsey announced as she joined Parker, Blair, and me at the crowded women's bar, Peppermint Patty's, where we had decided to meet a few weeks later. "Sam Adams," she told one of the bartenders, then stretched her neck from side to side and groaned. She turned to us. "Have you been waiting long?"

"Two drinks," Parker answered as she held up her empty cocktail glass and waved it at another bartender.

"Which translates into half a drink for me," I answered.

"I guess I'll order something to drink now," Blair said. "I wanted to wait until everyone was here."

"What'll it be?" Lindsey asked her.

"Um . . . Chardonnay, I think."

"And a Cardonnay," Lindsey called out to the bartender.

"What are you confused about?" I asked Lindsey.

"The judge," Lindsey answered as she tipped her head once more from side to side, then dropped a ten-dollar bill on the counter. She hefted the frosted mug and downed a few gulps of beer, then handed Blair's drink to her.

"Let's grab that corner table," Parker suggested as she swung off the bar stool and grabbed her third martini. Without waiting for a response, she forged a determined path through the shoulder-to-shoulder after-work crowd of professional women to the table. She reached the table at the same time as another group, glared at them, then pulled out a chair in front of them and sat down with her back to the women.

The group frowned at her, then turned on their heels.

We held back to see how Parker's encounter with the group would play out, then sat down around the table.

Parker raised her glass. "To getting together again," she toasted.

We clinked glasses, drank, then looked at Lindsey.

"So what are you confused about?" I asked her.

Lindsey shook her head, raised her hands in the air, then shook her head again.

"What?" Blair asked.

"So a few days after we last got together, there I am, outside the judge's chambers, waiting for her to come out, right?" she began.

"Literally, or figuratively?" Parker chuckled.

Lindsey showed Parker a grimace. "I was going to follow through on the agreement we made last time. I was going to ask her out. I figured I'd suggest coffee, or maybe a drink. But I was wondering if I should suggest a drink, since I know her professionally. As I'm going back and forth with this—coffee, drink, coffee, drink—she comes out—uh, walks out of her office—locks her door, turns and sees me sitting on the bench outside her office, and says, 'It's about time you showed up to see me.' "

"So she was interested in dating you, too," I said.

"Not necessarily," Lindsey replied. "You've got to hear the whole story. So I start to ask if she wants to grab a cup of coffee, and she turns to me, places a finger on my lips, and says, 'No words.' She presses the elevator button. The doors open, and we get onto the elevator in silence. We ride down five floors, again in silence. Then we walk out into the parking garage together. There are a few cars here and there, but pretty much it's deserted. So she says, 'Walk me to my car,' and I do. We stop by a black BMW. 'Get in the back,' she tells me as she unlocks the front door. I'm thinking to myself, *Get in the back? What's that all about?* But I do. So she follows me into the backseat, slams her door shut, and lunges at me."

"She punches you?" Blair exclaimed.

Lindsey shot Blair an impatient look. "She didn't *punch* me. She *lunged* at me. With her mouth. She put it on my mouth. No, wait. She *clamped* it on my mouth. Like she was one of those . . . those . . . what are those creatures called that suck right onto you?"

"Ticks?" Blair asked.

"No."

"Mosquitos?" I suggested.

"No, no."

"Leeches," Parker pronounced. She drained her cocktail glass, then plopped the green olive into her mouth.

"Exactly!" Lindsey exclaimed. She held one hand up in the air. "See? This is me. La, la, la, I'm in the backseat of the Beemer, minding my own business. And then," she said as she slapped her other hand onto the raised palm, "wham! The woman has locked her lips onto mine. I'm pressed against the door clear on the other side of the car, half lying down, half sitting up."

"What did you do?" Blair asked.

"What *could* I do?" Lindsey replied. "I was trapped. By this black-robed leech."

"She was still wearing her robe?" I asked.

Lindsey shook her head. "No, no. I was just saying that for effect."

"What was she wearing?" asked Blair.

"Who gives a shit what she was wearing?" Parker broke in. "So she's got you in a lip lock . . ." she prompted Lindsey.

"Right." Lindsey nodded. "And on top of that she rammed her tongue into my mouth and nearly down my throat. And she's squeezing my breasts. *Hard.* Like they're some sort of fruit in a market. All the while she's moaning, 'Do me. Do me.' "

"Oh, my," Blair declared. "Right then and there I would've slapped her and said—"

"I couldn't say a word," Lindsey broke in. "Remember? She had her mouth clamped on mine."

"Well, then I'd slap her," Blair continued.

"It happened too damn fast for me to react at all," Lindsey responded. "I mean, a few minutes earlier I had been think-ing—remember?—coffee or drink, coffee or drink. And then she's got her tongue rammed down my throat and has her hands gripped like vises around my breasts."

"Sounds like fun." Parker grinned.

"So what did you do?" I asked.

"What did I *do*?" Lindsey echoed. "I didn't have time to do anything, because then . . . well . . . um . . . a few minutes later . . . it was over."

"Here comes da judge." Parker laughed.

Blair stared at Parker. "What do you mean?"

"What I mean, oh, sweet, innocent one, is that the judge came," Parker explained. "As in, 'Oh, baby, do me, that's right, that's right, that feels good, oh, yeah, I'm coming, I'm coming—' "

"She *came*?" Blair cut in. "But how—?"

"Friction, Blair. Friction," I told her.

Lindsey shook her head. "What's up with that? I realize she's got my leg between hers and she's . . . she's . . . well, she's . . ."

"Humping it?" Parker asked.

Lindsey nodded.

"My goodness," Blair gasped, then took a quick sip of her drink.

"Goodness my ass," Lindsey hissed. "She comes while she's humping my leg and squeezing my tits so hard I thought they were going to pop. All the time with her goddamned tongue down my throat. I thought I was going to gag. And then she says, 'Okay, babes. Gotta go. Catch ya later.' "

"Huh?" I grunted in question.

"She said what?" Blair asked.

"Quote . . . 'Okay, babes. Gotta go. Catch ya later.' End quote," Lindsey answered.

"Well, that's kind of—" I began.

"Cheap," Blair broke in.

"Hot," Parker said at the same time.

"Disgusting!" Lindsey spat out, then took a swig of her beer. "I went home and brushed my teeth for half an hour. And brushed my tongue. I used half a bottle of mouthwash. I mean, really! After she spoke to me in the car, I just sat there—well, kind of lay there—staring at her in disbelief about what had just happened."

"All you wanted was coffee," Blair pointed out.

Lindsey nodded. "So she pats me on the leg and says, 'No time for you now. I gotta get home to my *girlfriend.*' I emphasize that because I want to be certain that you've all heard that. Let me repeat it. She had to get home to her *girlfriend.*"

"Well, you know the name of that game," Parker said.

"Cheat, cheat, never beat," Blair chanted.

Parker shook her head. "She's not a cheater. It doesn't matter that she has a girlfriend. Because in her mind, what she did with Lindsey wasn't cheating."

"Of course it was," Blair disagreed. "She came when—"

"She came without getting naked," Parker cut in. "She came without Lindsey touching her. Without Lindsey actually making love to her. In her mind, that's not cheating. That would be like getting off by yourself. It's just taking care of business. Lindsey didn't even have to be there."

Lindsey slumped a bit in her seat. "Thanks, Parker."

"That sucks," Blair commented.

"But she still *had sex* with another woman," I argued.

Parker shook her head. "Counselor, answer this question," she said as she looked at Lindsey. "Did you, or did you not, have *sexual relations* with that woman?"

"Why does this sound familiar?" Blair asked, then nodded. "Oh, yeah. Mr. Wild Bill."

"I don't know how to answer that," Lindsey replied.

"Neither did he," I commented.

"Counselor, I asked you a yes-or-no question," Parker persisted. "You need to tell me, 'Yes, I had sexual relations with that woman,' or 'No, I did not have sexual relations with that woman.'"

"I say yes," I answered for Lindsey. "Doesn't ramming your tongue down someone's throat and feeling them up qualify—"

Parker held up a finger. "No, no, no, that's not what I'm asking here," she said. "I asked Lindsey if she did or did not have sexual relations with that woman."

"It doesn't matter what Lindsey says," Blair pointed out. "The person who should really be answering that question is the judge."

"That's correct!" Parker beamed at Blair. "Because, you see, it really doesn't matter what Lindsey says. What matters is what that woman tells her girlfriend—if she tells her anything at all. It's what *she* believes in her mind happened. And Lindsey didn't touch her. Lindsey didn't make love to her. Lindsey was just a presence, a warm body—all that woman needed to get off."

"Gosh, I'm just feeling better and better," Lindsey moaned, then downed the rest of her beer.

"It's going to really suck the next time you see the judge in court," I pointed out.

Lindsey sighed, then sat back in her chair and crossed her arms. "Well, see. It didn't end there in the Beemer that night."

"What do you mean?" Blair asked.

"You see, I wanted to talk to her," Lindsey answered. "Of course I did. You can see that. I wanted to talk to her, to figure out what had gone on. I had . . . well . . . the car thing happened on Friday. I had all weekend to think about it. You know. To run it over and over in my mind. And it brought up some stuff for me. I wanted to tell her how I felt."

"Why do lesbians always have to talk about how they feel?" Parker asked as she shook her head. "They're always feeling mad, sad, happy, glad, pissed, horny, rejected, dejected, hurt—"

"Parker, we get the point," Blair cut in.

"—hungry, tired, needy, lonely, scared—"

"We get the point, Parker," I echoed.

"Okay, okay," she said, then flagged the attention of a nearby waitress. She made a circle with her hand to indicate another round of drinks.

"I think it's good to talk things out," Blair commented. "I would want to do the same thing, Lindsey. To talk it out with her. To figure out together what went on."

"What's to figure out?" Parker asked. "The judge saw, conquered, and came." She turned to me. "What about you, Gracy?

Let's process how you would *feel* if the situation had happened to you."

I shrugged my shoulders. "I guess if that had happened to me, I wouldn't want to see her again. And I'd pretty much figure that she wouldn't want to see me, either. It sounds like it might be an embarrassing situation. For both people."

"So you'd just let it go," Parker concluded. "Good for you."

"I didn't say I'd let it go," I corrected her. "It would really bother me. By the time Monday rolled around, though, I'd probably be pissed that she had taken advantage of me."

"That's how I felt," Lindsey said. "That was the stuff I was talking about. I'm tired of being taken advantage of in my relationships. I'm always the one giving, and my lover is always the one receiving. And I don't just mean in bed. But no matter. I didn't want to show the judge I was angry, even though I was. I just wanted to talk to her, to kind of smooth things over so there wouldn't be any hard feelings, any difficulties when we saw each other. I mean, she's a judge. I have to face her in court when she presides over my cases. I'm walking a fine line here."

"Honey, you're not walking any line," Parker sniffed, then placed her elbows on the table and rested her chin on her hands. "You're being led around on a leash by someone who has power over you, control over you." She sighed. "It's kind of erotic."

"Oh, please!" Blair moaned.

"Are you begging me?" Parker grinned at Blair.

"So you got together with her on Monday?" I broke in before Blair could reply.

Lindsey nodded. "And Tuesday. And Wednesday. And—"

"You what?" I nearly shouted.

"Good for you, girlfriend!" Parker beamed.

"Are you *crazy*, Lindsey?" Blair asked. "I mean, it sounds like you're getting involved with this woman. A woman who isn't available to you."

"It sounds like she's very available if she got together with you that much," Parker commented.

"Okay. Let me tell you what I was thinking," Lindsey began.

"It doesn't sound like you were thinking at all," Blair cut in.

"Things got hotter, right?" Parker asked, then pulled a twenty out of her purse and dropped it on the waitress's tray. The waitress set the next round of drinks on the table.

Lindsey ran a hand through her hair, then cradled her beer mug. "See, here's the thing. It's been a long time for me. You know. Being with someone. The judge is the first person who's shown an interest in me in years. And she touched me."

"She practically raped you," Blair pointed out.

"Which is even more erotic." Parker grinned. "It's like a women-in-prison scenario. I acted that out once with someone. It was a pretty intense—"

"Will you *stop!*" Blair cut her off.

"But she has a girlfriend," I protested.

"That's what I wanted to talk to her about," Lindsey answered. "I was wondering why she did what she did with me. So on Monday, I waited outside her chambers again. She steps out, sees me, and gives me this big smile. She shifts her head to the side and nods, indicating that she wants me to come in her office."

"So did you come in her office?" Parker chuckled.

Lindsey sighed and looked down at her drink.

"Oh, Lindsey!" Blair exclaimed. "What were you thinking?"

"In her office?" I asked. "Isn't there something ethically wrong with that?"

"Of course there is," Lindsey snapped.

"And that's what made it exciting, am I right?" Parker asked.

Lindsey raised her head and looked at Parker. A smile slowly formed on her face. "Oh, yeah. It made it *damn* exciting. Each time we're together, we do a little bit more. One late afternoon she called me on my cell phone as I was leaving the office. She said, 'I want you in my office *now,* Counselor.' So I went there. Knocked on the door. I didn't hear anything, so I knocked again. And then I turned the knob. The door was open. She was sitting behind her desk in her robe. She says, 'Lock the door, Counselor.' So I do. I turn back around to face her, and she has her robe open. And she has nothing on underneath the robe. She sits back in her leather chair, then slowly drapes a leg over each arm of the chair."

"I can't believe this," Blair moaned. "She's going to hurt you, Lindsey."

"Who cares?" Lindsey replied. "This is the hottest sex I've ever had."

"So what did you do when she was in the chair?" Parker asked as she leaned forward.

"I don't think we need to hear that," Blair commented. "Do we, Gracy?"

I opened my mouth, then shrugged my shoulders. "I'm kind of curious. The legal profession has always interested me."

Lindsey leaned forward and rapped a finger against the table. "I . . . went . . . down . . . on . . . her!"

I sucked in a quick breath of air, then took a sip of my drink.

"And then what happened?" Parker asked as she licked her full, flaming-red lips.

"Then she turns me around, pushes me against her desk, and pulls down my pants," Lindsey whispered. "She opens a desk drawer, reaches in, takes out a dildo—"

"TMI, TMI," Blair broke in as she placed her hands over her ears.

"The old dildo-in-the-drawer trick." Parker chuckled.

"What's TMI?" I asked Blair.

"Too much information," she answered. "I think we get the point, Lindsey."

"It . . . was . . . amazing!" Lindsey exclaimed.

"So what else have you done with her?" Parker asked.

"I think we get the *point*," Blair reiterated as she glared at Parker, then turned back to Lindsey. "You're continuing to have hot sex with a woman who's essentially your boss—"

"She's essentially God, in my profession," Lindsey broke in.

"Oh, that's even better," Blair muttered. "So you're having hot sex with the top of the organizational chart, who also has a girlfriend, who you claim pretty much took advantage of you in the backseat of a car in a garage owned by the State. Oh, and you also had sex with her in a courthouse, which was built and is operated by the Massachusetts taxpayers' money. Am I leaving anything out?"

Lindsey thought for a moment. "No. That's pretty much it."

"You do realize, Lindsey, that this woman is a dead-end street," I said.

"Oh, but what a street to be stuck on." Parker laughed.

"I can't have sex with someone unless I love them," Blair huffed. "Not that I'm judging you, Lindsey—"

"No pun intended," I joked.

"So I gather you haven't had sex since the New Year's Eve party," Parker said to Blair.

"No," she answered. "But I did ask someone out. As we *agreed*," she emphasized, glaring at Lindsey.

"Did you ask out that teacher at your school?" I asked Blair.

"Glue girl?" Parker grinned.

"Yes," Blair said. "And her name is Julia."

"So what did you do on your first date with Miss Julia?" Parker asked. "Make collages?"

Blair again glared at Parker. "No. We had coffee after work." Blair met Lindsey's eyes. "*Coffee*. And we *talked*. I don't think you know what that is, Lindsey. Or you, Parker. But it's when two people have a conversation and exchange information. So you can get to know one another."

"It sounds pretty boring," Parker commented, then faked a yawn.

Blair turned away from Parker. "Julia is a very nice person. And we have a lot in common, too. We had a wonderful conversation. A couple of days later, we had dinner out at a nice restaurant in Scituate. Right by the ocean. It was very romantic."

"Did you kiss her?" Parker asked.

"No, I did not kiss her," Blair replied. "Just because something's romantic doesn't mean it has to lead to something physical."

"So how long does it take you to actually kiss someone you're dating?" Parker asked. "A year? Two years? A decade?"

"For your information, we kissed on our third date. We went to see a movie. And no, Parker, it wasn't an erotic film. It was a beautiful French film that we had both wanted to see. We went out for dessert and coffee afterward—"

"And you talked some more," Parker mumbled as she tapped her lacquered fingernails impatiently on the tabletop.

"Yes, we talked some more," Blair responded. "Then I drove her home. I kissed her in the car before she got out."

"How 1950s." Lindsey grinned. "But I hope you both had protection. I hear that kissing with your mouth open—"

"Stop picking on Blair," I snapped at Lindsey. "I think her dates with Julia sound nice. I wish someone would take the time to get to know me—wish I could do the same with her—before we hopped into bed."

"It sounds pretty dull," Parker commented as she stretched her arms out and emitted a satisfied groan. "I prefer the physical to happen right away. And I rather that the only oral thing on a date be sex."

"Julia and I are not going to *have sex*," Blair told Parker. "If or when we do go to bed, we'll be *making love*."

"Will I still be alive then?" Parker asked. "I mean, I might live for another forty years or so, but I just want to be sure I'll be around *if and when* you and Julia make that big decision. We could throw you a party afterward. An I-finally-came party."

Blair stared at Parker. "You may think I'm old-fashioned or out of step with the times or whatever," she finally said to her. "But I don't admire anyone—man or woman—who looks at women or treats women as sex objects. Being a lesbian doesn't mean having sex with women. That's just part of it. Being a lesbian, to me, means loving another woman—loving other women. When was the last time you loved a woman, Parker?" she asked. "Wasn't it in the eighties?"

"Ye-ow!" Lindsey growled.

Parker slowly licked an index finger, then lowered it in the air. "Point for you, Miss Brown."

"I think Julia sounds nice," I told Blair. "Was it hard getting up the courage to ask her out?"

Blair stuck out her tongue at Parker, then turned to me. "It was. But I think it was good that we had this little assignment. I know I wouldn't have done anything if I hadn't gotten the push from this group. I knew I couldn't chicken out, because then what would I have to tell you guys?"

"Maybe something more interesting than your three dates with Glue Girl," Parker suggested.

"Oh, enough, Parker," Lindsey said. "I'm jealous, Blair. I wish I could be dating the judge, getting to know her, instead of—"

"Be serious, Lindsey!" Parker protested. "Hot sex is much better than sitting down over a cup of coffee and jawing."

"Well, I like it," Blair sniffed at Parker. "Maybe if you gave yourself a chance with someone, to really get to know her and to actually let her in your life so she could get to know you, you wouldn't still be hanging onto Ana Maria and your broken heart. I mean, how many centuries ago was that?"

Lindsey looked at Blair, then at Parker. "Are those fightin' words I hear?"

Parker crossed her arms and stared at Blair.

"I mean, get over it, Parker," she added.

Parker raised an eyebrow at Blair. "So your evil twin, Nancy Nasty, has surfaced."

"Hey, you started attacking me first, for who I am and how I do things," Blair responded. "I may be nice and polite and all that, but don't cross me. I'm a teacher. And teachers don't take shit from anyone."

Parker stared at Blair.

I laughed. "This just in, folks. Blair Brown has effectively silenced Parker Lowell. Details at eleven."

"So you think I should fall in love again and get my heart broken?" Parker asked Blair.

"The two don't necessarily go hand-in-hand," Blair replied. "You can fall in love. Period. A broken heart may or may not happen. But it's not a given, like you think it is. Having sex may feel good, Parker, but who's there when you want someone to talk to? Who's there when you just want to hang out? Or be held?"

"Okay, okay, Tiger," Parker said. "You can back off now. I get your point."

"You do your things your way," Blair continued. "I'll do things my way."

"Well, I tried your way," Parker told her, then looked around at us. "Yes, I did, folks. I did my assignment. What do you think about that?"

"What did you do?" Lindsey asked.

"I did not—I repeat—I did not ask anyone out since we met at the party. In fact, someone I had sex with in the past, who I guess really liked me for some strange reason and wanted to do that dating thing you're talking about, Blair, called me. She wanted to get together for dinner. And so we went out to dinner. At the end of the night, she went her way and I went mine."

"Good for you!" Blair said.

"But I'm still horny as hell," Parker muttered.

"Did you enjoy going out to dinner with her?" Blair asked.

Parker thought for a moment. "I guess. I mean, it was okay. It wasn't uncomfortable. It was, well, it was nice, I guess."

"So would you go out with her again?" I asked.

"I don't know," Parker said, then shook her head. "I think she really likes me."

"So?" Blair asked.

"What's not to like?" Lindsey added. "You're attractive, outgoing, humorous, rich—"

Parker flipped her hair back from her face, then held up a hand. "Okay, okay. Enough. We'll see. Now what happened with you, Gracy?"

I laughed. "You wouldn't believe it. Because I didn't."

"Tell us!" Blair encouraged.

"Well, I told you guys that I don't have much contact with people, since I work at home," I began. "I didn't know who I could ask out on a date. So I decided to look at personal ads." I immediately held up a hand. "I know, I know. We already talked about it. I went on-line to planetout.com. I looked through the ads and found someone I was interested in. So we started writing. This was maybe a day or so after the party. We wrote to each other every day, sometimes twice a day. Then she suggested we get together. We arranged to meet at a coffee shop in Cambridge—"

"What is it with you guys and coffee?" Parker cut in.

"Go on," Blair said.

"I get to the shop about fifteen minutes before the time I'm supposed to meet this woman," I continued. "All I know about her, besides the things we chatted about through our E-mails, is a basic physical description. Height. Weight. Hair color. Eye color. And she has the same information about me. I walk into the shop and spot my ex sitting at a table. I think, *This could be awkward*, because I haven't seen her since we broke up a couple of years ago, and it wasn't a very good breakup. In fact, she cheated on me and left me to be with this other woman. Who was a close friend of ours. But that's another story."

"That's the usual story, isn't it?" Lindsey asked.

I nodded. "I guess. Anyway, she recognizes me and waves a hand, so I go to her table and sit down. We chat for a bit. After a few minutes, I'm looking at my watch. She's looking at hers. I tell her I have to meet someone. She says the same thing—"

"Oh, no!" Blair cut in.

"Oh, yes," I answered with a grin. "It turns out we were waiting for each other."

"What did you do?" Lindsey asked.

"We sat and had coffee together," I answered.

Parker rolled her eyes. "Of course."

"And we had a really nice conversation," I continued. "We took a long walk afterward. As we said good-bye, she asked if she could call me. If we could get together again. It turns out the woman she dumped me for dumped her a few months after they had been together. She said she never should have done that to me and knew she had really hurt me. She told me that she had been alone ever since to kind of get herself together, and was only now feeling like she could date again."

"Was it nice to hear that she felt bad about dumping you?" Blair asked.

I nodded. "It was. And it was kind of nice knowing she got as hurt by someone else as I had by her. Not that I wish hurt upon anyone. But when someone puts the screws to you, sometimes it's a good feeling when you know that they've gotten a firsthand taste of what they did to you."

"What goes around, comes around," Lindsey quoted.

"So how did you leave things with her?" Parker asked.

"She asked if I wanted to go with her to a Boston University women's basketball game," I replied. "She used to play for the Terriers. So I told her, sure. Last week she called and told me the Terriers were playing my alma mater, UMaine. So we're going to the game this weekend."

"Oh, that's nice," Blair said. "A real date."

I smiled. "What makes it even better is that the Black Bears are undefeated this season. They'll probably trounce the Terriers, which will make me very happy."

"Well, we've all taken a dive in the dating pool," Parker concluded. "Of course, some of us have gotten wetter than others," she added, nodding at Lindsey. "But we've all taken that first step."

"Now what?" Lindsey asked.

"I think you should stop seeing the judge," I suggested.

"I don't," Parker said. "What's the harm? It's just sex."

"Well . . ." Lindsey began, then stopped.

Parker stared at her. "No! Don't tell me you're falling in love with her!"

"We see each other every day," Lindsey said defensively.

"How can she do that—and have a girlfriend?" I asked.

Lindsey shrugged her shoulders. "I don't know. But she does. And she sometimes buys me flowers or—"

"But how long will that last?" Blair asked. "I mean, after a while, the sex with her is going to grow old. As is the knowledge that she's going home every night to be with someone else."

Lindsey shrugged her shoulders. "Maybe by that time, she'll want to be with me. You know, *really* be with me."

"Oh, I don't know that those relationships work out," I said. "Look what happened to my ex. She dumped me for someone who only dumped her."

"Do you guys even talk when you're together?" Blair asked Lindsey.

"Not really."

"Do you go out with her and do things, like dinner or the movies?" I asked.

Lindsey shook her head.

"Then all it is *is* sex," Parker pointed out. "She just wants you for hot times. I doubt it's going to go anywhere else."

Blair nodded. "I agree. So if you're starting to feel for her, Lindsey, I say get out now while you can. Before you really get hurt."

"Ask someone else out," I suggested.

Lindsey ran her fingers through her hair. "Okay. I've heard what you had to say. Now let's talk about something else. Like when we're going to get together again. What we're going to do."

"I have a suggestion," Blair answered. "I want you all to save the last Saturday of the month. The women's center where I volunteer is having an all-day event, with workshops, crafts sales, music, food, and dancing. It's a benefit we hold each year to raise money for battered women's shelters around the city. I'd like you all to come with me." Blair paused, then glared at Parker. "To the event," she clarified.

Parker grinned and punched her lightly on the arm. "Okay, Cookie Pie. I'll be there."

"But it may not be your cup of tea, Parker," Blair added. "So I'll totally understand if you want to blow it off. I mean, it's kind of a mix of earthy crunchy lesbians and political dykes and New Age spiritual—"

"I said I'd be there, Snookums." Parker grinned.

Blair looked at her in surprise. "You will?"

"Don't you know who one of the major sponsors of your event has been for the past five years?" Parker asked.

Blair thought for a moment, then smiled. "Pier Lowell!"

"See, I'm not such a bad girl after all," she said, then grinned at Lindsey. "I'm nothing like Lindsey, the Lustful Lawyer."

"Oh, shut up," Lindsey muttered. "I only did what we agreed to do."

"We didn't tell you to boink a judge," I argued.

Blair wagged a finger at her. "Don't you be playing the

blame game with us, Lindsey. We asked you to find someone to date, not a fuck mate."

"Oh, my!" Parker exclaimed, then fanned her face. "Such language! It hurts my tender little ears."

"And I don't want you to bring the judge to this event," Blair said. "It's just going to be us girls."

"Girls?" Parker asked.

Blair waved a hand in the air. "Women. Just us girls. I mean women. Oh, you know what I mean."

Which Comes First: Sex, or Love?

Here's a question that's sure to stump most lesbians. Which happens first: falling in lust with someone, or falling in love? Some might argue that falling in love comes first, but women usually say that after *they've come with someone. And others will say, "It's the sex, baby," that has opened their hearts to feeling love for a person.*

After all, what makes two women want to start seeing each other as more than friends? It's invariably all about the physical attraction, which oftentimes negates any serious, analytical consideration about whether or not she'll be loyal, she'll take care of you, she'll keep a nice home, she has a good job, she'll always be there for you, she's someone your parents will like, and so on.

Here's what it all boils down to, then. Someone looks good to you, you look good to her, and the seeds of desire are planted. There's the desire to caress, to touch, to taste, to feel, to possess. So you start to see one another and get to know one another, with the ultimate goal of, hopefully, going to bed together. Sometimes that happens within an hour, but if not then, at least by the end of the week.

And then, usually at the moment you cry out, "Oh, God!" you fall in love.

To those of you who would protest this conclusion, who would say in no uncertain terms that you have to love a woman before you go to bed with her, I submit the following scenario. Two women meet online. They strike up an E-mail communication that lasts for months. Now let's just say that they are separated by a wide geographical distance that restricts their meeting up too quickly. After a while, they exchange phone numbers. They have wonderful conversations. Maybe, sometime after that point, one woman asks for the other woman's picture. They exchange photos via computer, and then the communication ceases from one person.

What's happened to that wonderful exchange they established in the past?

It's all about the physical attraction. Call it chemistry, if that makes you feel better. But to love someone, you have to lust for her. Lust, therefore, sets the stage for the potential of love.

But maybe, just maybe, there's another scenario. Maybe, like the great debate about which came first, the chicken or the egg, there's no way to truly distinguish which one must happen before *the other. Maybe lust grows love and love grows lust, at the same time. With that first brief brush of a hand against your arm—a brush that makes your hair stand on end and your heart beat faster—the seeds of love as well as the seeds of lust can be sown.*

Perhaps this is that thing called chemistry*—the subject that flummoxed you in school and still flummoxes you as you try to understand the role it plays in influencing an attraction to someone.*

So, in the garden of your heart, perhaps both lust and love can flourish. Hopefully, when the lustful desires weaken—as they so often do—the feelings of love will grow. But since that's not always the case, another debate is opened: which leaves first, the love or the lust?

Ah. Now that's a question for another day.

4

Secrets of the La-La Lesbian Sisterhood (Sisterhood Is Sumptin' Powerful!)

An hour before the start of Saturday's Righting Womyn's Wrongs Conference, three of us stood near the end of a long line of women—and a few brave men—that snaked several blocks from the entrance of the large high school auditorium, where the conference was to be held. We were waiting for Blair to show up with our all-day guest passes, and she was already a half hour late.

Parker cupped a Starbucks to-go large coffee underneath her nostrils and breathed in deeply and noisily. "French vanilla," she cooed in pleasure, then moved the cup away from her nose and took in a deep breath. "Patchouli," she determined as she wrinkled her nose. "Unbelievable! Don't lesbians know that there's a world of exquisite perfumes to choose from?"

"Yeah, at fifty dollars a pop," Lindsey commented as she shoved her hands deep into the pockets of her black jeans. "I'm a CK gal myself."

"I wear patchouli," I confessed.

"Yes, you *wear* it, Gracy," Parker answered. "But there's a difference between wearing it and taking a bath in it. *Every day.*" She sniffed the air around her. "I don't know. Maybe for lesbians patchouli courses through their bodies like garlic does. It just oozes out of their pores." She took another sip of her coffee. "Ah!"

A woman who was standing in line ahead of us turned

around to look at Parker. She glanced at the coffee cup. "I see you're drinking Starbucks coffee," she commented with a stern expression on her thin, pale face.

"Yes," Parker replied as she raised her eyebrows and peered down at the anorexic-looking woman, who was standing just shy of five feet tall and had a short buzz cut. "And I see you're wearing some sort of wrap."

The woman tightened her lips and flared the nostrils of her large nose. "It's called a magicka mai-mai. It's a traditional female dress from Guatemala. It's made of all-natural hemp and colored with dyes derived naturally from forest plants."

"In-ter-est-ing," Parker answered slowly. "Fashion with a history. I'm wearing an oh-my-my, feels-so-good-against-my-skin silk blouse and skirt imported from China."

"Made from exploited silkworms and underpaid women and children, I imagine," the woman sniffed. "As I mentioned, my dress is totally biodegradable."

"Then I guess you could probably eat it, too," Parker replied. "Or just wear it until it—poof!—disappears into thin air."

Lindsey let out a quick snort, then glimpsed the woman's tense expression and quickly cleared her throat.

"What plants make clothes dyes?" I asked the woman.

The woman tightened her lips. "I really don't think you'd be much interested in that."

"Well, if I wasn't interested, I wouldn't have asked," I countered.

The woman slowly took in the three of us and perused the outfits we were wearing. I had on a pair of khaki pants and a black cotton shirt, just the opposite color combo of Lindsey, who had on a tan shirt with her black jeans.

"There's nothing natural about what any of you have on," the woman concluded. "Like that's a big surprise. But if you're really as interested as you say you are about the issue of natural wear, you can certainly attend The Politics of Clothing seminar that's being offered today."

"I didn't know clothing had politics," Lindsey said, then grinned at me. "I wonder how the clothes I'm wearing would vote in the next election." She looked down at her pants. "Are you for or against an estate tax, Levis?"

I laughed and answered "Against" in a high-pitched voice.

"Republicans wear red, Democrats wear blue, and Independents wear white," Parker joked. "And, of course, the Green Party wears green."

The woman stared stone-faced at us.

Parker flittered a hand breezily in the air. "Oh, lighten up, honey. It was just a joke."

"I'm not your honey," the woman hissed through clenched teeth.

"Quite truthfully, that's fine by me," Parker replied.

"Whatever," the woman snapped. "But I think you need to hear what I have to say about the cup of Starbucks coffee you have in your hand."

"Do I have a choice?"

"There's a Starbucks about six blocks from here," Lindsey told the woman.

"I know where Starbucks *is*," the woman replied. "It's *her* coffee that concerns me."

"What did she say?" I asked Lindsey.

"Parker's coffee concerns this woman," Lindsey replied, then frowned. "Whatever that means."

The woman sneered at Lindsey. "I'll tell you what it means. I was one of the founders of the Boston-area protest against Starbucks last year," she boasted as she latched a hand onto her hip. "I'm sure you all saw the coverage of the protest in the *Boston Globe*."

"You must really hate coffee," Lindsey commented.

"Starbucks also sells tea," I pointed out. "Do you hate tea, too?"

Parker shook her head. "I don't really like hot tea. But I like iced tea."

Lindsey nodded. "Me, too. I like it with a little lemon and a lot of—"

"Hello?" the woman cut in with a wave of her arm. "I was talking here. Our protest was integral to raising consumer consciousness about Starbucks coffee," she forged ahead. "We've used the coverage we received in the *Globe* on our Web site and in many of our fliers."

"Well, good for you," Parker sniffed. "I guess I missed that issue. I might have used it to line my canary's cage." Parker then turned away from the woman and flashed Lindsey and me an expression that roughly translated into, *How do I get rid of this gnat?*

"What were you protesting?" Lindsey asked.

"Don't encourage her," Parker muttered.

The woman expelled an exaggerated sigh of exasperation and slowly shook her head. "Don't you women know that Starbucks is a *coffee colossus* that *exploits* people?"

Lindsey extracted a hand from her pocket and scratched her head. "Well, its prices are a little steep compared to other—"

"I'm not talking about what they're *charging* consumers," the woman cut in, then wagged a finger in the air at us. "I'm talking about the fact that they don't buy coffee beans from eco-friendly farmers who can then earn a living wage. By the year 2006, Starbucks plans to have its cash registers open at 10,000 more stores in sixty countries. Starbucks is one of the *prime offenders.*"

"Of what?" I asked.

"Not you, too," Parker mumbled, then took a sip of her coffee and stepped closer to me. "This woman is like the house pest—I mean, guest—who never leaves."

The woman emitted an impatient sigh. "Okay. I can see I have neophytes here. So let me say this in a way you all will understand."

Parker turned to her. "Oh, I love a woman who talks down to me," she sneered.

The woman ignored her. "Starbucks subordinates life values to commerce."

"Don't most businesses?" Lindsey countered. "I mean, the point to making money is to buy product as cheaply as possible and then turn it around for a profit."

"Why are you even bothering to engage this woman in conversation?" Parker asked Lindsey.

Lindsey shrugged her shoulders. "I enjoy a good argument."

"Who are you, the CEO of some wallet-sucking company?" the woman asked.

"I'm a lawyer," Lindsey snapped.

The woman raised both hands in the air. "Oh, well, that's just as exploitive. Your kind *sucks* bank accounts dry."

"My kind?" Lindsey echoed. "Listen, you little piece of—"

"I wonder where Blair is," I cut in as I grabbed Lindsey's arm, pulled it up, and glanced at her wristwatch. "She should be here any minute."

Parker took a long, slow, noisy sip of her coffee as she locked eyes with the woman. Then she smacked her lips. "And this . . . this subordination," she began. "This affects me how?"

The woman's eyes narrowed. "*You* should *not* be buying coffee from Starbucks. Can I make that any plainer?"

Parker smiled at the woman and shot her a quick wink. "Is that because *you* want to buy *me* coffee from Starbucks? I know that's what lesbians like to do."

The woman rapped a knuckle against Parker's coffee container, nearly knocking it out of her hands. "*No one* should be buying this brew of exploitation!"

"Hey!" Parker shouted at the woman.

"Now there's a flavor I haven't heard of." I chuckled nervously.

Parker straightened up to her full height and looked down at the shorter woman. "First of all, *honey,* take your finger off my coffee and put it away. Who knows whose nose you've been sticking that finger into besides mine. *Honey.* And, second of all, I can buy my coffee anywhere I want. Without your permission."

The woman started to wag her finger in the air, then looked at it and lowered her hand. "That's just the kind of attitude I'd expect from you."

"And who am I to you exactly?" Parker challenged as she took a step toward the woman.

"This is getting a little blown out of propor—" I began.

"You are part of the spendthrift population who doesn't give *a shit* where your high-end merchandise comes from, just as long as you can get what you want when you want it," the woman responded in an angry tone. Then she leaned forward and raised herself up on her toes in an attempt to place her face inches away from Parker's.

"Okay, okay," Lindsey broke in. "I think this has gone far—"

"Do you realize that I could effectively stomp you into the ground in these Ann & Taylor all-leather sandals," Parker sizzled between clenched teeth. "But I paid a lot of money for these, and I wouldn't want to get them soiled with your all-natural hemp bull—"

"I'd like to see you try it, you overpaid, overdressed—"

"Ladies, ladies, listen up," I cut in. "Maybe you both should—"

"Hey, look, Coffee Cop," Lindsey interrupted as she tapped the woman's shoulder and pointed to some lesbians who were crossing the street to join the line. "They're all drinking Starbucks coffee. Why don't you go and harass them?"

"In due time, you will all understand what I'm talking about," the woman replied as she glanced at the group, then shook her head. She turned back to us. "There's a Fair Trade for Fair Wages seminar today, which you would all benefit from attending."

"Will coffee be served at the seminar?" Parker asked with a straight face.

Lindsey broke into laughter. "Oh, that would be great. A Fair Trade for Fair Wages seminar that serves Starbucks coffee, gives discounts on Nike sneakers, has sandwiches made with undolphin-friendly tuna—"

I grinned and started to open my mouth to add to the list.

"Oh, you women think you're pretty funny, don't you?" the woman snapped.

"Of course we do," Parker answered. "We're a regular stand-up trio. We're called The Comedy Cunts. Coming soon to a playhouse near you."

The woman's jaw dropped. "How . . . how . . . how absolutely *despicable* that you would even call yourselves that . . . that word."

"What word?" Parker asked as she fought back a grin. "Comedy? What's the matter, Short Stuff? Why are you so offended? Are you really a fag in Guatemalan drag?"

"I see no humor in—"

"Well, now *there's* a surprise." Lindsey chortled. "You not only see no humor, but you wouldn't even know humor if you fell over it. When was the last time you cracked a smile? When they manufactured you in the all-natural lab?"

"So that seminar," Parker cut in. "Are you going to be at it, Tiny?"

"Of course I am!" the woman nearly shouted.

"Then I'm definitely *not* going to be there," Parker answered. "You see, it's people like you, Missy-Girl, who undermine your causes with this kind of belligerent, in-your-face, militant tactic. You think you're passing along your beliefs to others by doing what you're doing—which is essentially shoving your philosophies down peoples' throats—but you're only turning people off. You're making them want to go out and do just the opposite of what you want them to do. You're as bad as the PETA people, who do things like set hundreds of mink free from mink farms because they proclaim to believe in animal rights. Then they don't take any responsibility when nearly all of the mink die because they haven't a clue how to live in the wild."

"Oh, you want to talk PETA now, do you?" the woman shouted. "It just so happens that I'm a member of the—"

"Enough!" Lindsey cried out. "Why don't we just cool it. This isn't a court of law. We have differing opinions. Which, as you know," she began, then paused to throw a hard stare at the woman, "is fine."

"No, I don't think she knows that," Parker countered. "I think this woman couldn't hear an opposing point of view if IT WAS SCREAMED IN HER EAR!"

Several people ahead of us and behind us in line suddenly stopped talking.

"Hey!" I broke in and pointed. "There's Blair."

"Thank God." Lindsey sighed.

"You mean, 'Thank Goddess,' don't you?" the woman asked.

"Oh, please, let's not go there," I protested.

"Hi, guys!" Blair beamed as she joined us. "Sorry I'm late, but I had to juggle some of the seminar rooms because of a couple of last-minute changes to the workshop schedule. I hope you weren't too bored just standing here."

"Oh, this may be the highlight of my day," Parker declared as she raised her Starbucks cup at the woman, took a drink, then turned her back to her.

The woman raised her middle finger at Parker's back.

Blair stared at the woman's finger. "Excuse me?" she asked. "Would you put that finger down, please?"

The woman responded by rotating the finger in front of Blair's face. Blair tipped her head to the side and then emitted a short whistle. "Wow! You're really talented. When you grow up, maybe you can learn how to use the other four fingers on your hand."

"Spoken like a true teacher." Parker grinned as she caught the end of the exchange between the woman and Blair. Then she held out the Starbucks cup to the woman. "It's empty now, Coffee Cake. Do you want to use it to collect money for your Nuke Starbucks campaign?"

"I've got the perfect slogan for your fundraising," Lindsey added. "Brew hate, not coffee."

"Zing!" I laughed as I lightly punched Lindsey on the shoulder.

The woman shook her head and turned on her heels.

"Bye-bye, mai-mai." Parker giggled. "Don't be a stranger now, ya hear?"

"What was that all about?" Blair asked us.

I shrugged my shoulders. "It was pretty much a close encounter of the weird kind."

"I hope there aren't more of *those* la-la lesbian sisters at this conference," Parker commented as she nodded toward the woman. "She be one o' dem scary dykes."

"Well, there are some . . . um . . . interesting lesbians inside," Blair said. "As you know, the purpose of this conference is not just to benefit battered women's shelters, but also to provide a space for the diverse expression of women-identified values, politics, and community."

"So basically what you're saying is that we're in for an all-day big yawn?" Lindsey asked her. "It sounds like this event is going to require use of some of my brain cells."

"And that's another thing that drives me nuts about lesbians," Parker cut in before Blair could respond. "It's their *inclusiveness*. Of all makes and models of lesbians. It's like we're all part of this big lesbian village, but within this village are different tribes. And each tribe has its own philosophies, its own religion, its own habits, its own foods it likes to eat, its own peculiarities. If there are one million lesbians in this village, then there are a half a million different tribes." Parker paused. "And rather than shut anyone out, we've all got to get along."

"It's more than just getting along, though," I added. "It's like we've got to accept and embrace every different tribe as well as our own."

Parker nodded. "Well put, Gracy. When lesbians aren't spending their time focused on *issues*—which you know is another thing that I can't stand in this community—then they're dedicating themselves to *embracing* and *celebrating* everything female. Oh—whoops! Was I not supposed to use the term *female*? After all, it has the word *male* in it." She pressed her fingers against her mouth. "Have I committed a lesbian gaffe?"

"Some lesbians are just way too out there," I agreed.

Lindsey nodded. "Sometimes it gets to be too much. Some lesbians are so judgmental. I'm not saying everyone. But if you're too girly-girl, then you're judged as being too feminine. If you make a lot of money and have a lot of nice things, then you're judged as being too materialistic. If you want a career in the corporate world, then you're ignoring the plight of underpaid, undereducated women. If you—"

"If you're not inclusive of deaf Jewish vegetarian lesbians over fifty who drum during full moon cycles, then you're not one of *us*," I cut in with a grin. "You know, even though I've heard that sisterhood can be powerful, I just think it can be pretty perplexing. And frustrating. It's like lesbians belong to some sort of secret society, and in order to be accepted into this society you have to know the right words, the right way to dress, the right way to believe, the right way to behave—all of which are based on knowing the needs and desires of all the individual tribes in the lesbian village."

"But the rules change all the time," Lindsey complained. "Just when you think you're the most politically correct, all-inclusive lesbian you can be, some new cause, some new diversity, comes up and starts to demand your attention. It drives me buggy. Why can't we all just be?"

I grinned. "Free to be, you and me."

"I tell you, the gay boys are just not that way, chicks," Parker said. "First, they'd never have a conference like this one. They'd throw a confetti dance. They don't process anything ever—they simply party. And they wouldn't give a rat's ass what color you were or who or what you worshiped. Unless it was cock."

"Language, Parker," Blair scolded as some women who were standing behind us in line groaned at the word *cock*.

"Pardon me," Parker addressed the women. "I mean *penis*."

The women groaned again.

"I know what you mean, Parker," I responded. "It's like that show *Queer as Folk*. The men are always—*always*—out having a good time. Their lives are positively filled with adventure. But the lesbian couple on the show—"

"Lindsey and Melanie," Lindsey cut in.

"Right." I nodded. "All they do is experience a lot of angst. Or process ways to make them grow emotionally closer as a couple. They have a baby. They have a commitment ceremony. They convert their attic into an at-home office for Lindsey. Nothing ever really seems to happen to them. They don't pursue adventures or take chances the way the boys do. They don't even get out into the lesbian community."

"They don't even have a lesbian community on the show," Lindsey pointed out.

"And they should," Parker added. "If they brought the women out into the *real* lesbian world, they might at least be making fools of themselves in a bar, playing in a championship softball game, or even bed-hopping. At the very least, they could be more sexual together on the show. After all, the boys do it all the time. Every gay boy who watches the show probably thinks that lesbians don't have sex. At all."

"I'm not just talking about the sex," I replied. "I mean, it's like they don't even have a support network for themselves. Whereas the gay guys—Brian, Justin, Emmet, Michael, and Ted—all support one another in whatever they do: Start a new business. Meet a new guy. Experience homophobia. I wonder why that is—why gay men, who seem so focused on sex and chance encounters, can actually be there for one another, whereas women, who seem to be so focused on emotions and commitment, can't seem to devote any quality time and support to their friends."

"It's because there's too much separatism," Parker answered as she opened her pamphlet and tapped a finger on a page. "I mean, listen to all these different lesbian populations that either have workshops or 'intensive learning booths' at this conference: womyn of color, womyn with disabilities, crones—what's that?" she asked Blair.

"Essentially, women who are older," she answered.

"Why not just call them old biddies?" Parker asked. "And why do they have to have a separate group? A woman's a woman, no matter what her age. Gay men like the gay boys. Why don't older lesbians like the young girls?"

"How about some of the spiritual groups here today?" I asked as I flipped through the pages of my pamphlet. "Check this out. There are dharma dykes, a group called nice Jewish girls, which is for lesbian and bisexual women, orthodykes, for orthodox Jewish lesbians, sacred sisters, for lesbians interested in pagan spirituality, lesbian satsang—"

"What's that?" Lindsey asked.

"Uh," I paused while I flipped through the pamphlet.

"Here it is," Parker said as she looked at her pamphlet. "Satsang means 'association with truth,' and the group is for lesbians 'who follow a spiritual path of nonduality' . . . uh . . . Taoism, Buddhism, or Advaita Vendanta—"

"What's Advaita . . . uh . . . whatever you said?" I asked.

"It sounds like the name of a car." Lindsey grinned, then shifted into an announcer's voice. "The new Advaita Vendanta. For those who like lush interiors, a luxury ride, low maintenance—and lesbians."

"I don't think I'd ever link low maintenance with lesbians," Parker commented. She closed her pamphlet. "Okay, Blair. We're here, we're queer, and we're leery of this whole conference. But we're yours for the day. So, lead on, lady."

"First, here are your passes," she said as she handed out laminated cards to each of us. "Use these pieces of string to tie them around your neck."

"I'll like to tie this around her neck," Parker muttered as she nodded at the Starbucks-hating woman, who had now moved ahead of us in the line and was engaged in conversation with a similarly dressed woman. "Oh, look. She has a clone. Let's destroy them now, before more are produced, overthrow our capitalistic government, and ban caffeine."

"Let it go," Blair suggested.

"Is there anything at this conference that's not all touchy-feeling, issue, issue, issue, get-back-to-Mother-Earth, save the whales and the rain forests?" Parker asked as she finished tying the string and then looked down at her guest pass. "This is just not working with my outfit."

"Of course there is," Blair answered. "There are over a hundred artisans exhibiting their works today—you like art, don't you Parker?—musical, dance, and theatrical performances, hands-on activities, workshops, and lots of good food. You won't believe the wonderful aromas inside. Do you know that there's even a sweat lodge set up in there?"

"Perhaps that explains the aromas." Lindsey snickered.

"So what exactly happened with the woman who flipped you the bird?" Blair asked Parker.

"Nancy Nose-in-My-Business decided to take me to task for drinking Starbucks coffee."

"I love Starbucks coffee!" Blair exclaimed. "I sure wish I had some now. There are only decaffeinated teas and juices inside, and I sure would like a caffeine kick."

"Then I wish you had been standing here instead of me,"

Parker replied. "Because she tried to give me her own version of a caffeine kick. Are all the workshops today run by radical dykes like her, who are out for blood?"

Blair tipped her head to the side. "Well, there are a few, I'm sure. But there are so many other interesting workshops that aren't political like that at all. I'm interested in yoga and drumming, for instance. Gracy, maybe you'd be interested in the Writing from the Heart or the Journaling in Everyday Life seminars."

I gave Blair a halfhearted smile. "Writing is what I do every day, Blair. I really don't want to do it on the weekend, you know?"

"Oh, sure. I understand. Then you could do Singing in a Sacred Circle or Drumming for Heart and Lung Health or Salsa ain't No Sauce—It's a Dance or Making Art from Trash and Selling it for Cash."

"As interesting as all of those sound," Parker began, "I'm wondering if there are any, I don't know, *normal* seminars being offered today. Like investing for the future. Or how to choose the best highlights for your hair. How to keep your fingernails and toenails healthy. The proper care of dildo harnesses. How to murder a lesbian activist and get away with it. I'd also be interested in learning more about achieving orgasms simply from breast sucking and massaging."

"I think you're talking about a whole different conference." I smiled as I glanced through the pamphlet. "You could take belly dancing, Parker. That's somewhat near the breasts. Oh—wait! There's a workshop called Your Best Highlights."

"There is?" Parker asked as she glanced down at the page I had opened in my pamphlet.

"Ah, I see it," Lindsey nodded. "But it focuses on . . . uh . . . 'an exploration of your body auras and chakras.' "

Parker sighed. "Well, maybe there'll be some good food to eat. I'm getting pretty hungry."

"Oh, there's lots of food," Blair said, then waved her arm for us to follow her as she started walking past the line of women. "It's mostly vegan, of course."

"Of course?" Parker echoed. "Why of course? Don't lesbians eat meat? Or is the Vegan Tribe on kitchen duty today? I want to be at a conference where the I-Slay-Meat Tribe does the cooking. I could go for a nice pork roast right now. Or a thick slice of—"

"There are Not Dogs here," Blair called to her over her shoulder. "And Garden Burgers."

"I wouldn't call those meat products," Lindsey commented.

"Fuck me," Parker muttered as she strode past those who were waiting in line. "Nothing to do, nothing to eat." She shook her head, then stopped and peered back at the line of women. Her shoulders slumped. "And no one to look at. Good grief! Are we the only normal lesbians here?"

"Suck it up," Lindsey advised Parker.

"Go to your happy place," I added as I followed behind Lindsey.

Be the Best Lesbian Separatist You Can Be

In the lesbian community, the most important require-
ment for admission into the Lesbian Village is not who you
are but which diversities you can contribute to the village.
Are you a woman of color? Asian? Inuit or Native American?
Hispanic? Caucasian, while acceptable, is really quite dull.
So dig deep into your heritage. Try to locate an immigrant
somewhere in your bloodline, and milk this background for all
it's worth.

Who or what do you worship? If you're Catholic, that's
fine, but there are a lot of lesbian Catholics (both practicing
and recovering) in the Lesbian Village. Therefore, you need to
distinguish yourself from them in your way of worship. An
Orthodox Jew is a good choice. So is the study and practice of
Buddhism in any tradition or sharing a spiritual synchronic-
ity with goddesses and moon lore.

Are you bisexual? Well, that's okay, but it seems that more
and more lesbians are jumping on that bandwagon, and it's
getting mighty crowded. Transgendered is the way to go
nowadays.

It's okay to have been married in the past and to have children from this heterosexual relationship. After all, no lesbian
will fault you for finally discovering the error of your way
and bringing an end to that sorry time in your life where you
functioned as a sperm receptacle. But while female children
from marriages are embraced, boys have a harder time gaining acceptance in the Lesbian Village. (After all, males are
hunters and lesbians are vegans, so the males won't be doing
the lesbians any favors.)

Try taking your young son to any women's festival, and
chances are he's going to be housed at a different location,
with guards posted twenty-four hours a day so he can't wan-
der off and "infect" the rest of the population. Even though
little boys are cute and haven't started growing beards or

talking in deep voices, they do have penises (albeit tiny ones). And the testosterone that's coursing through their veins can cause near panic at a women's event.

Do you consider yourself to be a woman, or a womyn? A girl, or a grrrl? Do you believe that you are part of the large circle of womanhood or wimminhood? The more creatively you can spell your affiliation with feminism—not feminity, mind you, because that's a whole other story—the higher the ranking you will have in the Lesbian Village. And, if you are adept at eliminating any use of the words "men" or "male" in both your writing and your conversations, you may even be viewed as a role model.

Now, if you can combine your heritage, your religious beliefs, and your feminism with any sort of tribal skills—drumming, for instance, or chanting, or knowledge of herbal healing remedies, all the better. This is particularly important for Caucasian women, because they've got to do their best to convince other lesbians that while they're white on the outside, they can be ethnically awakened on the inside.

While many lesbians are sports-minded, it would be best to display interests in lesser-known sports whenever you're away from the softball field or basketball court and around large groups of lesbians. However, be sure to combine a lesser-known sport with some sort of philosophy. You could develop a talent as a Zen archer, for instance ("Feel the bull's-eye; be the bull's-eye"), or as a feng shui rock climber ("The rocks are alive, therefore the hills are alive, with the sound of music").

If you have a creative talent—poet, artist, musician, dancer, and so on—do not write, sing, or use art in any way that appears to be mainstream. You must be offbeat in your craft— even goofy—and show others that you're not out to make money from your talents but rather to make a political/spiritual/emotional statement. When talking about your creations, work into the conversation such words as "enlightenment," "empowerment," "sustainable universe," and "anger" to give your talents more value.

If you start to make money from your art, abandon your style quickly before you build up a bank account. A strug-

gling, starving, artistic lesbian has a viable and even revered place in the Village; an established, rich artist does not.

Finally, it's important to understand that while you're a sexual being and have probably had more orgasms with women than you've ever had when you were dating men or even married to one, sex is pretty much downplayed in the Lesbian Village. It's not that lesbians don't have sex; it's just never presented as any sort of big deal. To gain acceptance into the Lesbian Village, you have to act as if you don't see the breasts, shapely hips, and sensual buttocks all around you.

Also, you must abide by certain Lesbian Village sex rules:

Never flirt or be coy with someone who interests you. That's what heterosexual women do. You can, however, come on to another woman. (See next two items.)

Do not dress in skintight, low-cut, or sexy clothing. That's what heterosexual women and Britney Spears wannabes do. Since lesbians are politically opposed to such blatant visual seduction tactics, it's best to wear the typical lesbian outfit: a tank top with a sports bra underneath and a pair of baggy shorts. (Note: Grrly-grrls may wear nice tops and skirts, but must refrain from looking like a cheap hooker.) Acceptable underwear includes Hanes or Jockey briefs. Thongs are what you wear on your feet, not under your pants.

You can put the moves on a woman, but never, never can you come right out and ask her to go to bed with you. That's something a guy would do. Instead, assume that if she's interested in you and you're interested in her, you will end up in bed together. Of course this may take a while, since neither of you can actually voice your desire. But eventually you'll find yourselves wrestling together on the couch and then peeling your clothes off.

You must pay attention to creating the appropriate bedroom atmosphere when taking a lesbian to bed. Never, ever play any music sung by a man. Always light scented candles and have plenty of them on hand.

When you're having sex, never cry out, "Take it all, baby!" or "Who's your Mama?" Even if you don't like oral sex (either performed on you or doing it yourself), it simply is something a lesbian has to do at some point in her life. You're just going to have to lick it—uh—like it.

The use of sex toys such as dildos and dildo harnesses should never be discussed outside the bedroom (it would be like men talking about their cocks). Since dildos look strikingly like penises, choose colorful ones, give them feminine names, and then offhandedly suggest their use by saying something like, "Do you want Aphrodite to join us tonight?"

Although you might fantasize about fucking a woman or having a woman fuck you, remember that a lesbian is never reduced to such sexual perverseness. Women never "get off" with one another. You always "make love," even if you're drunk out of your mind and know that the only reason you're having sex at all is because answering machines hadn't been invented the last time you had sex.

You must always sleep over after sex (translation: making love). Even if you sober up after your orgasm and realize you've made a big, big mistake. Even if you're highly allergic to cats and she has six of them—who must share the bed with you all night. Even if her partner is expected home any moment. Lesbians love confrontation and its ensuing drama!

Lesbians revel in being as different from one another as much as the rich are dedicated to widening the gap between themselves and the poor.

So be as different as you dare to be. But keep in mind that with so much diversity in the Lesbian Village, interactions with other tribes may be difficult. Sadly, in the effort to celebrate and embrace diversities, lesbians have not created their own version of a perfect Babylon, but a modern-day Tower of Babel.

5

You Might As Well Admit It, You're Addicted to Love (You're the Worst Thang, Worst Thang . . .)

I was riding in the car with Leslie, my ex who was now my current. We had started dating after we had seen each other in the coffee shop while meeting our online dates—who turned out to be ourselves—and later that week had attended the Terriers-Black Bears basketball game. (The Bears ended up mauling the Terriers, much to my satisfaction.) At halftime, Les had purposely brushed her hand gently against mine and flashed me a smile that always used to make me melt—along with other things, like her athletically built body, which she kept tightly honed at the gym and through regular exercise, her light blond hair, her tan skin, courtesy of regular sessions in the tanning bed, and her sparkling sea-blue eyes.

She had disappeared at halftime while the BU band and cheerleaders entertained the crowd at The Roof, then returned with a Black Bears T-shirt from the concession stand for me, signed by none other than horror writer Stephen King, who tracked the Bears as relentlessly as he did the Boston Red Sox. Though thin and frail after his freak accident years ago, he went wherever the Bears roamed, and Les knew that I read whatever King wrote. I had once told her that he could write the copy for a cereal box, and I'd read it with the same fervor with which I devoured all of his novels.

It was a classy thing for her to do. It took a lot of nerve to work her way through the crowded stands on the Black Bears side of the court, sporting a BU Terriers basketball jersey and baseball cap, approach the famed author in a way that made him believe she wasn't some sort of crazed Kathy Bates–style stalker, hand him the T-shirt, and ask for his signature for a fan.

So, of course, I had asked her to spend the night.

Les and I had done more fun things together in the few months after that game than we had in the time when we had struggled to be together in a committed relationship. Maybe we had each discovered some vein of maturity within us since we had split, because now we could talk about anything under the sun and didn't shy away from the big issues as we had in the past—money, sex, squeezing the toothpaste from the middle of the tube rather than from the end. As a couple, talking had never been our forte; we were much better at bickering. Too, maybe we had both changed a little in our time apart: she, becoming a little less pushy with me and the time I needed to write, and me, becoming a little more relaxed about balancing working with having fun. At any rate, we were truly enjoying one another's company and were trying to take it slow.

Okay. Maybe not *that* slow. After all, lesbians don't know how to do slow—on a dance floor, yes—but not when dating (as if that *really* exists in the lesbian community) or in a relationship. You meet someone you like, you have sex, and then you're in it forever and ever. Or at least you think so, until the next head-turner comes along. Les and I had talked about how that had been the pattern for us the first time around, and so we set up a schedule for the times we would see each other and then stuck to it. That gave me the time and space I needed to write, without interruption and without the pressure of feeling like someone else needed my time and attention, and it gave us both a sense of separateness that we had never allowed ourselves to have before.

Lesbians love fusion; the more fused, the better. (I firmly believe that a lesbian invented Velcro so she always knew where her lover was; it took a man to realize that Velcro had more significant uses than simply keeping a lover in check.) When Les and I had been a fused couple, there had been little time for either one of us to pursue personal pastimes. Anything that took us away from each other was viewed as a source of conflict and competition rather than something that could complement our intertwined lives.

Les, who had always been a bit of a compulsive workout freak—I won't even get into how it annoyed the hell out of me the first go-round with her when she would get up at the crack of dawn every morning to go for a run and leave our warm bed (and me) behind—had become a certified kickboxing instructor. She was now leading classes at a studio two nights and Saturday mornings each week, making women punch, kick, and sweat. After we had started seeing each other again, I had watched her lead one of her classes. I saw her transformed into a confident, ferocious, warrior woman as she led her students for fifty intense, sweaty minutes. They loved her; the line to get into her classes would start forming a half hour before she cued her music, and sometimes people even had to be turned away. So Les was doing something she really liked to do, and what she got in return was positive validation from her dedicated students. This was a good thing for her, and I told her so after I had watched her.

When we had been together the first time, she—like me, because of my at-home work—didn't have many friends or outside activities. So the burden had always fallen on me to be her source of entertainment, her confidante in all matters, big and small, and her sole companion for whatever she wanted to do. After a day spent sucking my brain dry in front of a computer, my least-favorite question to hear from her was, "What do you want to do now?" More often than not, I'd say, "I don't really care" because, in fact, I really didn't. As William Styron once said about his profession, "Let's face it, writing is hell," a sentiment I shared with him. So anything that got me away from that hell was fine by me.

But then the least-favorite statement I wanted to hear after that was, "You never want to do *anything*, Gracy!" followed by the slamming of a door. After a while, trying to write and trying to be with Les had become hell for me. And for both of us, I guess, since she eventually looked elsewhere for love and attention.

Considering how well we were getting along now, I guess

maybe we had both matured. Too, maybe we had both changed a little. After all, it's not easy meeting someone you not only really like, but whom you care to know and understand. I think we considered ourselves lucky to have found each other again, and I knew, although we had never come right out and said it, that we really wanted to make it work this time around.

And so, Les was going to join me today at my get-together with The Girls. (Blair had reluctantly agreed to our calling ourselves that, "As long as it's fully understood that we aren't girls, but women." To which Parker had replied with her smug grin, "You go, girl!")

The Girls had gotten together about once every two weeks in the three months since we had attended the Saturday workshop, usually for dinner or drinks and a couple of times for Sunday brunch. One late Sunday morning, as we were sipping our mimosas and digging into plates stacked with all-you-can-eat brunch buffet offerings at a wharf restaurant overlooking Boston Harbor, Lindsey had fished some tickets out of her pocket and dropped them in the center of the table.

"What are those?" I asked.

Lindsey smiled. "Compliments of Judge." (She, and we, had started calling the cheating justice Judge. I'm sure the woman had a name, but either we had never heard it or we all just preferred to call her Judge.)

"What are they?" Blair asked.

Parker picked up the tickets and squinted as she peered at them. "Boston Breakers? What's that?"

"They're a professional women's soccer team," Lindsey answered. "Home turf for them is Nickerson Field at Boston University, and their season starts in late May. But these tickets are for an exhibition world soccer game. They're playing Spain at the Worcester Centrum."

"Oh-lay!" Parker exclaimed with a grin, then tossed the tickets on the table. "You do know how much I love those Spanish women. Do they wear really tight shorts and skimpy tank tops? Do they bend over a lot? Do they do little shake-your-booty dances after they kick the ball and score a touchdown?"

Blair rolled her eyes, then stabbed at her blueberry pancakes with a fork. "It's soccer, Parker, not football."

"But the point is still to score, right?" Parker asked as she smiled at Blair. "That's the only part about sports that I like."

"There's a surprise," Blair muttered.

"Why are there eight tickets?" I asked as I counted them.

"Judge suggested we each bring a date," Lindsey answered, and then nearly bounced up and down in her chair. "That means she's coming."

"Isn't she always coming?" Parker quipped.

Lindsey stuck out her tongue at her. "She's going to be coming with me."

"Don't say it," Blair warned Parker as she pointed her fork at her. She turned to Lindsey. "So Judge will be with you for this soccer game? Like on a date?"

Lindsey nodded. "Can you believe it? We're actually going to be seen out in public together after months of sneaking around. It was her idea, actually. I think—I really think—that she's heading in the direction of leaving her partner. For me, of course."

"I don't know about that, Lindsey," Blair cautioned with a frown. "It's not good to leave one person and head right into a relationship with someone else."

"It's not like that doesn't happen all the time in the Village," I answered. "After all, that's what Leslie did to me."

"But now you're back with her," Blair responded, then turned back to Lindsey. "I just don't want you to get your hopes up. I mean, her going to a Breakers game with you is one thing. Moving out from where she's been living with a partner is totally another."

"Well, it's a step in the right direction," Lindsey sniffed. "Anyway, I'm excited about this. So Judge will be with me. Blair, will you bring Julia?"

Blair nodded. "Sure. She likes sports."

"And will you bring Leslie?" she asked me.

"Absolutely," I answered. "I'm sure she'll love it."

"Now what about you, Parker?" Lindsey asked her.

"Well, you know how I feel about sports," Parker replied.

"The only thing I can relate to is the scoring. Unless you tell me what sport is being played, I don't know one from the other. Although I do know the difference between croquet and badminton." Parker thought for a moment. "At least I'm pretty sure I know the difference. Is croquet with the net or the wickets?"

"Are those even considered sports?" I asked.

"Some parts of the country think competitive hot-dog eating is a sport," Blair pointed out.

"I don't care how you *feel* about sports, Parker," Lindsey cut in. "Because you're going, whether you like sports or not. It's what The Girls will be doing. I'm just asking who you'll bring. What about that woman who likes you? Are you still dating her?"

"She keeps saying yes whenever I ask her to do anything—even if it's outside of the bedroom—so, yeah, I guess you can say that we're dating," Parker replied with a shrug.

"What's her name?" Blair asked.

"Cindi. That's spelled C-I-N-D-I. But she doesn't sign her name with little hearts over the *i*'s, and she'll snap your head off if you call her Cynthia," Parker answered. "She's . . . well . . . she's kind of butchy-femmy. So I think she definitely likes sports. I'll just have to see if she's free then. She works odd hours."

"What does she do?" Blair asked.

"Well," Parker paused, then grinned. "Sometimes she goes down on me. And sometimes I go down on her. Other times—"

"You do that just to annoy me, don't you?" Blair cut in.

Parker beamed and nodded. "And it works every time."

"So what *does* she do," Lindsey began, then added, "for a living? She's not a stripper, is she? Although I don't think that would be a bad thing."

"What made you think of that profession?" Blair asked her.

"I don't know." Lindsey shrugged. "The spelling of her name. The fact that she works odd hours. Her interest in Ms. Hot Pants here."

"She's a cop," Parker answered, then took a quick sip of her drink.

"A cop?" I echoed.

"A lady in blue?" Blair exclaimed, then shook her head. "Somehow, I just can't picture our own Ms. Scuzzy with a Ms. Fuzzy."

"That's pretty funny," I told Blair.

"She's a narc," Parker continued. "Officer Cindi—with an *i*—Morales. She works in the downtown precinct. Needless to say, being with her has cut down on my use of recreational drugs."

Blair's eyes widened. "You do drugs?" she asked Parker.

"Well, I used to," she answered. "In my younger days. Since I find it hard to accept that the age of forty is now a lot closer than thirty, I like to relive my wild and crazy days—at least in my mind."

"How the heck did you ever meet a cop?" I asked Parker.

"Funny thing about that," Parker began. "She and her partner had been tailing a known drug dealer, some dropout lowlife who sold pot and pills to kids. One night, short on cash, the guy had broken into my downtown store. He tried to bust into the safe, but the cops caught him before he could even twist the dial because I have a security system that's hooked into the police department. Of course, the cops had to call me down to the store so I could disengage the alarm.

"So I got dressed and drove to the store. One of the cops was a macho Mr. Studhead. The other was, well, one of us. My gaydar told me that right off the bat. We did a little flirting while her partner went to their cruiser to fill out a report. I asked her when she got off, and she said, 'Whenever you want me to. That is, if you do the right things.' Well, that sealed the deal for me. That, and the fact that she's a hot-looking Hispanic woman, with long, curly, dark hair and deep brown eyes. She handed me her card, and I handed her mine after I had written my home address on the back. I asked if she wouldn't mind checking out the security system in my place because," Parker paused, then batted her long, mascara-coated lashes, "I told her that I was *so scared* and *she looked so big and strong*. She came over that night after her shift ended. We had a sleepover. It was fun."

"And then she wanted to see you again?" I prompted her.

Parker nodded. "But more than see. She said she wanted to date me. That was all I needed to hear; I immediately rolled up the red carpet and began screening my calls. But she kept calling. At first a lot, and then every so often. She wasn't persistent to the point of being annoying. Not like a *Play Misty for Me* or a *Fatal Attraction* thing. She was just... well... being nice, I guess. Just wanted to talk. 'Shoot the breeze,' as she said. Like we were friends. She called during The Girls' dating trial— when I was told I couldn't have sex—and I got together with her for dinner. And so, now we are. Dating, that is." Parker peered at Blair. "We're doing things in and out of the bedroom, you'll be pleased to know. But, well, she's very different from me. I mean, she's a cop. She makes, like, two dollars a week. She lives in a tiny apartment in the city that she can barely afford that smells like cooked cabbage and fried onions. She wears a uniform and boots to work. She's into guns and violence. She's—"

"I bet she's a really nice person," Lindsey cut in.

"She's... um... how do I say it?" Parker paused. "She's protective of me. She looks out for me. I guess it's her cop instinct. But the really nice thing about being with her is that who I am, what I do, how much I'm worth, and how I live don't impress her at all. She's happy having a bowl of spaghetti with me at some cheap North End dive and then taking a walk by the harbor afterward. Most of the women I've been with expect more from me—the fancier restaurants, expensive gifts, hard-to-get theater tickets. I had always thought that was a good thing. Because, of course, I had wanted the women to *be* impressed. So I could get them in the sack. They expected me to wine them and dine them and buy them expensive gifts, and that's what I did. One former bedmate once suggested that we take a trip to Kittery, Maine. To shop at the outlets. You know how I feel about shopping. I mean, it's on par with sex. As we got out of the car in the parking lot, she handed me a list of things she wanted me to buy for her."

"Oh, that's cold," I said.

"What a jerk!" Blair agreed.

Parker shrugged. "It's something I'm used to, something I fostered. And I've never minded it before. Not really. But now I don't like it. I want to be . . . I don't know . . . seen for me, I guess. Cindi is not like anyone I've ever been with before. She's just really down to earth. In an *Ozzie and Harriet* kind of way. Except she does like sex."

"She sounds nice." Blair smiled. "I can't wait to meet her."

Parker grinned and eyed Blair. "And being with a woman who owns a set of handcuffs isn't bad, either."

Blair chuckled. "You know, Parker, say what you want. But I think you like Cindi."

Parker ran a fingernail along a tooth and extracted a piece of food. "Yeah, well, I don't know about that. Like is one of those four-letter words I prefer not to use. Now pass me those muffins, would you? *Those* I do like."

I called out the exit to Leslie, and she steered off the highway.

"We should be about fifteen minutes from Blair's apartment," I told her. "We'll pick her and Julia up there, then head out to Worcester. Lindsey and Parker will be meeting us there."

"So these gals are both schoolteachers?" she asked.

I nodded. "And now Julia wants to move in with Blair. Actually, she's been suggesting that they buy a house together. It's been about three months since they started seeing each other. That's about the right time for lesbians to talk about moving in together, wouldn't you say?"

Leslie slowly turned her head toward me. "Are you suggesting anything, Gracy?"

I opened my mouth, then closed it. "Am I—oh! You mean for us? To move in together?"

"It's something to think about."

"I'm not ready yet," I answered quickly, then placed my hand on her leg. "It's not that . . . well . . . I mean . . . when we were living together before . . . you know. We just had so many problems. And you, well, the cheating thing. I need to be sure that I'm who you want. I'm still a writer, and I will be until someone pries my cold, lifeless body out of my computer chair."

"We've talked about that, hon," Leslie answered as she reached down and took my hand in hers. "It was wrong of me to make you feel as if you were being pulled in two directions when we were together before. I made you feel like you had to choose between your profession and being with me. Now that I'm happier in my career—I finally have a job I love—and teaching kickboxing—something I also love—I understand how important those things can be in your life. I wasn't happy with myself before. And I think I resented your writing because it made you so happy."

"I appreciate that," I said. "But I'm also . . . well . . . I just want to be sure. About us. To be on firm ground. To trust that you're not going to move in with me and then want to be with someone else."

"I understand." She nodded. "Once burned—"

"Twice scared," I finished.

"But here's what I'm thinking," she began. "That we find a place—*eventually,* Gracy, not right away—that we both like. A place that's not yours. And not mine. Someplace that's ours. I think that's something that bothered me when we first got together—that I moved into your place, that is. It made me feel like I was invading your space. I don't want to do that again. I'd like to start out our new lives together in a neutral space. We can get something bigger. I know we can afford it. I'd like to get a place that's big enough for you to have an office that isn't taking up half of the living room. That way, you can go into your office any time you want, close the door, and I'll know that's your time for writing. I'll be less inclined to bug you then."

I looked down at the sheet of directions I had on my lap and called out the next turn.

"So? What do you think?" she asked as she raised my hand to her lips and gently kissed it. Then she wiggled her eyebrows at me and gnawed playfully on one of my knuckles.

"Let me sit with it for a while, okay?" I answered, then squeezed her hand and glanced down at the directions again.

I swallowed, and then realized my throat was dry. I knew what my answer would be. So why wouldn't I just say yes right now? What was holding me back? I thought about those questions for a few moments. What it boiled down to, I figured, was that I couldn't believe how my life had changed, for the better, since meeting The Girls on New Year's Eve. I now had new friends, a renewed relationship with someone I truly liked, and a newfound inspiration for my own writing. New, new, new. It was all exciting, but it was still new. And it was a bit much to take in all at the same time, a bit hard to believe. I think every lesbian wants to believe that fairy tales can come true. That everything, in the end, will be wonderful and happy and glorious. And yet, like most lesbians, I found myself wondering if the clock would start to chime midnight and the dream would disappear, just like the mice turning back into pumpkins.

But like the typical lesbian that I am—at least one who's loved and lost for a few decades—I didn't want to charge full-steam ahead.

Not for another two weeks—at least.

And not until I had priced U-Hauls.

Blair and Julia, who was a tall, thin African-American woman with cropped-short hair and model-like high cheekbones, sat in the backseat and took turns guiding Leslie on a shortcut to the highway that would lead us to Worcester. After a few minutes, our two backseat drivers had Leslie and me grinning as they finished each other's sentences or quickly apologized with, "Sorry about that, babes," whenever they spoke at the same time.

"So how's life as a couple?" I asked after Leslie had steered us onto the highway.

"I'm so happy," Blair cooed at the same time that Julia replied, "It couldn't be better.

"You know," Julia continued, "it's hard to believe that Blair and I spent so many years teaching across the hall from one another and we never even really gave each other the time of day."

"But I didn't think you *were*," Blair told her.

"And I didn't think *you* were," Julia replied. "I mean, you're so—"

"Tupperware, Mary Kay, Avon girly–girlish?" I asked as I turned to look at Blair, then tossed her a playful wink.

Julia flashed me a broad smile. "I mean, she's so fine, who could believe she's a lesbian? This is one fiiiinnnne woman."

"Oh, stop it!" Blair protested playfully, giggling like a schoolgirl.

"I won't stop it!" Julia giggled back at her, then tossed an arm around her shoulders. "So anyway, during one lunch period, I remember looking at Blair from across the tables in the cafeteria—we were both lunch monitors that day—and thinking to myself, 'Now there's a fine-looking woman. Why can't I be with someone like her?' But I'm shy, and she's even more shy, so I really didn't do anything about it. Blair was the one who made the first move."

"She completely denies that she had *dozens* of bottles of glue in her desk drawer when she asked to borrow *my* glue," Blair told us.

"I seriously wasn't coming on to you." Julia grinned at her. "Who knew I had so much glue!"

"Well, if glue's what it took to get us together," Blair began, "then maybe we'll stick together like glue for a long, long time. Because when you came into my life, my life truly began."

I started to laugh, then glanced over the backseat and noticed that Blair's comment had been delivered with heartfelt sincerity. At that moment, she and Julia were locked in a deep, passionate kiss.

I caught Leslie watching the activity in the backseat through the rearview mirror. "Is she for real?" she whispered to me.

I nodded and whispered back, "That's our Blair. The sweetest, nicest, kindest lesbian you'll ever meet."

"So they really *do* exist?" Leslie chuckled.

"Perhaps," I answered. "But The Girls have a theory that Blair is not made of flesh and blood, but steel and concrete. How else could she have made it this far in her life as a lesbian and still be so damned upbeat and positive after her heart's been broken a few times? Most of us end up with harder hearts because of that. Not our Blair."

"Now is it just me," Blair cut in to our whispering, "or is Lindsey talking about Judge *way* too much? It seems like none of us can say anything about anything without her somehow bringing Judge into the conversation. 'Oh, Judge would get a kick out of this seminar.' 'Judge was just talking about this the other day.' 'Do you think Judge would like these earrings?' I mean, I'm getting a little concerned about how focused she is on Judge. Especially since she told us that all that ever really happens between them is they have sex in some oddball place, and then Judge dashes off home to be with her girlfriend. Lindsey's getting way too wrapped up with this woman."

"Maybe she doesn't want anything more than what she's getting from Judge," I opined. "Maybe all Lindsey wants is to have someone to be with for a while. You know, someone who will take away the emptiness of her not having a girlfriend. Maybe being with Judge gives her something to look forward to."

"That's what I told Blair," Julia said.

"I don't think that's it," Blair replied. "She called me the other day, you know? She was crying. About Judge."

"What did she say?" I asked.

"She told me she was falling in love with Judge," Blair answered.

"She's *not* falling in love," I said dismissively. "She's falling in lust. Everyone does. You have some good sex, and you think you've finally met *the one*. She'll get over it."

Leslie turned to me. "So is that how you view *me*?" she asked with a feigned hurt look on her face. "Am I just . . . just an easy score?"

I shook my head. "Not at all, hot legs. But you have to know Lindsey . . . you have to have heard the circumstances of how they—"

"But she doesn't even have *good* sex with Judge," Blair argued. "Judge practically raped her that first time in the car. And Lindsey keeps going back for more. It's like . . . well . . . it's like she's possessed or something. She told me that she's doing things with Judge that are so totally out of her character. She said she feels like she's been cast under some sort of spell."

"I told you before, Blair," Julia said. "It's not voodoo that's making her do what she's doing. It's her vagina."

"But Lindsey's *so* upset," Blair countered. "She said that she asked Judge if she would ever leave her girlfriend. Judge responded, 'Why would I do that?' "

"Then what's she doing with Lindsey?" Leslie asked.

"She's having recreational sex," Julia answered.

"It'll die out," I said. "Eventually."

"Why aren't you as upset as I am about this?" Blair asked me. "Our Lindsey's going to get hurt."

"I think Judge is being very clear with her," I answered. "And so are we, you know. At least in our subtle ways. I mean, not one of us has flat-out screamed at Lindsey, 'Are you out of your fucking mind!' But that's definitely what we've all conveyed to her. I guess it's okay if Lindsey pays no attention to us. But if Lindsey truly can't hear what Judge is saying and recognize that this is something that's not ever going to be more than it is—"

"I think she's addicted to her," Blair broke in.

Julia sighed. "Oh, geesch, here we go again. I thought we already talked about this."

"I know you don't believe it, but I do," Blair told her, then reached forward, clutched the front seat in her hands, and pulled herself forward. "After Lindsey called me that night, I went on the Internet," she told us. "I looked up *love addiction*. Did you know that there's a self-help group called Sex and Love Addicts Anonymous? It's for people who live a pattern of sex and love addiction."

"Don't we all?" Julia asked.

I turned to Blair. "I don't think that Lindsey has a pattern of that. I think if anyone did, it would be Parker."

"I know," Blair agreed. "But then I went to a site that had questions. You know, for people to make a self-diagnosis of sex and love addiction."

"Do we have to talk about this?" Julia asked Blair. "We processed all of this before."

Blair turned to her. "Yes, we did. But you had formed your opinion before I could even say anything, honey-love. I want these guys to form their own."

"I don't know how accurate those types of questionnaires are," Leslie told Blair. "I think any one of us could answer those questions and think we were a sex or a love addict. The questionnaires that are put out by self-help groups are written in a way that makes you think you have a particular problem. That's because they're designed to recruit, not enlighten."

"Okay, fine," Blair replied as she reached down, opened up her purse, unfolded a batch of papers, and laid them out in front of her. "I'll just read off a few questions that I think apply to Lindsey, okay?"

"Okay," I told her.

" 'Do you ever find yourself unable to stop seeing a specific person even though you know that seeing this person is destructive to you?' That's Lindsey, for sure," Blair commented.

"Well, I agree with that," I said.

"And how about this one?" Blair asked. " 'Have you had sex at inappropriate times, in inappropriate places, and/or with inappropriate people?' That's another bingo-Lindsey question. 'Do you feel desperation or uneasiness when you are away from your lover or sexual partner?' "

"That's me!" Julia cut in. "I *desperately* want you whenever you're not around," she said in a breathless voice as she placed her hands on Blair's back and began rubbing it.

"Here's another Lindsey one," Blair went on, ignoring Julia. " 'Are you unable to concentrate on other areas of your life because of thoughts or feelings you are having about another person or about sex?' "

"Anyone who has ever fallen in love would answer yes to that," I said. "That has nothing to do with addiction. That's about feeling strongly for someone."

"Right," Julia agreed. "Thank you, Gracy. That is exactly what I told Blair last night when she showed me that list for the hundredth time. I said to her, 'You can't just pick and choose which questions you feel Lindsey might answer yes to and then make a diagnosis from that.' "

"Why was the lesbian sex addict not concerned when the power went out?" Leslie asked us.

"Huh?" I responded.

"Is this some sort of joke?" Blair asked.

"Why was the lesbian sex addict not concerned when the power went out?" Leslie repeated.

"I don't know," Julia said. "Why?"

"Because all her vibrators were battery operated," Leslie finished. "How many sex addicts does it take to change a lightbulb?"

"Another joke?" Blair asked. "I'm trying to be serious here."

"Okay, I'll bite," Julia answered. "How many?"

"Who wants to change a lightbulb when all those sex addicts are in one room? What do you call a bunch of lesbian sex addicts in a closet?"

"Why are you making jokes about this, Leslie?" Blair asked. "Lindsey is—"

"A licker cabinet," Leslie finished. "Do you know what this is?" she asked as she turned her head to the side and stuck out her tongue.

"No, what?" Julia asked.

"A lesbian sex addict with a hard-on."

I started to laugh. "Where did you hear these, Les?"

She winked at me. "A lesbian sex addict goes to her gynecologist—"

Blair groaned. "You have *more*?"

"The gynecologist examines her and says, 'My, but it's immaculate in here. What do you do to keep yourself so hygienically clean?' The lesbian sex addict smiles and tells her, 'I have a woman in three times a week.' "

Julia laughed out loud. "Boy, I sure wish you had found *this* Web site," she told Blair.

"I'm trying to make a point here," Blair told us.

"A lesbian sex addict is sitting in a crowded bar on a weekend night when a beautiful woman walks in—"

"Where is this coming from?" I broke in and stared at Leslie. "I never took you for a comedienne."

"These aren't all mine. This one's Lea Delaria's, with a slight modification," she explained.

"So the lesbian sex addict is in a crowded bar—" Julia prompted her.

"Right." Leslie nodded. "And a sexy woman walks in. The sex addict walks up to her, brushes her hands lightly around her own face, and says, 'Let me clear a place for you to sit on.' "

Julia and I laughed out loud.

"Well, that's certainly a little bit raunchy," Blair commented.

"Did you hear about the new running shoe that was invented by a lesbian sex addict?"

Julia and I started to giggle in anticipation of the punch line.

"It's called Dykey," Leslie finished. "It has an extra long tongue and it only takes one finger to get off."

Blair burst into laughter. "Dykey! How cute is that?"

We all grinned, then looked at Leslie.

Leslie hit her blinker and changed lanes.

"That's it?" I asked her.

She raised a palm in the air. "That's all I know, babes. There are probably a lot more, but those are the ones I can remember. I heard them in the lesbian Sex and Love Addicts meetings I attended."

"You?" Blair asked.

"Get out!" Julia exclaimed.

"What?" I added.

"S-L-A-A." Leslie nodded, then cleared her throat. "Hi, everybody. My name is Leslie, and I'm a sex addict."

"Are you really?" Blair asked in a breathless voice.

Leslie shook her head. "Not a chance. But after I had left Gracy for one of our closest friends—and then got dumped by the friend—I was miserable. I went out drinking more than I should have and had a few one-night stands. One morning, I woke up next to a woman who closely resembled a beached whale. I had no recollection of meeting her, let alone who she was or what I had done with her the night before. I was worried about my behavior, so I went to a therapist."

"Hey! I tried to get us to go to one before you left me," I chastised her in a hurt voice.

Leslie nodded. "I know. Gracy, I was messed up to leave you, and I stayed messed up for a while. Anyway, I needed to go to a therapist when I was ready to go. So I did. This woman spent all of fifteen minutes with me before she decided that I was a sex addict. She told me that my assignment was to go to one meeting a day for one month. I learned more about sex and love addicts than I ever cared to know by attending those meetings. I also discovered that I was in no way, shape, or form a sex or love addict. So, while I don't consider myself to be an expert, Blair," she said as she glanced up in the rearview mirror and met Blair's eyes, "I will tell you this. Sex and love addicts are compulsive. More often than not, it's not about having sex with one person or even falling in love with someone. It's about having *as much* sex as possible with *as many* people as possible, and then equating that with making love. Sex addicts are compulsive masturbators, have repetitive one-night stands, multiple sex partners, have phone sex or cybersex. It goes on and on. Basically what I'm telling you is that Lindsey isn't a sex addict. Maybe Judge is—I don't know if Lindsey is her only partner, or if she has a number of lovers hanging onto her. But I definitely think that Judge is using Lindsey and doing whatever she can to string her along. My guess is that she's not going to show up today. I mean, can you imagine, doing what she's doing—cheating on her partner with one of your friends—and then showing up to meet you? Believe me, she knows she's not going to be embraced into welcoming arms. So my money's on her not being here today."

"That would be a good thing," Julia said as she patted Blair on the leg.

"But it will *devastate* Lindsey," Blair replied. "I think she's been hurt enough by Judge."

"Maybe Lindsey needs to be devastated," I suggested to Blair. "Sometimes that's what it takes to end something that's really bad. But I don't think she will be. Lindsey's a smart woman. I don't think she'll put up with being treated badly for too long. "

* * *

"We've been here for two hours already," Parker pointed out to Lindsey as she leaned back against Cindi's shoulder in the large corner booth we were sitting in at a Worcester sports bar after the Breakers game. "Are you sure this is where Judge said she'd meet you?"

Lindsey glanced down at her watch, then nodded. "This is the place."

"Are you sure about the time she said that she was meeting up with us?" Blair asked as she crumpled her napkin on the table.

Lindsey sighed. "Maybe . . . traffic," she muttered.

"How much longer do you want us to wait?" I asked Lindsey.

She shrugged her shoulders. "Half an hour?" she asked. "Can you guys stay with me for another thirty minutes?"

"Sure we can," Cindi reassured her. "I've really enjoyed this day today. The game. Getting to meet all of you. Having a nice dinner. I think you guys—"

"Oh!" Lindsey suddenly exclaimed, then glanced down at the pager she had clipped to her belt. "It's her," she informed us with a smile, then reached into her jacket pocket and pulled out her cell phone. "She's probably just stuck in traffic," she told us as she punched in some numbers. "Or maybe she got a flat tire. Those things happen, you know?" She placed a finger over one ear and her cell on the other.

"Hey," we heard her say. "Oh? What do you mean?" Lindsey glanced at us, shook her head, then squeezed out of the booth. "But I thought—" she began, then walked away from us, out of hearing range.

"She's not coming," Leslie concluded as she watched Lindsey walk away.

"You called that one," Julia told her.

"What a shit!" Parker huffed. "First she gives Lindsey the tickets and says she'll be at the game. Then we meet up with Lindsey at the Centrum, and she tells us Judge said to meet us here after the game because she can't get away until later. She can't get away from what—that she doesn't say. I mean, it's Saturday. Now we've been waiting here for hours—"

"And she gets a damned phone call," Blair finished.

"Here she comes," I whispered as I watched Lindsey head back to the table.

Lindsey shoved the cell phone into her jacket pocket, then slid back into the booth. "Well," she began, then placed her hands on the table. "I guess we should square up the bill." She waved her hand in the direction of our waitress.

"So she's not coming?" I asked Lindsey.

Lindsey frowned. "I should've expected it," she told me. "Sometimes I think it's never going to change. That it's always going to be like this. Even when she leaves Brenda." Lindsey paused and looked at us. "That's the name of her lover. And yes, she *is* going to leave her. She's working hard to do that. And it's not something she's telling me just to keep me hanging on."

"Are you sure?" Parker asked her. "I mean, how hard is it just to say to someone, 'Listen, I've met someone else.' "

I sighed. "Not too hard," I said as I glanced at Leslie.

Leslie showed me a sad smile, then looked at Lindsey. "The thing is, Judge has simply got to walk away from Brenda. She can't keep hurting her."

Lindsey nodded. "The problem is, well, Brenda's got some problems. She gets anxious. I mean, she has anxiety attacks. She hasn't been able to hold a job as a result. She kind of fell apart when some sort of tragedy or catastrophe or something happened a few years back. They haven't really had a relationship since then. It's been more like a caretaking thing, with Judge as the mother and Brenda as the child. So it's no wonder that Judge wants me, wants something normal."

"I don't know that I'd call what you have with her normal," Blair pointed out.

"Well, you know what I mean," Lindsey answered. "Normal as in companionship. Normal as in physical closeness. Normal as in being able to laugh and have a good time. Judge told me that sometimes she'll come home from work and find Brenda sitting on the floor in a corner of a room. Just sitting. Apparently, that's all she's done all day. What Judge has been trying to do for several months now is to locate some member

of Brenda's family who can intercede, who can take some responsibility for Brenda. Otherwise, what can Judge do? She
can't just walk out on someone who's that messed up. And she
can't kick her out, because she's just going to end up on the
street. The complicating factor is that Brenda's family doesn't
live in this country."

"I didn't know all this," Blair said.

Lindsey shrugged her shoulders. "That's because I never
told you. It's my problem. Not yours."

"No, it's *our* problem," Parker corrected her. "Because it affects you. And what affects you affects us. Now, don't get me
wrong. It's too bad about Brenda. But Judge is the one who's
choosing to stay in that situation."

"She did love her, Parker," Lindsey answered. "She did
love her once. How can she just walk away?"

"*You* could just walk away," Blair suggested. "Look at you,
Linds. You're miserable."

Lindsey looked down at the table.

"She can't give you what you need," I pointed out as Blair
gently rubbed Lindsey's arm. "At least not right now."

Lindsey raised her head and looked at us. "It's just that you
all have someone now. Someone to be with. I want to be part of
that group. I want to have someone in my life, too."

"But not someone like that," Blair argued. "Not someone
who can't be there for you. My guess is that Judge is just using
you, Linds."

"I know," Lindsey agreed. "But maybe . . . maybe I'm using
her, too. So I can have someone there. Because I've been thinking that eventually I'll just be left behind. You are all going to
be spending more time with your lovers, and then pretty soon
The Girls won't be getting together at all."

"There's no way that's going to happen," Parker told her.
"You, Blair, Gracy, and me. We're a team. No one's going to
break that up."

Julia nodded. "That's what Blair told me from day one.
That no matter what, her plans with The Girls always take pri-
ority."

"It has to be that way," Cindi added. "You guys are important to each other—more important than any lover could ever be. Friends are the deepest, most intimate relationship of any that you can have in your life. Heck, some of the friends I have go way back—even to high school. They're never going out of my life, no matter what, and I'm always going to be there for them, whether I'm in a relationship or I'm single. So there's no way in hell that I would ever expect Parker to turn her back on any one of you, even just once. And especially not for me."

"It doesn't matter whether or not you and Judge end up together or you find someone else or you're single for a while," Blair said as she placed her hand on top of Lindsey's. "Because you're never going to be alone. You'll always have me. And Parker. And Gracy. We're stronger and better than any relationship you can ever have. We'll always be there for you. We're always going to be there for each other. And that's a promise."

Twenty Reasons Why Girl Friends
Are Better Than Girlfriends

1. It doesn't matter if she has her period.
2. You can take her home to Mom and Dad without causing a problem.
3. She will remember your name in the morning.
4. She will always take your side.
5. She doesn't care about the actual date you first became friends.
6. She can have countless bad habits and they'll never bother you.
7. She will tell you when you've gained weight or when your new hairstyle makes you look like a squirrel.
8. She won't get jealous of your ex-lovers.
9. She won't want to dress like you.
10. Being away from her doesn't make you feel guilty.
11. She doesn't need to hear the word commitment.
12. She doesn't have rules.
13. You can have a lot of them, and you won't get a bad reputation.
14. You never have to fake it with her.
15. She won't get mad if you say you have to work late or are too tired.
16. She doesn't expect you to bring her flowers.
17. She never asks, "Why are you looking at that woman?"
18. She never compares herself to your other friends.
19. She won't say to you, "You never listen to me."
20. She's satisfied with a hug and a quick kiss.

6

No One Thinks She's Going to Be Meg Ryan in the Deli ("I'll have what *she's* having.")

"What's going on with you tonight?" Lindsey asked Blair as we watched her drain her third drink in less than thirty minutes.

"Noth . . . ing," she answered slowly as she stared down into her empty glass. Then she tipped her head back and shook the remaining drops left in her glass into her open mouth.

"That's attractive," Lindsey mumbled as she watched her.

Blair lowered her head and grinned at Lindsey. " 'Ank you." She giggled, then tipped her head and the glass back again.

"I think you've got it all, Blair," I told her, then shot a quick glance at Parker and Lindsey.

Parker raised her eyebrows at me in return. Lindsey shrugged a shoulder.

Blair smiled at me. "Oh . . . kay, Grashy," she said in a little girl's voice as she carefully placed the glass on the table with both hands. "I got it all. Alllll done. Blair drank it alllll up. Yum, yum. Blair's a good little girl, isn't she?"

"Welcome to our nightmare," Lindsey mumbled.

"Excuse me, miss," Parker cut in as she rapped her knuckles on the table to get Blair's attention. "But you look remarkably like another one of my friends. We call her Miss Two-Drinks Maximum. In an entire evening. She'll even fight you tooth and nail for the role of designated driver. You don't happen to know who I'm talking about, do you?"

"She's ah . . . way for the ev . . . en . . . ing," Blair answered slowly, then wiped her mouth with the back of her hand, sighed, hiccupped, and wagged a finger in the direction of one of the harried waitresses in the packed downtown bar.

"The same?" the waitress shouted to Blair over the din of the Thursday evening crowd of professional gay men and women. Casey's was one of the more popular after-work gay bars—although not the most intimate or elegant—because the prices of everything from drinks to food were cheap and there was something for everybody. The lesbians had their pool table and a juke box near it that blared out such all-time sisterhood-bonding favorites as "We Are Family" and "Bad Girls." The gay men had for years staked their claim in a corner room off the bar that was adorned with ferns and other hanging plants and had a gorgeous, Adonis look-alike piano player who took both tips and tricks. And the karaoke stage area didn't much care who plunked down money and made a fool of themselves in front of other people. A soused young gay boy could warble a Barry Manilow love song to his flame du jour just as well as some butch could loudly proclaim to the room in a gravelly, off-key voice that she had Bette Davis eyes.

"Two, please," Blair called back to the waitress as she held up three fingers and hiccupped again.

"Maybe you should take a break," I suggested to Blair.

"Maybe you should go to an AA meeting," Lindsey added.

"Maybe you all should . . . should . . . jus' back . . . off," Blair told us. "Off. Off, off, off!" she repeated as she shook her head. Some strands of hair pulled loose from her scrunchie as she tossed her head about and ended up hovering in front of her left eye. Blair rolled her eyes up to look at the hair, then blew out a puff of air. The strand rose up slightly, then flopped back down in front of her eye. Blair air-puffed the hair again, then shrugged her shoulders as it settled back into place. "You know, shomtimes a girl's jus' gotta get herself drunk."

"Well, it's good to have a goal," Lindsey responded.

"Why does a girl just gotta do that?" I asked her.

"Becaush," Blair answered.

"Because . . . ?" Lindsey prompted her.

"Becaush," Blair repeated. "Becaush . . . becaush . . . becaush. Becaush of the wonderful things he dosh. Hey! What's that from?"

"*The Wizard of Oz,*" I told her.

Blair clapped her hands together. "Grashy wins! So what prize do you want to claim, Ms. Grashy Maynard?"

"Why don't you tell us why you're getting drunk tonight?" I asked her.

"I will. *I will,*" Blair emphasized. "I jus' can't get into it right now. Not right now. I need to build up my cour . . . age. It'sh a big thing I need to shay. But mark my words," she proclaimed as she sat up taller in her chair and shook a finger in the air, "I *will* get into it. Yesh, I will. I need jus' a couple more drinky-poosh, and then I'll be—"

"Under the table and no good to anyone," Lindsey finished.

"Why don't you just tell us what's going on now," I suggested.

"Before you black out," Lindsey added.

"Black out?" Blair echoed. She stared at Lindsey for a few seconds, then covered her mouth with a hand and started laughing loudly.

Parker, Lindsey, and I quickly swept our eyes in each other's direction.

"What's so funny?" I asked Blair after several seconds had passed.

Blair removed the hand from her mouth, then started making snorting noises.

Lindsey scratched her chin as she stared at Blair. "Well, this is going to be a long, interesting evening. What the hell is she drinking?"

"It'sh . . . it'sh . . . an inside joke." Blair giggled, then took in a deep breath of air. "But I'll let you in on thish inside joke. Becaush you are my very, very, *very* besch friends."

"I think she's drinking whiskey sours," I answered Lindsey. "Or, as Blair might put it, whishkey sourshs."

"Oh-kay, ever'body. Here it ish. Ready?" Blair asked us.

"For what?" Parker asked her.

"The funny *thing*, Pah . . . ka," Blair answered, then rolled her eyes at us. "What I'm laughing *at*. Duhhh!"

"Just tell us," I told Blair.

"Okay. This ish . . . are you ready?"

"We're ready!" Lindsey answered in a loud voice.

Blair widened her eyes at Lindsey. "Well, my goodnesh. You don't have to get all huffy 'bout it."

Lindsey sighed. "Go ahead, Blair."

Blair broke into a smile. "Ohkay. Ohkay. Are you ready?"

"Good Lord!" Parker declared as she sat back in her chair and crossed her arms over her chest. "This better be worth the wait."

"We've been ready for a week," Lindsey growled.

Blair snorted once more, then sucked in another deep breath of air. "Ready?"

"I'm going to add *aim* and *fire* to that word if you don't hurry up and just spit out what's making you behave like a loony," Parker told her.

Blair sucked in her cheeks and rocked her head back and forth as she stared at Parker. "Well, whose schtick is up your damn butt? At leascht I have a sense of humor."

Parker locked eyes with Blair. "No. You have a sense of drunken hysteria."

"So shoo me," Blair huffed at her. She tapped on the tabletop in front of Lindsey. "Lindsh. Draw up the papersh, would you?"

"So what's so funny, Blair?" I cut in, trying to redirect the conversation.

Blair turned to me. " 'Bout what?"

I shrugged my shoulders. "Never mind."

"Oh!" Blair cried out, then grabbed my arm. "Oh, Graschy! *That* funny. It's funny. It really ish."

"Okay," I said. "Then what is it?"

"Are you ready?" Blair asked us.

Parker opened her mouth to respond, but Lindsey quickly reached out and grabbed her forearm, then pinched the skin between her fingers. Parker glared at Lindsey, clenched her jaw, and then forced a smile and an attentive look in Blair's direction.

"How can I *black out*?" Blair asked us. "I *am* black! So maybe I *white out*! You know. Like that offisch supply liquid thingy." Blair slapped her palms against the table and resumed her snorting.

"You want to know what I'm thinking?" Parker asked as she turned to Lindsey and me. "I think there's trouble in paradise. Something's clearly amiss in Blair and Julia's Garden of Eatin'."

"It ish not!" Blair responded.

"Garden of Eatin'—that's a good one," Lindsey repeated with a chuckle.

"I can't think of anything else that might make our little Girl Scout hit the bottle, can you?" she asked Lindsey and me.

"Now she here, Pah . . . ka," Blair cut in. "What makesh you think that having a teensy weensy bit more lick . . . ker has any . . . fing to do with Ju . . . la?"

"Roughly translated," I told Lindsey and Parker, "she's upset about something to do with Julia. But she doesn't want to talk about it."

Blair stared at me in feigned shock. "Grashy! Grashy, Grashy. I nev . . . er said anything 'bout Ju . . . la."

"You don't have to," Lindsey replied. "You've been upset about things before—your job, gaining a few pounds, the dead baby birds you seem to find whenever you go out for a walk—but you've never gotten drunk over those things. So it has to be something to do with your relationship with Julia."

"I schware ta God—"

The waitress came up behind Blair at that moment. Blair turned to her, then smiled. "Oh, good. You're here. I want to order. Two more drinksh, pleasch."

The waitress glanced quickly at us, shrugged her shoulders, and then placed the drinks in front of Blair.

"And a large mug of your hottest, blackest, strongest coffee, please," Parker told the waitress. "Make it a bucket. Pronto on that."

The waitress nodded, then turned and was swallowed up by the crowd.

"Wow! That woman isch fast!" Blair told us. "I'm gonna give her a good tip. A really, really, really good tip. I mean, I was jus' thinking about two more drinksh and—ta da!—here they are. It'sh like magic."

Parker rose up from her chair, reached across the table, and slid the drinks away from Blair.

"Hey!" Blair cried out in protest.

Parker raised one glass in front of Blair's face. "You get this one after you tell us what's going on. And I'm drinking the second one. Because until you can start talking more clearly, you're too drunk to even be a passenger in a car tonight."

"I'm not—!" Blair started to protest, then hiccupped three times. "Oh . . . kay. Perhaps I am a weensy bit teensy. I mean . . . tipshe."

"So?" Lindsey asked. "What gives?"

Blair placed her elbows on the table, and then slowly leaned against them. "I love her immenshly. I love my Jujubee with all of my heart."

"Jujubee?" Parker muttered, then shook her head.

Blair slowly leaned back in her chair and then pressed the palms of her hands against her chest. "With all of my heart. *All of it.* You hear me? You know what I'm shaying?"

"I'm trying to keep up with the translation," I responded. "But, yes, I think we know what you're saying."

Blair reached out for my hand and patted it. "Oh, Graschy. Thank you. Thank you soooo much for being so . . . being so . . . I don't know . . . being so . . . being so . . ."

"Will someone please stomp on the floor?" Lindsey asked. "The record's skipping."

"So you love Julia," I prompted Blair.

Blair nodded her head vigorously. "Yesch, yesch, yesch. I do. I mean that sinsherly. Ju . . . la has schtolen my heart away."

"Gosh, this is taking a long time," Lindsey said, then waved a hand in circles in the air in front of Blair. "Can we just pick up the pace here? Tell us what's got you so upset?"

"Well . . . now . . . I'm getting to that," Blair told her.

"Let's hope she doesn't pass out before she gets to it," Parker said.

"Everything about . . . her," Blair continued. "It'sh so wonderful, you know?" She sighed and sat silently in her chair, wearing a dreamy expression on her face.

Parker snapped her fingers in front of Blair's face. "Got it. You love her. Now what's the problem?"

Blair sucked in a deep breath of air, then exhaled it in a loud burst. Her chin started to quiver.

"Oh, no, she's going to cry," Parker muttered. "I don't like weepy drunks."

"I did someshing really, really, *really* bad," Blair mumbled.

"What?" Lindsey and I questioned at the same time.

"Buy me a Coke," Lindsey quipped as she delivered a playful punch to my arm, and turned her attention back to Blair.

"Well . . . I did someshing . . . and I'm . . . I'm not proud of it," Blair continued. "It'sh like I'm lying to Juju. And I don't think that'sha good thing."

"What did you do?" I asked her.

Blair leaned forward, placing her chest against the edge of the table, then beckoned us to come closer by waving a finger in the air.

When we had each drawn closer to her, Blair rubbed her nose, sniffed, and then whispered, "I faked it."

"You faked what?" Lindsey whispered back.

Blair blinked her eyes a couple of times at Lindsey. "You know. *It.*"

"It?" Lindsey repeated in a soft voice.

"She faked an orgasm," Parker blurted out.

"Shhhh!" Blair cautioned Parker as she placed a finger on her lips.

"There's nothing to be hush-hush about," Parker assured her as she leaned back in her chair. "Every woman—straight and lesbian—has faked an orgasm at least once in their lives."

"Really?" I asked, then thought for a moment. "Yeah. I guess you're right."

"More than once I think is the case," Lindsey added. "I've faked it a few times with Judge. And with people before that."

"But that'sh not the shame thing," Blair told Lindsey. "You 'n Judge are bunnies. Sinch the beginning. You came together, so you could come together. Which you've done. And I'm sure a lot. Of coming. So it'sh okay not to come, you know, if you're always coming. You know?"

Lindsey shrugged her shoulders. "I guess. To whatever point you're trying to make."

"The point," Blair answered as she raised a finger in the air, "ish that I'm just starting out. And . . . okay, okay . . . you shee, I've dug myself into a hole. Because I faked it in the beginning with her and now . . . and now . . ."

"You're still faking it," Parker finished for her.

" 'Zactly!" Blair exclaimed. "Now how do I shtop faking and shtart coming? And that'sh really the thing. 'Caush I— oops!" she cut herself off as the waitress arrived at the table with two mugs of steaming coffee. Blair pressed her fingers against her lips.

"It's okay to talk about it," Parker told her, then handed a twenty to the waitress. "Have you ever faked an orgasm?" she asked the waitress.

"Parker!" Blair cried out in protest.

"She does this every time we're in a public place," I muttered to Lindsey.

The waitress tucked the twenty in her pocket, placed the empty tray on the table, and leaned a hip against the table. "Of course I have," she answered. "Nothin' wrong with that."

"See, Blair," Parker beamed across the table at her. "I bet if we surveyed every woman in this room—"

"—which I hope to God you're not going to do," Lindsey spoke up.

"—every woman would say she's faked an orgasm at least once," Parker finished.

The waitress nodded. "You're right about that."

"Hey! Over heah!" yelled a butch-looking woman sitting a few tables away from ours.

The waitress slowly directed a glance over her shoulder.

"Yeah, you know I'm talkin' ta you, Chris. Get yer butt ovah heah. You're supposed ta be takin' ordahs, not pickin' up chicks."

"Cool your fuckin' jets, T. J.," the waitress yelled back at her. "I'm havin' a *conversation*. Not that you'd know what that means." The waitress turned her back to T. J. "An ex," she explained to us. "*What was I thinking*, you're probably wondering, right? What can I say? It was just one of those times of desperation. But it only lasted three months. And"—the waitress grinned down at us—"I didn't come once with her."

"Well, converse on your own damn time," T. J. yelled back. "Where's our frickin' food?"

"Like she fuckin' needs it," the waitress told us. "Anyway, I've faked it with others, besides that lowlife over there. Sometimes a girl's just gotta do what she's gotta do. There's no harm in it. You fake it once, you come a few times after that. It's a small price to pay." She rapped her knuckles on the table. "Gotta go, ladies."

"So here's a question," I began after the waitress left. I placed my hands flat on the table. "If, let's say, every woman in this room has faked an orgasm at least once, then that means that she must've been faked out herself. By at least one woman she made love to."

Parker nodded.

I turned to Blair. "See? You're not alone. And maybe Julia has faked an orgasm with you."

Blair stared at me for a few seconds, then slumped in her seat. "Oh, God! I can't come with her and she can't come with me! I'm a horrible, horrible lover!"

"Well done, Gracy." Parker frowned at me.

"That's not what I meant," I said in a defensive tone. "I thought if she knew that—"

"I know you meant well," Parker broke in, "but we've got to get her sobered up first. She can't hear anything we tell her without overreacting. Right now, she doesn't know her ass from her elbow."

"Oh, yeah?" Blair asked as she jutted out her chin at us. "Elbow," she said, pointing to the seat of her chair. "And ash." She beamed, pointing to her arm.

Lindsey sighed. "You're right, Parker. The big ash doesn't know her ash from her elbow."

"Drink up," I encouraged Blair as I slid one of the coffee mugs closer to her.

"So who wants to go first?" Parker asked as we sat in a coffee shop eight blocks from Casey's. Blair was working on her third cup of coffee and that, combined with the brisk walk we had taken in the cool night air, had helped Blair return to her more normal—and more sober—self.

"What? We're going to tell stories about how we've faked it?" Lindsey asked Parker.

"I don't know that that's what I need to hear," Blair muttered as she rubbed her eyes. "I guess I must be able to fake it okay, because Julia thinks I've had orgasms with her. But I'm clear now. I understand that every woman fakes it at least once with a partner. The difference between me and every other woman, however, is that's all I've been doing. Faking it. With Julia . . . and . . . well, with other people I've been with. My problem is," she paused, then let out a long, loud sigh. "My problem is much bigger than that. Than faking it with a lover. I'm thirty-six years old, right? And I don't think I've ever . . . ever . . . had one."

"One what?" I asked.

"An orgasm?" Lindsey guessed.

Blair nodded.

I stared at Blair. "Not one? Not even one?"

Blair shook her head.

Parker placed an elbow on the table and rested her chin on it. "I've read about people like you."

Blair met Parker's eyes, then hung her head. "There's something wrong with me if I'm in some sort of book."

Parker immediately reached across the table and took Blair's hand in hers. "No, no, honey. That's not what I'm saying. There's nothing wrong with you. It's just, well, you're a late bloomer. That's all. You're just like a lot of other women who achieve first orgasms later on in life."

"But I'm thirty-six," Blair moaned. "How old were you when you first had one?"

"Wasn't it in the womb?" Lindsey joked.

Parker's lips curled up in a half smile. "Not quite as early as that, Linds. But I was very young when I started exploring my body, and I did it happily and quite frequently." She paused as she surveyed us, then shrugged her shoulders. "Hey, I was an only child, and I grew up in a pretty wealthy home. There wasn't much else to do. And riding horses has a way of putting you in touch with what's between your legs."

"Ah, the old 'But Dad, I really want a pony' plea from a young girl." Lindsey grinned.

"Which is why dykes like bikes so much," I added. "It's like spreading your legs around one big vibrator!"

Parker chuckled, then patted Blair's hand. "I think I had my first orgasm by my own hand, so to speak, just before I started my period. And my first orgasm with a woman—actually, a girl—was in the gym locker room in the eighth grade."

Blair frowned. "You were *that* young?"

"Let's hear it for gym class." Lindsey grinned.

"Have you always had an orgasm, with everyone you've been with?" Blair asked Parker.

Parker shook her head. "Of course not. Sometimes, no matter how good a lover someone is or how turned on you think you are, your body or your mind just can't get into it. I remember I went for almost a month not coming with any lovers because my business was going through a bit of a down cycle. I couldn't seem to shut that off."

"But I'm not thinking about work when I'm with Julia," Blair told her.

"It doesn't have to be about work or anything else that's on your mind," Lindsey said. "It can just be your body doesn't want to go there. No matter how much you want to. It's like . . . well . . . I guess it's like a man not being able to get it up."

"I think I have a hard time coming when a lover isn't doing what I want her to do," I offered. "But sometimes it's difficult to interrupt, to redirect her, when she's on her mission. It's hard to work up the courage to tap her on the shoulder in the middle of it all, when she's clearly enjoying herself way more than you are, and tell her, 'Uh, can you touch me here and do it like this.' What makes it even worse is when you need to reposition her again two minutes later. But even when she's doing everything that you're asking her to do, it doesn't always get you where you want to go. It's no one's fault. It's just the way it is."

"But you *do* need to know what you want," Parker added.

"True," I agreed.

Blair shrugged her shoulders. "The women I've been with have been good lovers, I think. So it must be me. I don't know. Maybe I *have* had an orgasm and I just don't know it."

Parker shook her head. "No, you'd know it, Blair. You would definitely know the difference between having an orgasm and not having one."

"Well, it makes me very sad." Blair sighed. "I don't know anyone else who's this old and hasn't had an orgasm yet."

"But you've had one with yourself, right?" Lindsey asked. "So you at least know what it feels like."

Blair looked at each of us, then lowered her eyes and began playing with her coffee mug.

"Seriously?" Lindsey asked her.

Blair nodded.

"*There's* your problem!" Parker exclaimed. "You gotta *have* it first before you can have it. If you know what I mean."

"We need to take her horseback riding." Lindsey chuckled.

"It's not funny, Lindsey," Blair sniffed.

"I know, I know," Lindsey replied. "Sorry. But it's a totally natural thing to do, Blair. Everyone does it. And if they haven't, they should."

"Well, I haven't," Blair blurted out, then gripped her coffee mug with both hands. "I don't want to talk about this anymore. I want to go home."

"But why not?" I asked Blair. "Why haven't you ever masturbated?"

"I just said I wanted to go home," she snapped, then reached behind her and grabbed her jacket from the back of her chair.

"You can go home, hon, but that's not going to help," Parker told her. "You're still going to have this issue in your life and in your relationship with Julia. It's something that we, your friends, understand. We can help you with it. We *want* to help you with it. In a way that Julia probably can't. We want you to have your first orgasm. We want to know what that's like for you. And we want to know we had something to do with it."

Lindsey and I stared at Parker.

"We do?" I asked.

Blair dropped her jacket on her lap and narrowed her eyes at Parker. "Listen, lady, there's no way I'm going to let you—or any one of you, no offense—get into bed with me just so you can give me an orgasm."

"Oh, for God's sake, that's not what I'm saying," Parker told her. "What I'm saying is we—your *friends*—can help *facilitate*—I mean by talking and making suggestions—your first experience of an orgasm. Your first coming, so to speak. We can help take you there."

"We'll take you there," Lindsey sang and snapped her fingers.

Blair glared at Lindsey. "Again. Not funny."

"Sorry," Lindsey mumbled.

"Now tell me, sweetie," Parker resumed, "have you ever masturbated? Have you ever tried?"

"I am *so* embarrassed!" Blair wailed. "I wish I had never brought this whole topic up."

"I have," Lindsey answered. "And even though Judge is in my life, I still do."

"Me, too," I told Blair.

Parker smiled at her. "And you know what my answer is. So, have you masturbated?"

Blair sighed. "Of course I've tried," she answered. "Several times. But I always end up feeling the same way I do when someone is making love to me. It feels very good at the beginning, then it just feels good for a while, and then it just feels okay. It never gets better than it was at the beginning. It just . . . well . . . it just kind of dwindles down and then stays at that level until I get too frustrated and think, *What's the point?* And then, after a while, it's like I can't feel anything. Anything pleasurable anymore, I mean." She shook her head. "I don't know. Maybe I'm frigid."

"What have you done, exactly, when you've masturbated?" Parker asked.

"Dr. Ruth is in the house," Lindsey muttered.

Blair leaned forward in her chair. "Do we have to talk about this *here*?" she asked in a whisper as her eyes wandered around the coffee shop.

"They're not listening," Lindsey told her as she surveyed the handful of people who were engaged in quiet conversation in the small shop.

"So what have you done, exactly, when you've masturbated?" Parker repeated.

"I've . . . well . . . touched myself," Blair whispered.

"Just outside? On the inside as well?" Parker asked.

"How would I—no, just the outside."

"With your fingers? With a vibrator? Did you find you liked a particular side of the clitoris—one that you found was more responsive?"

Blair widened her eyes at Parker. "Can you keep your voice down?" she asked.

"There's nothing to be ashamed about, hon," Parker replied. "It's nature, babes. It's how you get to know your body."

"Well, it's work for me," Blair answered. "And it's very embarrassing to talk about."

"Have you ever used a vibrator?" Lindsey asked. "I have one, and I get off every time."

Blair shook her head.

Lindsey made a low humming noise and then started rotating her hips in the chair. "Oh, yeah," she moaned. "Oh, yeah. Right there. *Right there.*"

"Lindsey!" Blair cried out.

"Oh, that feels so good," Lindsey groaned as she tipped her head back.

"Will you *shut up!*" Blair hissed at her.

"How about a dildo?" Parker asked Blair.

"Yeah, stick it in me!" Lindsey cried out.

"Cool it!" I warned as I glanced over at some customers who were looking in our direction.

Blair wrinkled her nose at Parker. "You mean a fake penis?"

"No," Parker replied. "I mean something that feels mighty good when it's inside you. It makes your orgasms stronger because your muscles are squeezing against it."

"Oh, it's sooo big," Lindsey moaned. "But it feels so good. *So good,*" she panted.

I turned to Lindsey. "What *is* your problem?"

She turned her head and smiled at me. "Are you my mama?"

"No, I'm not your mama!" I answered her indignantly.

"But I *want* you to be my mama," Lindsey persisted. "Oh, I *love it* when you lick me all over. Do you like to hear me moan, baby? I'll moan for you."

Parker raised her eyebrows at Lindsey and began to grin.

I shifted my chair a few inches away from Lindsey and turned to Blair.

"I have a dildo," I confessed to her.

"Do you like what I'm doing to you now, to your breasts?" Parker asked Lindsey.

Blair and I stared at each other.

I cleared my throat as two sets of moans started up. "Les and I bought it when we first got together," I told Blair.

"Oh?" she asked.

"Yes," I answered. "We had a lot of fun with it."

"I want to pin your hands above your head and rub my wetness all over you," Parker told Lindsey. "Would you like that?"

"So, we started using it again," I told Blair. "You know, now that we're together."

"Oh yes, baby, I'd like that," Lindsey answered her. "Rub your body all over mine."

"We had to start all over again in getting to know each other's bodies," I continued.

"I can understand that." Blair nodded. "Because you hadn't been with each other for a while."

"Do you want me inside you?" Parker asked.

I nodded at Blair. "That's why I faked it with her a couple of times. I never really liked oral sex, but she loves doing that."

"You know I want it!" Lindsey cried out. "I want it now! *Now!*"

"I like oral sex," Blair said.

"Are you going to come for me, baby?" Parker asked.

"But everything's okay between you guys now, right?" Blair asked, then raised her eyes as she glanced over my shoulder. "People are starting to look at our table," she whispered to me.

I nodded as I looked over her shoulder at the people who were sitting behind Blair.

"I'm . . . I'm . . . coming!" Lindsey gasped as she started banging her fists on the table.

"I'm coming with you! I'm coming with you!" Parker cried out, then joined in with Lindsey's moans and started waving her hands in the air and shaking her hips.

The blending of their cries got louder.

"I can't tell you how happy I am that I brought up this topic tonight," Blair told me in a voice loud enough for me to hear over the background noises provided by Parker and Lindsey.

The coffee mugs and spoons began to dance on the tabletop.

I nodded. "Well, it was certainly worth a shot, seeing what kind of feedback you'd get from us," I said as I reached a hand out and rescued a mug that was making its way to the edge of the table.

Parker's and Lindsey's cries grew louder.

"Oh, *yes!*" Lindsey screamed.

"And another thing I'm happy about is that I'm sober right now," Blair stated.

"There's absolutely no way that we can stand up and leave, is there?" I asked her.

Parker let out a long, loud scream of *"Oh . . . God! Oh . . . my . . . God!"*

Blair shook her head. "If we had thought about doing that sooner, we might have been able to distance ourselves from them. Now we're just the two other weirdos at the table."

Blair and I stared at each other as Lindsey and Parker stopped their vocalizing and the coffee shop grew unearthly still.

Seconds passed.

Blair kept her eyes on me as she hissed at Lindsey and Parker, "I hope you two are damn proud of yourselves."

"Proud?" Lindsey echoed as she licked her lips. "Heck, I'm embarrassed as all hell."

"Believe it or not, so am I," Parker said as she pinched the front of her silk blouse and flapped it away from her body. "Whew! It's hot in here! But, you know, we did that for you, Blair."

Blair slowly swiveled her head to look at Parker. "You did that for *me*? Well aren't you just the most fucking thoughtful person in the world!"

"Hmmm. Blair said the *F* word," Lindsey stated.

"I was already uncomfortable bringing this whole subject up," Blair continued. "But now you've humiliated *me*. In public. And you've humiliated Gracy as well."

"We didn't humiliate *you*," Lindsey disagreed. "Or Gracy. We humiliated ourselves. So you'd see that sex isn't something to be embarrassed about. Heck, if we can make fools of ourselves faking an orgasm in public, it should be a piece of cake for you to do so in the privacy of your own bedroom."

"I mean, just think about it, Blair," Parker cut in. "Just close your eyes for a moment and imagine that you're at home now, in bed, and you want to experiment a little with your body."

"I don't—" Blair began.

"Just try it," Lindsey urged her.

Blair closed her eyes.

"Can you see yourself reaching under the covers and touching yourself?" Parker asked.

Blair nodded.

"How do you feel now about touching yourself?" Lindsey asked.

Blair thought for a moment, and then smiled. "Compared to what you guys just did, and in a public place, no less, it's not so bad."

"Not as difficult as it was before, right?" Parker asked. "Before Lindsey and I made asses of ourselves, pretending we were Meg Ryan in the deli. In that movie *When Harry Met Sally*."

"Oh, is *that* what we were doing?" Lindsey asked. "Gosh. And here I thought that you really wanted me, P."

Blair slowly opened her eyes. "I think I feel better about the whole subject already. More relaxed."

"You don't have to thank us," Lindsey told Blair.

Blair sucked on a tooth, then shook her head. "I wasn't planning on it."

Lindsey wiped her forehead with the back of her hand and grinned at Parker. "You know, Parker, I'm a little turned on."

"Well, don't look at me, girlfriend," Parker snapped. "I'm not some cheap little whore who you can pick up in some out-of-the-way coffee shop. I prefer to be picked up in a dark, damp, disgusting alley."

Blair started to laugh, then shook her head. "You guys were awful!"

"Awfully loud," I added. "Hell, I haven't ever come that loud."

"Well, remember, we're professional orgasm fakers," Parker answered. "Do not attempt this at home or serious complications may result."

"As well as certain side effects," Lindsey added. "Some orgasm fakers may experience light-headedness, sore throat or hoarseness, back spasms, sleep disorders—"

"Enough!" Blair cut in. "Okay, okay. So you've made me feel more relaxed about getting to know my body better. I'll try, um, my hand at it again."

"How about a little more help than that?" Parker asked as she glanced at her watch. "Come on. We still have time to get there before it closes."

"I don't need any more help," Blair moaned. "It's getting late. I have to work tomorrow. We all do."

Parker stood up. "Just one more hour, Blair," she pleaded as slipped her coat on. "And then I promise you that coming will never be a problem for you again."

* * *

Blair hesitated outside the door of Guilty Pleasure, a sex toy and accessories shop that was located in the basement of a building that housed the largest and oldest men's bar in Boston.

"Come on," Parker said as she grabbed Blair's arm.

"Just give me a minute," Blair replied as she shrank back.

"This isn't a roller coaster ride," Lindsey told her. "It's not scary or anything like that."

"Excuse me," said a deep male voice from behind us.

We turned to see two dark-haired, unshaven men who were decked out from head to toe in black leather. Both were sporting thick jet-black moustaches and displayed tree trunk–size muscular, tattooed arms that appeared to have been forced through the armholes of their fringed leather vests.

"Nothin' to be afraid of, ladies," one of the men said as he surveyed us, then nodded at the door to Guilty Pleasure. "There's somethin' for everyone in there."

The other man grinned at us. "Just look at us, girls. We used to be preppy, skinny Ivy Leaguers. This shop has changed our lives. As the saying goes, 'You can never have enough sex toys.' "

The two men laughed in unison, then creaked their way past us in their skin-tight leather outfits and opened the door.

Blair leaned her body to the side and peeked into the interior of the store. "Oh, my!" she exclaimed as the door slammed shut. She turned to us. "Did you see? In there they had . . . there's . . . one of them was—"

"You're not in Kansas anymore, Dorothy," Lindsey cut in with a grin.

"Come on," Parker urged as she put her arm across Blair's shoulders and started to step to the entrance. "Let's go see a wizard about some oz-some toys."

Blair rolled her eyes at Parker, then looked at me.

"Don't worry, I'm going in there, too," I reassured her. "I think I might buy a new dildo. Break it in with Les. Celebrate our reconnection. And maybe we'll find something for you, okay?"

* * *

Thirty minutes later, Blair and Parker were tucked in a corner of the crowded shop. Lindsey and I watched from a few feet away as Parker showed Blair each of the toys she had picked out for her and how to use them. Blair's facial expressions changed with each thrust Parker made with the dildo and every rotation of the head of the vibrators she had in her hands. At one point Parker tried to hand the dildo to Blair, but she immediately held up her hands and took two steps away from it. Parker shook her head, and motioned with the dildo for Blair to come closer to her.

Slowly, a dildo exchange was made between the two women.

A few minutes later, Blair had a small vibrator in her right hand and the dildo in the other.

Ten minutes later, Blair had the dildo, two vibrators, and two bottles of Astroglide tucked underneath one arm while she stood in front of the dildo harness rack with Parker. Blair chose a harness, then handed it to Parker.

Parker slipped the dildo through the hole, then showed Blair how to put it on by modeling it. She finished her presentation to Blair with a few quick thrusts of her hips.

Blair stared down at Parker's waist, with the dildo flopping in the air, and then turned to look at us.

"Can you believe this?" she called out to us.

Lindsey and I gave her a thumbs-up.

"Gracy?" Leslie mumbled as I lay on my stomach in the bed with an arm and a leg flung on top of her body.

"Hmmm?"

"The phone."

"Huh?"

"The phone. It's ringing."

I turned my head and squinted at the alarm clock. "It's three A.M."

"Better answer it," Leslie said. "There's never any good news at this time of night. The morning."

"All the more reason to ignore it," I mumbled.

"Answer it, hon."

I reached an arm out and fumbled for the receiver. " 'Lo?"

"Gracy?"

"Ummm."

"It's Blair."

"Hey."

"I came!"

"Huh?"

"I said I came! I came, I came, I came!"

I pushed an arm underneath me and sat up in bed. "You did?"

"I did!"

"And how was it?"

"It was great! Awesome! Powerful! Scary! Exciting!"

I smiled. "Pretty good then, is what you're saying."

"Yeah."

"Good."

"Thanks, Gracy. For all your help. Now I'm exhausted, though. Do you get this tired after an orgasm?"

"Oh, yeah," I answered. "But just wait until you have one with Julia."

"I can't wait," Blair said, then yawned. "Okay. I'm going to sleep now."

"Good night," I said, then pressed the OFF button on the phone. I thought for a moment, touched the ON button, and punched in some numbers. After eight rings, Parker picked up the phone.

"She came," I told her. "Tell Lindsey, would you?"

Parker let out a soft, sleepy chuckle. "Our little Blair. She's a big girl now. I'll tell Linds. Say, did you use your new toy yet?"

I glanced over my shoulder and surveyed Leslie's naked body. "I'm just about to," I said, and hung up the phone.

Mission to Venus

In the lesbian days of yore, when some of the women were women but most were men, making love was so much easier than it is today. First off, the roles were clearly delineated. You were either butch, or you were femme. The one who wore the pants, the tailored shirts, and the shit-kicker boots in the relationship was the giver; the one who wore the skirt, the perfume, and the makeup was the receiver. (Kind of like football.) The receiver received. The giver gave. Whatever style the giver had in bed was what the receiver got. No ifs, ands, or buts.

Ah, it was so much simpler in those days. Beebo Brinker had it soooo easy!

Now fast-forward to today. For the most part, lesbians have morphed into women. No matter how you choose to spell their gender, lesbians now bring home the bacon, fry it up in the pan, and expect to have mutually satisfying orgasms with their partners. Today's lesbians are both givers and receivers, and that's what complicates all things sexual.

Some lesbians were once straight and married and are used to one thing in bed. Other lesbians are bisexual, which means they can take it—and give it—any way they want. Some lesbians frown upon any sort of penetration during lovemaking because they think it's too male-centric. Others have difficulty with oral sex because there's more metal in their mouths—and on their clits—than in the Table of the Elements. Still others like the S, but without the M, or the M, but without the S. Some sisters swoon to tantric sex, which is having an orgasm with a partner not by touching her body, but her mind. There are lesbians who frown upon sex toys and some who can't have an orgasm without them. And there are even lesbians who are bound and determined to be virgins for the rest of their lives, or at least until they rub up against a woman on the dance floor, descend into a night of passionate, *wild lovemaking, and during their seventh lovemaking session with her, declare, "I don't know what the hell I was thinking!"*

Is it any wonder, then, that many lesbians throw their hands in the air in sexual frustration and exasperation and cry out, "Women! What do they want?"

Lesbian lovemaking has become an experience that involves all five senses and also the sixth, because a lot of the time you have to be a mind reader. Let's say you're in bed with someone you've been dating. You begin making love to her by kissing her on the neck. She moans. Ah! you think. She likes that. You start to kiss her harder and more passionately on her neck, but then she pushes her head to the side, squeezing your head out of neck-kissing position. You make a mental note: She doesn't like this anymore.

You move on to more promising places. You start by massaging her breasts, and then her nipples. She places a hand over one of yours and pushes it into her breast. Good, you think. Green light. You squeeze a little harder, and she starts to move her hips. Good, good, good.

Now you put your mouth on a nipple. She quickly shifts her body and places the other nipple in your mouth. Likes left breast sucked on first, you tell yourself. You run your tongue around her nipple, and she moans and starts breathing heavier. That's right, that's right, you mentally urge her on, and then think, Am I good or what?

You slide a hand off of one of her breasts and start to move it down the side of her body. You trace a hip with your fingers, and then slide your fingers across one of her legs. You slowly ease your hand between her legs and begin to gently touch her clitoris. She closes her legs and clears her throat. Not happy with that, I guess, you surmise. You slowly extricate your hand from the vise-like grip her thighs have on it—Thighmasters really do work, you think—shake it out so the blood resumes circulation, and return it to her breast.

But she takes this hand off of her breast, pulls it to her mouth, and slowly starts sucking on two of your fingers. Then she pulls in a third and runs her tongue up and down your fingers like

*she's licking and sucking on a lollipop. Quick! What's the mes-
sage here? you ask yourself. Sucking on fingers, sucking on
fingers—what does it mean?*

*She takes little nibbles on the tips of your fingers. You
don't like the sensation, but you know there's some sort of
message here that you're supposed to be interpreting.*

*Then she slowly pulls your fingers out of her mouth and
guides your hand between her legs, which are now spread
wide open. Ah, you think. She doesn't get really wet. Be sure
to bring the lubricant next time.*

*You slowly push two fingers inside her, and she gasps and
pushes her hips up against you. Good, good. That's a clear
signal, you think. She likes two. Let's try three fingers, then.*

*"Um, um," she mumble-moans as you start to insert the
third finger. You're not quite sure what this means. Three fingers okay? Three fingers not okay? You leave the third finger
hovering around the other two and force it not to do much of
anything except watch what the other two fingers are doing.*

*Slowly, your lips make their way from her breasts down to
her belly, and then to the top of her pubic hair. You use the tip
of your tongue to trace little circles through her hair as you
move closer and closer to her clitoris.*

*But as soon as you start to encircle the engorgement with
your tongue and lips, she suddenly clamps a hand down on
the back of your head, crushing your nose against her warm
wetness and effectively cutting off any possibility of nasal
breathing. You open your mouth to suck in air before you pass
out, and she cries out, "Oh, I love it when you blow on me!"*

*You continue to gasp for air like a fish out of water, which
apparently turns her on even more, which then makes her
clamp her hand down on the back of your head even harder.
You're now breathing in minute molecules of air, part of your
third finger, and a couple of detached pubic hairs which, as
they always do, settle in on the roof of your mouth and tickle
your throat. You can't swallow now without coughing the
hair up, but you also can't swallow because your mouth is
clamped between her legs.*

At the moment when you're close to complete oxygen de-

privation and see your life flashing before your eyes—Grandma, is that you? Uncle Dell? Fluffy?—she grinds her hips in quick circles, barks out three short yips, and then relaxes her grip on the back of your head.

Your body slumps next to hers as you take in deep breaths of air.

"Come here, you," she tenderly growls to you, and you slowly fight off the light-headedness as you crawl up to the pillows, where you collapse on top of her.

"That was amazing," she tells you.

You mumble something incoherent as your heart rate finally returns to normal and you think, Heck, I'm pretty good at making love to a woman.

"Let's do it again," she says after a few minutes and starts to push your head down her body, down to what you know now to be the Death Zone.

But this time you're ready. You take in three deep, lung-filling breaths, and then suck in a fourth. You plunge in. Just like at the YWCA swimming pool, where you've practiced holding your breath underwater.

"No, not like that again," she stops you. "I want to do something completely different."

And so it begins again. Finding out just what it is a woman wants. Every lesbian's dilemma.

7

Take a Swim in Lake You ("There's No U in TEAM")

"I have a question to ask everyone," Parker announced as we sat in a shady garden on a glorious spring afternoon, waiting for the scheduled time when a museum guide would lead us through Wellesley College's current exhibit, African-American Women in the Arts, located at the college's Davis Museum. The exhibit had taken years to pull together and had to clear numerous political and financial hurdles along the way.

The exhibit was the offspring of a small 1998 Tuskegee University art show, entitled American Art from Black Colleges and Universities, which received some national newspaper coverage. Their collection of a handful of pieces by African-American artists, both male and female, had been loaned from predominantly black colleges and universities and placed on display at Tuskegee for a few months. Art history students and faculty at Wellesley had visited the virtual gallery of the exhibit online and subsequently started a petition on campus urging Wellesley to pull together a similar exhibit of its own, but featuring the works of African-American women.

Once the college's administration had given the go-ahead, Davis Museum curators had contacted numerous colleges and universities that owned or displayed loaned works by African-American women artists in the hopes that they could put together, on a much larger scale, an exhibit focused solely on the work of black women. The curators spent nearly three years researching the location of various pieces that could be placed in the exhibit, worked out loan arrangements with the institutions that housed the works, arranged for transportation of the pieces to Massachusetts, and then assembled the collection for its first display, which would be the only showing of the art in the New England area. The exhibit was then slated to travel for two years across the country to other colleges and universities.

Lindsey had gotten us tickets for the show's opening week, which featured a private guided tour before the exhibit opened to the public, courtesy of Keystone Investments, a large corporate client she represented at her firm and one of the sponsors of the exhibit.

Blair was overjoyed when Lindsey told us over dinner one night that she could get us tickets to the exhibit. The opening would be at Davis in a month, had been hyped to the public, and almost immediately had generated a lengthy waiting list of ticket hopefuls.

"I minored in art history in college," Blair told us as our meals arrived. "Of course, there are no jobs in the real world that make good use of an art history education, so I got my teaching certificate. But my minor was a disappointment because all we studied in our classes were white artists. Usually white male artists," she added. "This is the first time so many pieces created by African-American women artists will be on display in one location. Just let me know the day everyone can go, and I'll get a substitute in for me."

"I once slept with an African woman," Parker piped in as she dropped a dollop of sour cream on her baked potato. "She was African-American, of course, but she was from Africa. Also, I've slept with several Asian-American women—one was from Korea, two were Taiwanese, and the rest were Chinese or Japanese. I've slept with one woman who claimed to be a Native American, a Canadian, a woman from Brazil, and—"

"Who cares?" Lindsey interrupted as she speared a cherry tomato in her salad with a fork. "We were talking about the *ex-*

hibit of African-American *artists,*" she emphasized. "And Blair was talking about the fact that *she* was an *art history* major. Neither has anything to do with the nationalities of the women you've seduced."

"I heard what we were talking about," Parker answered as she sawed a knife through her thick slice of rare roast beef. "And that's great, Blair, about the minor in art history. That's just like me. Who would've imagined that I, a successful business-woman, would've studied biology in college. I actually thought I wanted to be a researcher in my freshman year before I opted for the business path. But that's water under the bridge. I just told you about the women I've slept with because I thought you guys would be interested in what I call my "it's-a-small-world-after-all" period of past conquests. And we talk about sex a lot. I just wanted to contribute to the conversation."

"No, *you* talk about sex a lot," Lindsey snapped.

"I think we all talk about sex a lot," I quickly chimed in. "I wouldn't say there's anything wrong with that, but in this case—"

"Excuse me, ma'am," Parker broke in as she waved her knife in the air and peered at Lindsey. "But weren't you the one who started out a conversation the last time we got together with 'I was denuded and delighted?' And didn't we then spend the rest of the evening talking about you and Judge and every position you've tried out? Suddenly, you and Judge are back on track and back in the sack. I swear, Linds, I can't keep up with you."

"Let's get back to talking about the exhibit," I suggested.

"Yes," Blair agreed. "What—"

"No, let's not," Lindsey broke in as she glared at Parker. "The difference between you and me and between you and the rest of the world, Parker, is that at least I'm trying to make a re-lationship work because *I care.* You don't really care about *any-one* you sleep with. Black, white, rich, poor—who cares? It's just a conquest to you, some little notch for you to carve into the headboard of your bed."

"How did we get a conversation going in this direction?" Blair asked. "I mean, cool it, you guys."

Lindsey laid her fork down on her plate. "And what difference should it make anyway—to anyone—whether you've slept with an African woman, an African-American woman—"

"I've had some brown sugar in my time." Parker grinned.

Blair scowled at Parker. "Come on! Even in jest, I don't think that's funny."

Parker shrugged. "Fine. So I guess no one wants to hear about the hot time I spent with the Hawaiian woman I met last week on a buying trip to the island."

"Aren't you with Cindi?" I asked Parker.

"I don't know that I'm *with* her, at least in the context you're implying," Parker answered. "But I *see* her. Pretty regularly. And we have this understanding. We have an open-dating plan."

"That sounds like some sort of medical insurance choice," I commented, then lowered my voice. "With our open-dating plan, you can see as many doctors as you like in a year and not be penalized."

Parker chuckled. "That's pretty much the way it is with Cindi and me. I don't believe in monogamy—no surprises there, I guess—mostly because I equate monogamy with monotony. I can sleep with whomever I want, and Cindi can do the same."

"I doubt that she is," Lindsey muttered. "That woman really likes you."

"Then that's her choice," Parker answered. "She knows the drill because, as those touchy-feely lesbians say, 'I've been very *open* with my feelings. We've *processed* what we needed to process and *brought closure* to what we need to close.' "

"You're going to lose her if you keep sleeping around," Blair warned Parker. "She's not going to put up with that for very long."

"Are you willing to risk losing her?" I asked Parker.

Parker laid down her knife and stared at us. "Why did this conversation suddenly turn to me? All I said, about fifteen years ago now, was that I had slept with a lot of women from different countries. I thought that was relatively interesting and fit in with the African-American woman theme we were striving for, but what I said was apparently racist—"

"More like annoying," Lindsey broke in.

"What...ev...errr, Linds," Parker drawled. "Anyhow, the point that I'm trying to make is that what goes on between Cindi and me is our own business. We are way too early in this ...whatever it is...for it even to be called a relationship." Parker feigned a full-body shiver. "Eww! I don't even like saying that word, so I can't imagine that I'd even enjoy being in one."

"Then what do you call it?" Lindsey asked. "Is Cindi just the flavor of the week? Or the fuck-of-the-month choice?"

Parker raised her eyebrows. "That comment is just a wee tad nasty, don't you think?" she asked. "No, Cindi is not the flavor of the week or the fuck of the month." She paused. "But what if she was, Linds? That's my choice. What does it matter to you?"

Lindsey pushed her plate forward and leaned her chest against the edge of the table. "Maybe because I see you with someone who's really nice and who wants to be with you, P. And that doesn't...I don't know...that doesn't affect you in the least. You treat Cindi like you could take her or leave her."

"That's not how I feel," Parker responded. "But what if it was?"

Lindsey sighed and sat back in her chair. "I guess...well... I guess the way you treat Cindi is too much like the way Judge treats me sometimes. Not all the time, mind you. But sometimes. And I know how *I* feel in that situation. So I can't imagine that Cindi is feeling any better."

"Oh, for crying out loud," Parker grumbled as she jabbed a hunk of butter into her baked potato and mixed it in with the sour cream. "Will you stop comparing you and Judge to everyone else. You made your choice with Judge. You've either got to stop fighting the reality of the situation or walk away from it. Just like Cindi's got to accept what I can give her, or she's going to have to find someone else."

"Are you sure that's what you want?" Blair asked. "I've gotten the impression that you really like Cindi. Maybe more than most of the other women you've been with."

Parker sampled a bite from her potato, then licked her fork. "Maybe I do. Maybe I don't. I haven't really thought about it."

"Of course you've thought about it," I argued. "Otherwise, why would you be setting parameters with her, rules with her, limits with her?"

"There you go again, Gracy," Parker said with a sigh. "Therapizing again."

I grinned at her. "I minored in psychology in college. I have to put it to some use. So answer my question."

Parker tipped her head to the side. "Answer your question, Dr. Maynard? Okay. It's just that sometimes . . . well . . . sometimes she comes on to me like she wants more, and she knows I don't like that. I don't like it when she wants us to be an *us*. To do that settling-down thing. Like I said, it's too early to be doing stuff like that."

"It kind of freaks you out, right?" I asked.

"Is *freaks out* a clinical term?" Parker countered.

"Julia and I started looking at homes last week," Blair informed Parker. "We've been going together for the same amount of time as you and Cindi have. We didn't think it was too early."

I nodded. "Les and I are apartment hunting, and we think that it's the right time for us to do that."

"I'm thinking about moving into Judge's backyard and stalking her," Lindsey added, then cracked a smile. "I'm just kidding."

"So? So? So?" Parker asked as she looked at each of us. "That's the way you each choose to run your relationships. Doing that U-Haul, let's-be-together-forever-and-ever, monogamous thing. That's not my style."

"Are you still going to be saying that with such bravado when you're fifty-five?" Lindsey asked.

Parker beamed at her. "Of course I will. Then I'll be going through my midlife crisis. I'll buy a sports car—a little red Corvette, baby you're much too fast—and date women who are in college."

"Cindi is a wonderful person," I told Parker. "You should

start thinking about what you can do to hold onto her. Not push her away. Because once she's gone—"

"She's gone," Lindsey finished.

Blair nodded. "Nice people don't come along every day, Parker. People can look for years for the right person to—"

"Oh, pa-leeze!" Parker cut in. "Let's stop with the Lifetime for Women sappy stuff. Maybe I'm just not the settling-down kind. Maybe that's not right for me. Maybe I'm happy living alone. Maybe I like having my own space. Maybe I like having things the way I want them. Maybe I like being able to go to the fridge and know that the last piece of Simply Divine chocolate cheesecake is still there. And, lest you girls forget, I sleep alone only when I *choose* to. I'm not keeping the other side of the bed preserved as a shrine like you girls did before you met your current flames. I'm not waiting for Ms. Right to walk into my life so my life can finally begin. This is the life I *want*. Right here. Right now."

"You're truly happy sleeping with as many women as you do?" Lindsey asked.

Parker nodded. "Of course I am. Why else would I do it?"

"Oh, I don't know, let's see," I began as I scratched my head. "Fear of intimacy? Fear of abandonment? Fear of trust? Fear of—"

"It's you gals who are afraid," Parker cut in. "You're afraid that if you look at another woman when you're with someone, it'll be the end of the world. You're afraid that if you act on your attraction to someone else, you'll end up being alone for the rest of your lives. Sometimes having sex—not making love, mind you—but having sex outside of a relationship is a good thing."

I rolled my eyes. "Oh, God, no, don't say that. Don't even think that! It kills a relationship. It drives you apart and—"

"That's because Leslie *fell in love* with someone she was just supposed to fuck," Parker cut in. "And since you couldn't forgive her for that, *you* got fucked. Actually, you fucked yourself, Gracy, but not being open to her just getting a little pussy on the side."

"How dare you . . ." I began, then stopped. I clenched my fists and my jaw as my face turned beet red.

Blair glanced at me, then slammed her napkin on the table. "Sometimes, Parker, you are too crude. And too unfeeling. Gracy is your friend. She's never been mean or nasty to you, so why be that way with her?"

"I wasn't being mean or nasty," Parker countered, then shrugged her shoulders. "Hey, I'm just being honest. This is who I am. This is my life. If you don't like it, then don't live it. Live your own lives. But me, I'm getting what I want. And someday, who knows, maybe I'll write a titillating tale about all of my conquests and it'll fly to the top of the best-seller list."

"With men, perhaps," Lindsey quipped. "I don't know a single lesbian who would want to read such a book."

"How about every woman I've ever slept with?" Parker asked. "And now, let's see, the count is up to—"

"Parker, you are definitely more than just relationship-challenged," I cut in. "There's something not quite right about a person who cares more about the next bedmate than finding a soul mate."

Parker let out a quick snort. "Oh, now there's a term I adore. Soul mate! A soul *sister,* I might understand," she said as she glanced at Blair. "Which brings us back to where we started. Going to Wellesley College to see the works of your sister friends. I'm in for that. Who else is?"

I shook my head. "Nice deflection, Parker."

Parker closed her eyes, gave a slight bow in my direction, then opened her eyes. "Thank you very much, Gracy. And now I'd like to eat my dinner before it gets cold."

It took us nearly two weeks of back-and-forth communication before we settled on a day during the week that would work out best for each of us to attend the exhibit. Parker's schedule seemed to be the hardest to accommodate. She either had work-related obligations or a slew of previously scheduled personal appointments: the hairdresser for a perm and highlights, the masseuse for her weekly rub down, the spa for her facial and manicure, the first day of a sale at a pricy clothing store on Newbury Street. "I cannot possibly reschedule with some of these people—they book appointments *weeks* in advance," she told us during the fifth round of our negotiations. "And I certainly would be committing fashion *suicide* if I wasn't there the second the doors opened on sale day."

Finally, we settled on Thursday afternoon during the exhibit's opening week.

"I guess that'll have to do," Parker huffed as we each let out a deep sigh and closed our appointment books after one of our Sunday brunches.

"It *will* do," Lindsey informed her with a steely glare.

"It has to." Blair nodded. "I can't just ask for a sub on one day and then expect to be able to switch to another."

"Okay, okay," Parker agreed. "That's the date. End of discussion. Now, I don't know how you girls feel, but I'm getting really tired of having our Sunday brunches here. I want to go to La Scala's next time."

"That's the hardest restaurant in Boston to get into," Lindsey pointed out.

Parker waved a hand lightly in the air. "Not for me it's not."

Blair cleared her throat. "Um, I think it's a little out of my budget. I mean, I could swing it, but—"

"Me, too," I agreed. "I work from job to job, check to check, and one brunch there would cost me about two day's worth of copyediting and proofreading."

"But it's *worth* it," Parker argued. "The food is divine. The atmosphere is exquisite. The—"

"There's nothing on the menu that's even priced close to what we pay here for an enormous buffet brunch and drinks," Lindsey cut in. "Unless it's a cup of coffee. It's not that I can't afford it, P. But if Blair and Gracy can't swing it, then I say *no* along with them."

"Well, money shouldn't be the sticking point," Parker argued. "It'll be my treat. How's that?"

Blair shook her head. "I'm not comfortable with that."

"Me neither," I agreed.

Parker let out a sigh. "Okay, okay. But I'm the one making a *huge* sacrifice here. What are you guys going to do for me?"

"Not kill you?" I suggested.

"Gracy!" Lindsey exclaimed. "You're being far too nice."

"We'll continue to be your friends," Blair answered. "Your cheap, but accepting, friends."

On Thursday we met in the parking lot of the museum and walked to the garden and patio area that was set up outside the museum's entrance. It was a beautiful spring day—one of the finest of the season—with a bright blue cloudless sky overhead, a warming sun, and a gentle breeze.

Parker surveyed the concrete benches as we entered the shady garden and walked up to one. She pulled a handkerchief out of her purse, brushed leaves, tiny twigs, and bird droppings from one side of the concrete slab to the other, and then sat down.

Lindsey stared at the other half of the concrete bench for a few seconds, then looked at Parker. "Why didn't you clean off the entire bench?" she asked.

"I don't *need* the entire bench," Parker informed her in a huff. "I know I'm a large woman, but I'm not *that* large."

"I wasn't commenting on your size," Lindsey answered. "I'm commenting on the fact that there are three other people here who need to sit down and you clearly have the ability to clean the benches. Why not do it for everyone?"

"What am I, the janitor?" Parker asked. "Clean your own bench."

"It's not a problem," I said as I swept a hand over the other half of Parker's bench and sat down. I looked up at Lindsey. "It's no big deal."

Parker looked up at Lindsey. "You heard the woman."

Lindsey shook her head at Parker, then helped Blair brush off another concrete bench.

"I can't believe all the great artists who have works here," Blair said as she opened the brochure for the exhibit. "Edmonia

Lewis, for instance. A sculptor whose *Forever Free*, a statue in marble, was sculpted in 1867. Lois Mailou Jones, who was born in Boston and then studied in Paris in the 1930s. Her early exhibits in the United States were met with criticism. Listen to this," she said as she held up the brochure. "Alain Lock, a Rhodes scholar and poet, wrote to her in 1939. He said, 'We expect more from the Negro artist, a vigorous and intimate documentation of Negro life itself.' After she received that letter, she changed her imagery and—"

"So when does this tour get started?" Parker cut in as she fanned her face with her brochure, using it as a blackfly deflector.

"Two o'clock," I told her.

"I know nothing about any of these women," Lindsey commented as she flipped through the brochure. "But their works are beautiful."

"I wonder if any of the lovely Wellesley College gals will be at this exhibit." Parker grinned. "I once set a goal of dating a woman from each of the sister colleges. I dated a Smithie and someone from Mount Holyoke. I dated two women from Skidmore before I realized that Skidoo isn't one of the sister colleges. I thought it was. Can you gals name the seven sister colleges?"

"Oh—here's Elizabeth Catlett," Blair exclaimed as she pointed to a page in the brochure. "I have a print of this, of her. *Latch Key Child*. She was one of a group of printmakers who used their art to promote social change."

"I have a question to ask everyone," Parker cut in.

"And look—Carrie Mae Weems," Blair continued. "Oh, I love this work of hers. *You Became Mammie, Mama, Mother & Then, Yes, Confidant*—Ha. Look at the expression on the woman's face."

"Is anyone listening to me?" Parker asked.

"What?" Lindsey answered.

"I said I have a question to ask everyone."

"Okay," Lindsey said. "Then ask."

"Do you think I'm selfish?"

Lindsey let out a quick snort and then pointed to the bench Parker was sitting on. "Hello? Do you recall what you did before you sat down?"

"Forget about the bench, Linds," Parker answered. "What I want to know is, am I selfish? The reason I ask is because Cindi said something to me last night. We actually had a bit of a fight."

"Oh? Trouble in the Garden of Eatin'?" Lindsey quipped.

Parker flashed Lindsey a quick fake smile, and then resumed talking. "Before she stormed out the door she turned to me and yelled, 'Why don't you take a swim in lake u!' I asked her, 'What Lake U? What's a Lake U?' and she answered, 'You, Parker. As in Y-O-U. That's where you should take a swim. In Lake You. Because *you* are the most important thing to *you*. Got it?' And then she slammed the door and left."

Lindsey held her arms out from her body and made circular motions with them. "Go Cindi, go Cindi."

"Hey, I'm trying to be serious here," Parker snapped at Lindsey.

"Oh, and like we aren't ever trying to be serious when we talk about things that bother us with you?" Lindsey replied.

"Let's not start an argument," Blair cut in.

"What do you think Cindi meant by what she said, P.?" I asked. "What do you think she was trying to tell you?"

Parker grinned and wagged a finger at me. "Uh-uh, Gracy. Don't you be pulling that therapist shit with me. 'What do *you* think she meant?' I'm not falling for that." She looked at Blair. "What do you think, sister friend? I trust you to be honest. You're honest in a nice way. You don't stick a knife in people like Lindsey does."

Blair took in a deep breath as she carefully folded the pages of her brochure. "Well, Parker," she began, then paused and sighed. "Maybe sometimes you're a little . . . um . . . pushy. And—"

Lindsey let out another snort.

"Let her finish," Parker told Lindsey, then waved a hand at Blair. "Go on."

"Well . . . um . . . I guess everyone can be a little pushy from time to time. It doesn't always mean that—"

"See, well, there you are," Parker broke in as she surveyed us. "You want to know what I think? I think Cindi was just having a bad night. Maybe she was PMS-ing. Or maybe she was upset about something at work and just taking it out on me. I don't think that I'm in any way—"

"Yes!" Lindsey cut in loudly. "Yes, yes, *yes*! Yes, you *are* selfish, Parker."

Parker stared at Lindsey. "There's that knife, Linds."

Lindsey leaned forward. "P., we're friends. All of us," she said as she swept an arm to include each of us. "We accept each other's quirks and personality traits. Mostly because we don't have to deal with them twenty-four, seven. But with someone who cares about you as much as Cindi does, I would imagine it must be pretty hard for her. To deal with your selfishness, I mean. You expect people to work around you, to go along with you, even to adhere to what you want. Sometimes you don't take other people's feelings into account. Sometimes you're not even aware that other people do, in fact, have feelings."

"So you're saying that I'm selfish," Parker concluded. "I thought you'd feel that way." She looked at Blair. "Is that what *you* think?"

Blair swallowed, then nodded. "Your world is small, Parker," she said.

"Small!" Parker nearly bellowed. "I travel the world. My world is in no way small."

"She's not saying that the world is small," I told Parker. "Blair's saying that *your world*—the world that you consider to be your own space—is small."

"Meaning what exactly, Gracy?" Parker demanded.

I held a hand up to her. "Hey, don't be getting mad at me. Because you asked us a question. And we're giving you an honest answer. Remember? You like to be honest."

Parker cleared her throat. "Go on," she told me.

I shifted my position on the bench so I could face Parker. "I think what Cindi meant is that you think a lot about yourself.

Maybe too much. And while that may not be a problem with your friends—"

"Although you *have* been selfish with us at times," Lindsey cut in.

"—it's certainly a problem when you're involved with someone," I finished.

"Cindi has her needs, Parker, just as you have yours," Blair jumped in. "When you're involved with someone, you have to listen to her needs, accept her needs, even try to meet those needs when you can. Maybe you even have to let her have the last piece of Simply Divine chocolate cheesecake, for instance."

Parker widened her eyes and clutched her chest. "Horrors! Not my cheesecake!"

"What does Cindi say she wants from you?" I asked her.

Parker sighed. "Time. Time. And more time."

"And do you give that to her?" Blair asked.

"Sure I do. As much as I can give her, I mean."

"Except when you're making dates with other women," Lindsey scoffed.

"Not while I'm here," Parker mumbled, then stared down at her lacquered fingernails.

"What's that?" Lindsey asked.

Parker blew on her fingernails, then looked at Lindsey. "I said, not while I'm here. Around her, I mean," she answered. "I only do that when I'm traveling. Sometimes. Not all the time. Not as much as I used to."

"Why not?" I asked.

Parker shrugged her shoulders and shifted her position on the bench. "Because I talk to Cindi a lot on the phone. When I'm away from her. And then when I'm home . . . well . . . I'm with her. I don't have time to see other women. Because she's taking up all of my time."

"That's a Martha Stewart," Lindsey commented.

"A what?" Blair asked.

"A good thing," Lindsey smiled. "It's good that Cindi's taking up all of your time, P."

"But then she wants *more* time from me," Parker complained. "I mean, how can you make more time out of a finite amount of time? There are only seven days in a week. Twenty-four hours in a day. Sixty minutes in an hour. Sixty seconds in each—"

"What else does Cindi need besides time?" Blair cut in.

Parker sighed and turned to me. "Speaking of time, what time does this tour start?"

"We have half an hour," I answered.

"Then let's go for a walk or something," she suggested.

"Parker, what else does Cindi need?" Blair persisted.

Parker shook her head, then tossed an arm in the air. "Women! They need, they need, they *need*. They need to process everything. Every gosh darn little thing. 'How are you feeling?' 'What are you thinking?' 'What do you feel like having for dinner?' 'How do I compare to your other lovers?' On and on it goes. Why does everything have to be a discussion, or a barter, or a compromise? Why can't things just be . . . just be . . ." Parker's voice trailed off as she looked at us, then sighed.

"My way," she finished.

"And so she answers her own question," Lindsey said.

"Because that's not *her* way," Blair answered. "You have to be two people when you're with someone, when you're together. You can't be two people who are thinking and acting and doing with just one person in mind. There has to be a balance, an equilibrium, that accounts for both people getting their needs met."

"Well put," Lindsey commended her.

I nodded. "I know what Leslie needs, and she knows what I need. And because we know this about each other, it makes it so much easier to be together."

"What does she need?" Parker asked.

I smiled. "Besides the big things—trust, honesty, and commitment, which both of us need—there are so many little things that make her who she is. Those little things help me to understand her and help me to—and I know you're going to hate this word, Parker—but to *acknowledge* her presence in my life."

"So what does she need?" Parker asked again. "Expensive

gifts? A night out on the town every week? Sex three times a week?"

"Oh, so you want tangibles," I answered. "Okay. She needs chocolate every day. Whenever I buy her one of her favorite chocolate bars, she's very happy."

"Julia's a fiend for salty and spicy foods," Blair piped in. "She can't watch sports on TV—especially football—without chips and salsa. Mexican food is her favorite. So whenever I know she's going to want to sit in front of the TV for hours, I'll go out and get her favorite Mexican dishes for her."

"Judge loves sharp Vermont cheddar and Triscuits," Lindsey added. "And she loves those Kraft macaroni and cheese dinners. She likes bubble baths and foot massages and the poems of Emily Dickinson—"

"Okay, okay," Parker cut in.

"So what does Cindi like to eat?" I asked Parker.

"Everything, I guess," she answered. "She likes just about everything."

"Are there any foods she doesn't like?" Lindsey asked.

Parker thought for a moment. "I don't think so."

"Another thing that Leslie needs is to decompress at the end of a workday with music," I said. "For at least half an hour. Then we can talk about our day."

"Judge loves having her feet massaged at the end of the day," Lindsey said.

"For Julia, it's a run," Blair added. "It doesn't matter what the weather is."

"How does Cindi end her workday?" Lindsey asked Parker.

Parker thought for a moment. "She comes over to see me, I guess."

"I can't open any magazine we get in the mail until Julia's looked at it first." Blair giggled. "She hates looking at magazines that have already been read. She wants 'virgin magazines,' she tells me."

"Leslie loves the soaps," I said. "She's already told me that when we move into our apartment, our cable package has got to include the Soap Network."

"Judge needs a nap every day," Lindsey stated. "Sometimes

she calls for a fifteen-minute recess during an afternoon trial just so she can take a nap in her chambers. I think I'm the only one who knows that."

"Julia needs me to drive whenever we go on day trips," Blair said. "I drive, and she buys me whatever I want to eat during the day."

"Leslie needs to sit at the end of the aisle when we're at the movies," I added.

"Julia needs to wear socks to bed." Blair giggled. "Even when it's hot out."

"Judge needs—"

"Okay, okay, I get it," Parker broke in.

"I bet Cindi knows what *you* need, P.," Lindsey pointed out. "I mean, you are pretty good at vocalizing what you want."

"But you need to know what Cindi needs," Blair added.

"How do I do that?" Parker asked.

"Just ask her," I suggested. "That's one way to find out. And pay attention to her. Watch the way she does things. That can tell you a lot about what she likes." I glanced down at my watch. "I guess we should get going to the museum. The tour leaves in about ten minutes."

Parker remained on the bench while the rest of us stood up.

"Aren't you coming?" I asked her.

She chewed on a corner of her lip, then nodded. "I will, Gracy. In a minute. I think I'll . . . well . . . I think I'll just give Cindi a quick call. You know, to check in. No big deal. Go on. Go ahead," she told us as she reached into her purse and pulled out her cell phone. "I'll be along in a few."

Blair, Lindsey, and I walked away a few steps, then stopped and looked at Parker.

Parker had her back turned to us. "It's me," we heard her say into the phone. "Nothing. No, nothing's wrong. I'm just calling. I just . . . well . . . I just thought you might like to think about . . . well . . . about what you'd like to do tonight. Huh? . . . It doesn't matter to me . . . No, really. How about, well, didn't you say you liked Chinese food as much as Italian? That was you, right? . . . Yeah, I remember you told me that once . . . Of course I pay attention to you. Do you want to try out that new

Chinese restaurant you said opened up downtown? . . . I don't care what the atmosphere is like . . . That's fine . . . Really . . . Yes, really. I told you nothing's wrong . . . I just, well, I just miss you, okay? . . . What's that? . . . Very funny. Then pick yourself up off the floor and get your work done. And I was wondering, um, what's your favorite flower?"

These Are a Few of My Favorite Needs

One of my former college buds—someone with whom I've remained friends for many, many years—admitted to me once that she was "somewhat addicted" to filling out personal ad profile forms on a Web site for single lesbians.

"I'm not doing it to meet someone new," she assured me. She knew that I considered her to be my "relationship role model," having spent a decade and counting with the same woman.

She does this, she told me, because she enjoys identifying the things she likes and doesn't like in a public forum. It's the thrill, she says, of knowing that someone, somewhere, might be interested in the things she considers to be her passions, as well as the things she dislikes.

She told me she gets "jazzed up" thinking of a perfect stranger reading her profile and learning a little bit more about her. "Because," she said, "it's knowing the little things about a person that makes a big difference in a relationship.

"I miss the stages of first getting to know someone," she confessed. "That's the time when you ask a potential love interest a lot of questions about themselves: what they like and dislike, what their goals and dreams are, how they see themselves in the world.

"When my partner and I were first dating, we would E-mail each other once a day with a list of ten questions we wanted answered. Sometimes the questions were really simple or mundane, like 'What magazines do you subscribe to?' Sometimes they were flirtatious and personal, like 'What part of your body is the most sexually responsive?' And sometimes they were more philosophical, like 'What do you think happens to you after you die?'

"I loved those first few months of questioning," she told me, then let out a deep sigh. "It made me feel as if someone

was truly paying attention to me. But now, well . . ." Her voice trailed off and she was quiet for a few moments.

"Now it's like my partner and I are sailing through our connected lives, but we're not on the same ship. She wants to do what she wants to do, and I either have to go along with whatever she wants or find my own things to do."

So one day, she told me, when she was feeling a bit rejected by her partner, a bit blue over the rift between them that was gradually widening with the passage of time, and a bit lonely even though she was in a committed, monogamous relationship, she visited a popular gay matchmaking Web site. She opened up the personals section to browse and found herself propelled into a universe in which sharing and discovery were the sole means of communication.

She didn't reply to any of the profiles at first, although she admitted to me that she was "tempted" to respond to a few who seemed to "be me."

But she thought it might be "a hoot" to fill out a profile of her own.

She started by naming her profile "This is Me." She filled out the basic information—age, body type, height, weight, geographical location, gender, ethnicity, a physical description, whether she was a smoker or nonsmoker, drinker or non-drinker, drug user or nondrug user, whether she had piercings and tattoos, pets, kids or no kids, and how out she was to friends, to family, and to the world. She assigned herself the member name, "memyselfI."

Then, she said, "I revealed everything about me that was important to me. What books I liked to read. My favorite movies. Music I love to listen to, and music I hate. How I feel about myself at this point in my life. What my desires are for the future. Where I fit my passions into my life. I wrote, and wrote, and wrote."

That was six months ago, she said. "Now I have six profiles on the site—all with different screen names, of course. Because I'm always changing, always evolving, and always interested in trying new things—which my partner is not. So I've composed a variety of profiles that fit certain aspects of my personality, that convey how I'm feeling at that particular moment in my life.

"I feel like I'm finally myself again," she told me. "I feel like I'm able to share once again who I am with the world. And the world listens. That, in turn, makes me feel happy and secure."

This conversation took place five months ago. I lost touch with my friend afterward—we each went our separate ways, I guess, as some of us do.

But then, by chance, we ran into each other last week. She was bubbly and giddy and full of smiles. She had left her long-time partner, she told me, for a woman who had responded to one of her profiles.

"And now," she said, "we've started our own Web site for women who don't want a lover or a partner or even a friend, but who just want to share with the world who they are." She smiled at me. "It's called memyselfI.com, and right now we have over three hundred profiles from women all around the world. We get over a thousand hits a day! Can you believe it? My life has taken such a dramatic, but such a wonderful turn. All because I was with someone who seemed more interested in herself than she was in me.

"It's been said," she told me, "that selfishness is the ruin of the human heart. That those who are self-absorbed are incapable of truly loving someone else. I believe this. I really do."

She told me more about her life—where she was living now, a new puppy she and her lover had adopted "just a few weeks ago," how her family was, and dozens of other things.

Then we parted. As I walked away from her, I thought about what an interesting turn my friend's life had taken, how happy she was, and how her passion for her new life had made her glow with excitement and pride.

And then I realized something else.

She hadn't asked me one question about myself or my life.

8

Living with Your Material Girl
(You Mean We Actually Paid
to Move *This?*)

"Check this out," Lindsey announced as she walked into the living room of her Beacon Hill condo. She carefully placed an object on the floor in the middle of where we were relaxing, and then sat down in front of the couch and crossed her legs.

We slowly and reluctantly leaned forward. We had been sprawled, nearly comatose, on the floor, our bodies propped up against numerous oversized pillows after finishing off a four-course gourmet takeout dinner followed by a rich, delicious dessert, courtesy of the Queens of Cuisine, a gay-owned catering service in Boston.

Parker blinked her eyes and groaned. "It's not something to eat, is it?" she asked as she sat up, unbuckled her jeweled belt, and unbuttoned the top button on her silk pants.

"Hardly," Lindsey answered. "Call this part of The Girls' evening, The Parlor Game."

"Please, not Pictionary," I moaned. "If I go to one more potluck that has groups of lesbians playing Pictionary, I'm going to convert to heterosexuality. And I don't want to play Scrabble. Or any other word game. Words are work for me, not fun. Don't lesbians know how to play Clue? Cribbage? Crazy Eights? Old Maid?"

"Honey, we're *all* old maids—or eventually *will* be." Parker chuckled.

"I like easy games like that," I went on. "I used to play Battleship all the time. And G.I. Joe. Oh—and I played with those little plastic toy soldiers. All the kids in my neighborhood would get together, pool their toy soldiers, and we'd stage these massive mock battles."

"Did you make all those boy-noises when you played?" Blair asked. "You know, the sound of machine guns shooting and grenades exploding and Army tank engines? I could never make those noises."

"I used to pin baseball cards with clothespins near the spokes on my bicycle," Lindsey said. "That made some pretty good noise."

"My family was into chess," Parker told us. "Since that involved way too much thinking for me, I'd beg out of the matches. Instead, I'd go to my room and make collages out of pictures I'd cut out of the stacks of magazines my mother and I subscribed to. I'd pick pictures that captured what I thought my future would be like. I'd imagine, *Here's where I'll be living. Here's what I'll be wearing. Here's what I'll be driving.* The mansions were huge, the clothes were expensive, and the cars were luxury models."

"That's not too far from the truth," I pointed out. "Your clothes are from the most fashionable stores on Newbury Street, your car is a brand-new Lexus, and you live in the penthouse of a downtown high-rise."

"I guess visualization really does work," Lindsey said. "If only I hadn't wasted so much time in my childhood just, well, being a kid."

"I liked playing with dolls," Blair confessed. "Barbie was my favorite, but I had a lot of other dolls, too. From different countries—well, I mean, they were *dressed* like they were from different countries. Sometimes I'd take them all out, prop them up on my bed, and pretend to talk to them in their foreign tongue."

"Even back then, Blair was giving tongue," Parker joked. "Did you have an Easy Bake Oven, too?"

"Of course I did," Blair answered. "I used it so much that my mother had to stock up on those little packages of mixes. I had a miniature pantry set up in my room."

"You mean you actually *ate* that stuff?" I asked.

Blair nodded. "That's how I acquired my taste to this day for Snowballs. And Twinkies. And I also like those gooey little—"

"Ladies!" Lindsey cut in. "Enough with the childhood reminiscences. I have a project for you here," she said as she pointed to the object in front of us.

"And no more talking about food," I added.

"I want you to check out this . . . um . . . thing," Lindsey said.

We each stared at the object for several seconds.

"What is it?" Blair finally asked.

"You tell me," Lindsey answered.

"It's a . . ." Parker began, then stopped and crawled forward on her hands and knees to assess the object from a closer vantage point.

"It looks old," I observed. "Is it an antique?"

Lindsey shrugged her shoulders.

"Well, it's made out of wood," Blair noted. "All those tall things sticking up on it. Whatever they are. They look like castle turrets. They're wood. Maybe pine. Maybe maple. Could be oak. I don't know. I'm guessing. I know nothing about wood, but I'm acting like I do."

"Don't expect Bob Vila to call on you, then," Parker told her.

"Who's he?" she asked.

Parker shook her head. "Never mind."

"It's made out of wood *and* little chunks of pink and green metal—see?" Lindsey pointed out as she tapped a metallic part of the object.

"Are those little doorways or something?" I asked as I leaned forward and poked my baby finger into an opening. "See? There are little holes here—all around it, as a matter of fact—like they're entrances to something."

"Maybe it's a teeny, tiny apartment building," Parker offered. "For bugs or something."

"Like one of those ant farms?" I asked.

"Sure." Parker grinned. "But it's a *private* bug home. For rich bugs. Because you can't see how they spend their time in there."

"Wouldn't bugs eat the wood?" Blair asked. "And who would want a bug house in their apartment?"

Parker stared at her.

"What?" Blair asked.

"I was only kidding."

"Oh," Blair responded, then looked at Lindsey. "What do you do with it?"

"Pretty much, I move it around a lot," she answered. "Judge gave it to me a few weeks ago. Whenever I know she's coming over, I make sure to put it out, on that shelf over there," she said, pointing to a floor-to-ceiling entertainment center that was set against a living room wall. "Then, when she leaves, I put it back in a closet. Or in the spare room. Anywhere out of sight."

"What did Judge say it was?" Parker asked.

Lindsey smiled. "That's just it. She didn't. She came here one night with a big box in her hands, all nicely wrapped. I got really excited when I saw that, because she had never brought me a gift before. Flowers, occasionally. Take-out food, sure. Handcuffs and a blindfold, yeah. But never a *gift* gift. You know, something just because. It was big. And it was wrapped."

"And so you opened it up . . ." I prompted her and raised my eyebrows to wait for a response.

"So I opened it up," Lindsey picked up. "I took it out of the box, looked at it, and said to her, 'Wow!' Because I didn't know what else to say. I couldn't say, 'Hey, look, it's a what's-it. Just what I've always wanted.' Or, 'How did you know this was exactly what I've been looking for?' So I just smiled at her, like this was the best thing to happen to me since I figured out that I was gay in college. Judge put her arm around me, gave me a kiss, and said, 'I knew you'd like it, honey. The minute I saw it, I knew it was *you*. I couldn't wait to give it to you.' "

Blair squinted her eyes at the object. "How is this supposed to be you?"

Lindsey shrugged her shoulders. "Beats me."

"Maybe she thinks you're an enigma," I suggested. "Like this whatchamacallit."

"Hey, that's a good name for it!" Blair said.

Parker leaned back on her arms and crossed her legs in front of her. "It's not Chinese. Or Turkish. Not South American. Maybe it's German. It could be Indian. It could even be Scandinavian. I'm not sure. I see a lot of objects from different countries, and I know my imports really well. But I've never seen anything like this before."

"What does it do?" I asked Lindsey.

Lindsey stared at the object, then sighed. "Pretty much, it does what you're seeing right now. Nothing."

"So it's an *objet d'art*," Blair concluded.

"What does that mean?" Lindsey asked.

"It's an object that's valued for its artistry," she answered.

"I think *objet what the fuck* would be more appropriate," I quipped.

"I don't know what value this would have," Parker said.

Lindsey cleared her throat. "According to Judge, it cost her 'a bootle.' But, as she told me, 'You're worth it.' "

We started to giggle.

"What?" Lindsey asked as she looked at us.

"It's just so . . . so . . ." Blair paused as she sucked in a breath of air. Then, through another set of giggles, she choked out, "It's just so *weird*, don't you think? It's just so *indescribable*. It's just so—" Blair dissolved into giggles again, then wiped her eyes. "But you're *worth it*, Linds! Whatever the heck it is, *you're worth it!*"

"It's indescribably indescribable." I chuckled. "If I had to write the copy to sell this item, I wouldn't know where to begin."

"How about, 'For the woman who has everything, here's something that's really nothing that'll have her guessing for years,' " Parker suggested.

"Not bad," I commented.

"It's a *big* thing, isn't it?" Blair asked. "Wide and tall and— gosh, there's a lot of it."

"Tell me about it," Lindsey mumbled. "From the size of the box it was in, I thought Judge had gotten me a bread maker. Now *that* I could put to good use, even though I'm not much of a cook. I hear you just wham all the ingredients in it, and the machine does everything. I think that's the type of cooking appliance even the toughest dykes would deem politically correct."

Blair nodded. "I've had a bread maker for years, and I just love it. You can make variations, too, on the recipes. Cinnamon raisin bread, apple spice—"

"I thought we weren't going to talk about food," I cut in.

Parker waved a finger at the object. "Whatever it *is*, Linds, it's making some kind of statement. Or at least it did to Judge when she saw it."

"What did you say when you thanked Judge?" I asked. "Did you say, 'Thank you for The Thing. The Thing is great. I'm always going to treasure The Thing?' "

Lindsey grinned and shook her head. "No. I just pretty much stopped at 'Thank you.' "

"Smart move," Parker said.

"Did Judge say where she bought it?" Blair asked.

Lindsey shook her head. "Funny thing about that. After Judge told me that she had spent a bootle on it, she added, 'And I'm not telling you where I got it. Because I don't want you to go there and check out what I paid. Next thing you know, you'll be asking me to take you on a trip to the Riviera.' "

"I think all it's worth is a trip up the road to Revere," I joked.

"Maybe she got it as part of a divorce settlement," Parker suggested. "You know, the wife takes Judge aside before she raps her gavel and says, 'I know I can't bribe a judge, but if you grant me everything I want, then I'll give you something that my husband gave me years ago as a wedding present. It's worth a bootle!' "

"Maybe it's some sort of family heirloom, and that's why it's worth a lot of money," Blair suggested.

"Maybe there's some sort of treasure hidden inside the object," Parker said. "Kind of like a Cracker Jacks box. We could take a hammer and break it open."

"Does it even open?" I asked Lindsey.

"It will with a hammer," Parker answered.

Lindsey shook her head. "I told you. It does nothing. If I left it out on the shelf all the time, it would collect dust. Which, I suppose, means that it at least would *do* something."

Parker crawled over to the object again, sat back on her heels, and wrapped her arms around it. "Did you shake it, Linds?" she asked, and then tried to lift it. Parker gritted her teeth, then dropped her arms. "My God, this sucker is heavy!" She tapped her fingernails against the object. "It sounds pretty solid."

"Maybe it's a door stop," I suggested, then added, "To a castle door."

"Maybe it's a paperweight for Paul Bunyan's office," Blair said with a smile.

"Who's Paul Bunyan?" Lindsey asked.

"Don't bother," I told Blair as she opened her mouth. "The joke's gone if you have to explain the story to her."

"More likely it's an anchor," Parker concluded as she turned around, readjusted a few throw pillows behind her, and then flopped back against them. "But there's one thing I know for certain about this thing of yours, Linds. If there's a fire in this building, this won't be high on your list of things you want to save."

"Even if the building burned to the ground, I think this would survive," Lindsey said.

"Have you looked in any books to find something similar to it?" I asked Lindsey. "Or maybe you could take a snapshot of it and then take the photo around to some antique dealers in the area. See if they can tell you what it is."

Lindsey shook her head. "It's not worth making that much of an effort over it. I guess it will just have to forever remain a mysterious thing in my life."

"Maybe you should give it a name," Blair suggested. "That way, you can at least think of it as *something*."

"A name?" Lindsey asked. "How can I name it? I don't even know what it is."

"Did it have any stickers or markings on it, to indicate where it was from or where it was made?" Parker asked.

"Not a one," Lindsey answered.

"It's like an orphan it," I stated.

"It *is* what *it* is," Parker joked.

"If you gave it a name, Linds, maybe you'd feel better about it," Blair continued. "Like Tom Hanks did in *Cast Away.* Remember? He named the soccer ball Wilson. Wilson was his friend."

"But Wilson was the *name* of the soccer ball," I clarified. "At least, it was the brand name. It was right on the box."

"And he thought Wilson was *talking* to him," Parker added. "I don't think Lindsey wants this whatever it is to be talking to her."

"Unless it can tell me what it is," Lindsey answered.

"We could shine bright lights on it and interrogate it," I suggested. I twitched one side of my upper lip, pointed a finger at the object, and then struggled with a Humphrey Bogart voice. "Okay, it. It's time to tell us what your name is. Cooperate, and we'll go easy on you. Keep clammed up, and we're gonna get rough with you. We'll get the ax. That's right, sucka. The ax. Then you'll be singing like a boid."

"Let's call it . . ." Blair began, and then stopped and furrowed her brow.

"I don't think you should name it," Parker warned. "You give something a name and, well, it's like giving a puppy a name. Once you do that, you own it."

"Lindsey *does* own it," Blair argued.

"But I don't think Lindsey *wants* to own it," Parker countered. "Without a name, she could easily give it away."

"Oh, it's mine all right," Lindsey admitted. "But I don't know what I should do with it. Everything else I own is *something.* And because it's something, then it has its place. But this . . ."

"Isn't very feng shui, is it?" I asked as I peered at the object, then looked around the room. "And it really doesn't match your furniture. Your own knickknacks."

"That's why it keeps going back into the closet," Lindsey told us. "Can you imagine, though, if Judge and I were living together? This thing would have to be at the epicenter of the living room all the time. How awful would that be? After a while, I think I would say, 'Listen Judge, it's either what's-it, or me. You choose. Because this condo ain't big enough for both of us.' "

"There are some things I'd love to ask Julia to get rid of," Blair said. "Now that we're living together, our space is filled with her stuff and mine. I love the woman, don't get me wrong. But her taste—yikes! I now have a rather large orange uphol-stered chair in the living room. *Orange!* It's like a constant blinding sunset inside the house. If you look at it for too long, and then look at an off-white wall, the wall starts to take on an orange tint. One day I asked her, 'Hon, don't you think that chair is a bit . . . well . . . *orange?*' And she said to me, 'It's not orange. I *hate* the color orange. The chair is *salmon.*' I told her, 'Salmon is pink. This chair is definitely orange.' " Blair shook her head, and then sighed. "That was our first argument. Over the orange-salmon chair." She flashed us a half smile. "But do you know what I did?"

"Tossed it out in the trash?" Parker asked.

"Covered it with a blanket?" I offered.

"No," Blair answered. "I went out to a paint store later on that week and got some paint samples. Of various shades of or-ange. And pink." She paused. "After comparing the samples to the chair, I was relieved to know that, indeed, the chair was most definitely orange. So I showed Jules the paint samples when she got home." Blair started to laugh. "That was our sec-ond argument. 'Is that all you have to do with your time?' she yelled at me. 'Try to prove me wrong? Who gives a crap whether the chair is salmon or orange? It's *my* favorite chair, and it's staying. Unless, of course, you'd like me to leave. 'Cuz if you ask me to leave, that chair's going right out the door with me. And neither one of us is coming back.' "

"Well, at least she said she'd take the chair with her," Parker pointed out. "That's better than her leaving you *and* the chair."

"So how do you feel about the orange chair now?" I asked her.

Blair shrugged her shoulders. "It's still orange," she answered. "It still bugs the heck out of me. From time to time, just to annoy Jules, I'll walk into the living room wearing sunglasses. Or, just before Halloween I'll suggest we put the chair out on the porch instead of a pumpkin." She laughed, then shook her head. "But it also reminds me of her. There are times when she curls up in that chair to read a book at night, and I'll look over and see that she's fallen asleep in it. She looks so cute, snoozing away in her god-awful orange chair. I guess I've just accepted it as part of her, part of our household."

" 'Love me, love my chair.' " Parker chuckled. "Or, how's this one. 'What do you want? Good sex, or good taste?' "

"That's the dilemma," I answered. "When you live with someone, you have to take them *and* their stuff. Leslie is a collector. Not a pack rat, because she can throw things out. But she has these collections she started when she was a kid. She collected all kinds of things. Football cards. Anything to do with the television series, *Wild, Wild West*. She loved, loved, *loved* Robert Conrad, the actor who played James West. Now she collects old soda bottles. Funky ashtrays. Metal advertising signs. The list goes on and on. Of course, she cherishes all of these collections. She has the football cards organized in a notebook. The old soda bottles line the wall in our front room. The metal advertising signs are set up in the spare bedroom, which she's taken over as her extra room. Just when I think I've seen everything she's collected and still collects, there's some new collection I stumble upon. Last week, I opened up a box that was tucked in the back of the hall closet and discovered hundreds of old *Mad* magazines. I dragged the box out of the closet and started looking through the magazines. She came out of the bathroom then, saw what I was doing, and went berserk on me. 'Don't touch those!' she shouted. 'Those are in order!' Then she raced over to the box, pushed me aside, closed the box back up, and started dragging it down the hall. 'Where are you going with that?' I asked. She let go of the box, placed her hands on her hips, and gave me this really annoyed look. 'They are going, missy, where all my other stuff is. You know, you just can't be messing with someone else's stuff.' I told her I wasn't messing with it. 'And anyway,' I added, 'it's just magazines.' Well, that was all she needed to hear. She launched into a forty-five-minute lecture on the history of *Mad* magazine, biographies of the contributors—both the illustrators and the writers—circulation figures, the issues that created the biggest public interest, and so on. When she was done, I pointed out how much room in our apartment was taken up with her collections. 'Oh, so, *you* don't have any collections, Gracy?' she asked me. 'What about your fountain pen collection? Huh? What about that?'

"I said, 'Those are pens, Les, and they take up half of a drawer in my desk. Your stuff is all over the place. The signs. The bottles.' "

Blair grinned. "That sounds like my fight with Julia. Round two."

I rolled my eyes. "It gets better. Then she started to cry. She said that I must not love her because the things she collects are *a part* of her. They're *important* to her. And, through her sobs, she asks me, 'Aren't I important to you, Gracy? Don't you love me—every part of me?' On and on it went. Then, when I thought I had her calmed down, when I thought I had said all the right things, she marched into the kitchen. I heard her open up a cabinet, and so I followed her. She took a plate from the shelf, waved it in front of me, and launched into a counterattack. 'I *hate* these plates of yours,' she told me. 'I hated them when we were together before, and I hate them now. Perhaps I even hate them *more*. Did you ever ask me if I wanted to eat off of these plates? Did you ever suggest we get place settings of our own?' " I paused and shook my head.

"So how did you guys resolve the whole thing?" Lindsey asked.

I smiled. "We had great make-up sex a few minutes later on the kitchen floor. I told her that I loved her and all of her collections."

"Of course you did," Parker said. "Before or after your orgasm?"

I thought for a moment. "During, I think."

"Oh, boy," Parker said. "Those collections are never going anywhere now."

I nodded. "I know. It wasn't the time to say something like that."

"And then did she say that she really did like your plates after all?" Blair asked.

I shook my head. "No. That was the end of the plate discussion. The next day we went out and bought new place settings. I boxed up the old set."

"Why?" Parker asked. "If you liked them, then why give in just because she didn't like them?"

I looked at her. "Because sometimes you do things to keep the peace, P. Sometimes you do things because you love her *that much*. Sometimes you do things because you don't much care whether you eat off of china or paper plates." I paused and showed everyone a sly grin. "And, sometimes, you do things for the future. So anytime she points out to you that you're selfish or that you don't ever consider her needs, you have something to fall back on, something to remind her of what you once did *for her*."

Lindsey grinned. "Smart investment, Gracy."

"A woman with a plan. I like that," Parker said.

"I think that's kind of devious, don't you, Gracy?" Blair asked.

I shrugged my shoulders. "A girl's gotta do what a girl's gotta do. You know, those collections really do drive me nuts. Probably in the same way that orange chair of Julia's does—"

"Orange Julius," Parker cut in with a grin. "Sorry. I just had to say it. I have that drink every time I go to the mall. You know the drink I'm talking about? It's made out of—"

"We know the drink," Lindsey broke in. "And we got the joke. As bad as it was."

"Does Cindi keep anything at your place that you don't like?" Blair asked Parker.

"Oh, yeah." Parker nodded. "Besides the clothes, which she never hangs up properly—I mean, there's a reason *why* hangers were invented—and the cans of Coors that take up so much space in the fridge—it truly bothers me that such cheap booze is next to my expensive bottles of champagne—and all of her sleeping attire, which consists of anything with the logo 'Boston Police Department' on it—apparently you can't have enough navy blue or gray T-shirts and matching workout shorts—there's one thing she has in my place that I don't particularly like."

"Okay, that only took a week," Lindsey grumbled.

"What's that?" I asked Parker.

"She has this, well, I call it her mumbo-jumbo shrine—it really bugs her whenever I call it that—which she's set up in a corner of my den," Parker answered. "It's where she goes to meditate every night before she goes to bed. And I mean, *every* night. We can't do *anything* until she's paid her shrine a visit. She's got a wooden statue of some woman with snakes crawling all over her set up there. And there's this little altar she's placed in front of the Lady of the Snakes, which she's covered with a velvet cloth. She has candles on the altar and little . . . I don't know what you'd call them. Trinkets, I guess. Stones and crystals and feathers and all sorts of things. Sometimes she'll find a cracked bird's egg in the spring and she'll put it on the altar. That has to be *completely* unsanitary. And then, right before she's going to meditate, she lights some incense cones while I run around the place opening up all the windows. She rings a bell a few times, which is my cue to jam on my headphones and crank up my music. And then she starts chanting, which at first turned me on a little but now does nothing for me. This goes on for . . . oh . . . a good half hour to an hour, depending on what kind of day she's had at work."

"Well, at least she's dealing with the stress of being a police officer in a good way," Blair pointed out.

"With bird's eggs and feathers she finds on the *ground*?" Parker countered. "Aren't birds *crawling* with mites? I probably have them all over my place now."

"But you *do* accept her having this shrine at your place, don't you?" Lindsey asked.

"Sure I do." Parker nodded. "Like each of you has said, you accept the things even though you're not wild about them. And just to prove how accepting I am, one time—I thought I was doing something nice for her, mind you—I went to one of those nature stores in the mall. Talk about another world. They were playing CDs of loon calls and wolf howls and the rumbling of thunder. Can you say cuckoo? And why, may I ask, would someone want to buy one of those contraptions with water that trickles constantly? I guess it's supposed to be soothing. But it would make me pee all the time."

"And so, on with the story," Lindsey sighed.

"I'm getting there," Parker answered. "So. I thought that I might be able to find Cindi something nice in there, something she could put in her shrine. I noticed once that she had placed some rocks on her altar—where they came from, I didn't even want to ask. Anyway, I bought her every stone that was in that shop. They were polished and kind of pretty. I gave them to her and said, 'These are for your altar, hon.' She looked at them and then said that I was really sweet to have done that, but the things she had on her altar had to be 'found objects'—things she discovered on her own. I told her I could hide them around my place and she could *find* them, but she said that wasn't the same. She said that they had to have an energy that 'called out to her.' Whatever that means."

"I think it means—" Lindsey began.

"Oh, for crying out loud, I *know* what it means," Parker cut in. "I may not *get it* in the big scheme of things, but I do get it. Anyway, I returned the stones the next day. But I spent a couple of hours that night, before we went to bed, bringing things into the bedroom—a can of Coors, a spoon, a book—and giving them voices, pretending that they were calling out to her. 'Cindi, this is your can of Coors. I'm calling out to you. Cindi, I'm your spoon. Please worship me. Cindi, this is—' "

"That's mean," Blair scolded Parker.

"I was doing it to be funny," Parker said. "And I actually had her laughing so hard she was crying."

"So what do you do when Cindi's meditating?" I asked.

Parker shrugged her shoulders. "Paint my toenails. Pluck

my eyebrows. Read fashion magazines. Play with myself. I mean, what else *can* I do?"

"Maybe you could meditate with her," Lindsey suggested. "Judge and I once went to hear this woman, Pema Chodron, who teaches a Tibetan Buddhist form of meditation. We bought one of her tapes after the lecture and listen to it from time to time. It's great. Very relaxing."

"And you wonder why Judge bought you this thing," Parker commented as she swept an arm in the direction of the object.

"It sounds like Judge includes you in a lot of her life, even though she's with someone else," Blair told her.

Lindsey nodded. "The situation with her has improved. I think she's finally realized that she's not Brenda's keeper, and so we're able to spend a lot more time together. And she did finally make contact with one of Brenda's siblings, who is planning to fly here in a few weeks to see Brenda's mental condition for himself. It could be, Judge has told me, that the brother takes Brenda home with him."

"That sounds pretty promising," I told her.

"It is. And I know you guys have never really been all for me seeing Judge, but—"

"Well, think of how you two began," Blair cut in. "I mean, would you have said to yourself at the time she was attacking you in the backseat of her car, 'Yeah, here's a woman I could fall in love with.'"

Lindsey smiled. "No. Of course not. But I'm glad you guys didn't give it to me too hard. I'm glad that you just let me be with my decision to hang in there with her."

"That's what friends are for," I told her.

"As trite as that sounds, I agree with Gracy," Parker said. "Of course you guys have been relentless in your disapproval of me and how I handle my relationships."

"You just give us so much to work with, P." Blair grinned at her.

"Now Judge and I do a lot of things together," Lindsey continued. "It's not just about sex. Or at least it hasn't been for the past month or so. I do hate being the other woman, though, de-

spite the fact that I know she and Brenda aren't in a lover relationship. In the past, whenever a friend would confide in me
that she was cheating on her partner, or seeing someone who
was in a relationship, I'd think, *God, you're such a little shit.* Now
that I'm on the other side—I'm that little shit—I can see how
easy it is to get caught up with someone else."

"That it is." I nodded. "But in Leslie's case, it didn't take her
very long to leave me after she had slept with the woman who
shall remain nameless. You've been with Judge for months now."

"I wonder if Judge's girlfriend has the same thing that you
have," Blair posed to Lindsey.

"You think she's got her own honey on the side?" Parker
asked.

"I don't mean an affair," Blair answered. "I mean that
thing," she said as she pointed to the object on the floor.

"If someone gave me that, I'd leave them for sure." Parker
chuckled. "I mean, no offense, Linds, but what kind of taste
does Judge have? If this gift is any indication, I'd say the
woman is out in left field in the home decorating department.
You'd better be careful if you ever start living together."

"What about someone who displays metal signs and old
soda bottles all over the apartment?" I asked Parker. "Or collects *Mad* magazines?"

"Well, that's strange, too," she answered. "I mean, what's
the point? Here's a bottle. Okay. Here's a sign, okay. Do you
have to keep looking at them? And the magazines—well—
after you've read them, you're done with them. Why hang onto
them? Unless—are they worth anything?"

"She's thinks they're worth something," I answered. "She
told me once that she could go on e-Bay and make a lot of
money selling the entire collection." I laughed. "I told her that I
was hoping she'd leave them to me in her will so I could live
out my years as a rich widian. That's a lesbian widow. I told
her, 'You'd do that for me if you were really *mad* about me.' "

"Big groan," Lindsey muttered.

"Well, the collections are Leslie's thing," Blair pointed out.
"Just as the orange chair is Julia's thing. *Love them, love their pos-*

sessions is what you have to think. You can't let little things like chairs or collections or plates or shrines interfere with your relationship. Because a relationship is about the bigger things— love and trust and honesty and—"

"Do I hear a swell of music in the background?" Parker cut in as she cupped a hand over one ear.

"Make fun of me all you want," Blair sniffed at her. "But you still have a shrine in your place, don't you? And that's going to be there for as long as you're with Cindi, right? We all have things we put up with."

"I just wish I knew what my thing was," Lindsey commented as she stared at the object.

"Maybe you should drive it out to the suburbs and release it into the wild," Parker suggested. "Then, if it finds its way back here, you'll know that it belongs with you."

"But then maybe Cindi will find it and bring it back to your place, P.," I joked. "She'll add it to the collection on her altar, and you'll be stuck with the thing in your place."

Blair giggled. "That would be good, because then the mites in your place would at least have somewhere to live."

"All kidding aside," Lindsey said, "I'm still stuck not knowing what it is."

"It's an object of Judge's love and affection," I told her.

"Well put, Gracy," Blair said.

Lindsey stared at the object for a few minutes. "Object of her love and affection. Object of her love and affection," she murmured. "Object. Love. Affection." A smile slowly formed on her face. "Hello, OLA," she said to the object, and then patted it.

"Oh, geesch, she's named it," Parker moaned. "Now it's really yours, Linds."

"That's fine," Lindsey said. "You know, I think I'm not going to put OLA away anymore. OLA is going to stay right on that shelf over there. Right OLA?"

"Brenda may not be the only mixed-up one in Judge's life," Parker muttered.

"Oh, go find a bird feather," Lindsey told her.

Blair stood up and stretched. "I think it's time for me to get home to the orange chair."

Parker nodded and slowly hoisted herself up from the floor. "Time for the altar."

"Time for the flea market," I said as I spread my arms over my head. "Good night, OLA. Oh, and good night to you, Linds."

Possessions are Nine-Tenths of a Lover

"*You wanna know some 'a the crazy, off-beat stuff we've moved?*" asked the rough-and-tough, no-nonsense owner of Macha Movers, whose slogan, "*We haul so U don't*" had made her moving company the number one choice for relocating lesbians in the greater Boston area.

"*First off, let me tell ya 'bout some 'a the basic things we move for jus' about every dyke,*" she said. "*Every one 'a them has at least one box 'a sports equipment. Basketballs, softballs, bats, gloves, cleats, soccer balls, tennis rackets, golf clubs. Them's standard.*

"*And then ya usually have a box or two 'a trophies from the tomboy days.*

"*Then there's the posters. Framed movie posters from lesbian classics. Desert Hearts, Lianna, Personal Best. Just ta name a few. Then there's some framed posters 'a naked women—not porno, mind you—'cuz they have them sappy little slogans or poetry. I seen a lot 'a Chris Williamson pics—you know, posed out in the desert. From The Changer and the Changed album cover, I think.*

"*Ya also got funky lamps and lampshades. Lesbians love 'em. Pink flamingos. Naked women. Or they cover up the lampshades in bumpa stickahs.*

"*And then them earthy-crunchies got a ton 'a kitchen stuff. On account 'a they do so much damn cookin' of veggies and tofu and other stuff that looks like what's in ya mulch bag afta ya mow the lawn.*

"*So them stuff is standard. Oh, yeah. And then ya always got the gals with a ton 'a sex toys. And no mattah how many times ya tell 'em, 'Take out the batteries,' they go 'n leave 'em in. One couple—man, they must 'a had a ton 'a vibrators. 'Cuz we start slidin' some boxes 'round in the truck ta fit some other stuff 'a theirs in. Suddenly, from way in the back 'a the truck, behind a wall 'a boxes we'd already packed in, it's like we whacked a hornet's nest. That buzzin' did not stop for a long, long time, too. Made us laugh like the devil.*

"Some chicks got some nice power tools they want us ta move. I like those chicks. I like seein' them chain saws. Circular saws. Workbenches. Them's my kind 'a gals.

"Then the rest 'a the stuff we load up, well, I gotta tell ya. It's all kinda strange ta me. Some couples must 'a collected all their stuff from yard sales and sidewalk trash piles. Some others got the fancy moldy-oldie furniture, and all we hear from them is the warnin's—'Oh, pleeeze be careful 'a that Queen Anne's doo-da.' Or, 'Be careful 'a that box. It's filled with Depression glass.' Which I don't get. Why move something that's a bummer ta begin with?

"Anyhootle, what I say is, there's no accountin' fer taste. What one woman likes, another wrinkles her nose at. I seen a lot 'a arguments happen after we've gone from one place packing in a woman's stuff and then show up at her partner's place. We open the doors ta the van and her partner cries out, 'Oh, tell me you don't want to move that!' And then they're off and runnin' 'bout who's got the most annoyin' stuff.

"But hey, I don't give a crap. 'Cuz they're payin' me by the hour, not by the job. Learned my lesson once, when a couple was havin' a standoff 'bout what was stayin' in the van and what was gonna be hauled out ta the sidewalk. That's when I was pricin' by the job, not the hour. Well, I watched the sun set that day, then the moon and the stars come out. All we was doin' was just sittin' around outside the van, half the stuff in, half the stuff out. I smoked a half a pack until I finally stood up and told 'em, 'If it's all the same ta you, I'm gonna lock up the van and take a taxi home. You gals need ta figure this out by six A.M. tomorrow mornin', 'cuz I got another job lined up and you're eatin' inta that time.

"Once they heard that, they were ready to snap to. They didn't want ta hafta find some otha sucka movah. 'Sorry, sorry, sorry,' they said to each other. Not ta me, mind ya. Sob, sob, sob, they goes. Hug. Hug. Hug. Then I hear, 'I love you, I love you, I love you.' Not ta me, 'a course.

"In the end, the gals gripe and complain and stamp their

feet and throw up their hands in horror at some 'a the things they see goin' in the van, some 'a the things they know they got to live with along down the road.

"But they do it. 'Cuz finally," she said as she smiles, "they see that livin' together ain't about what you possess, but about how ya feel 'bout one 'n other. Love can conquer the strangest things. Even a stuffed moose head with a sign 'round its neck that says, "Oops, I guess I didn't move fast enough." I thought that was a hoot. Now that I could 'a lived with!"

9

The Joy of Lesbian Ex (How Can I Miss You If You Won't Go Away?)

On a hot July morning, Lindsey and Parker waited in the car as I scaled the cement steps outside Blair and Julia's small house in Arlington—a white ranch trimmed with green shutters that had been plunked down about fifty years ago on a small patch of land at the end of a quiet, dead-end side street. I pressed the bell and waited for Blair to open the door.

Weeks before making an offer on the house, Blair and Julia had invited The Girls to see it—purportedly to give them our opinions about it—even though, as Blair had told us at the time, "It's a done deal. This is what we want, and we're going to be very happy here. I just know it."

"But it's so tiny," Parker commented after we had followed Blair and Julia through the front door, down a short hallway, and into a kitchen that was crammed full of appliances, furniture, and racks of knickknacks.

"It's teeny tiny," Parker continued as she squeezed her bulk into the space between the refrigerator and the stove so the rest of us could get a glimpse of the kitchen. She relocated her shoulder purse, then righted a few bottles of spices that she had knocked over in the process. "I'm not just saying that because I'm a large woman. But it's so . . . it's so . . . ."

"I think it's cute as a button," Lindsey cut in as she glanced at Blair's look of disappointment at Parker's comments. Then she turned to take a look around the kitchen and stepped on Julia's foot. "Sorry."

"Well, it's certainly the *size* of a button," Parker replied as she plunked her suitcase-size purse down on the stovetop and knocked over the same spice bottles.

"It's not *that* small," I pointed out. "It's just full. Of stuff."

Julia nodded. "That's it exactly."

"It's cozy," Lindsey told Blair. "It's homey. It's just, well, a little house."

I turned and knocked shoulders with Lindsey. " 'Little House in the City,' " I quipped.

"Are Ma and Pa gonna stay here, too?" Lindsey asked with a grin.

"Not in a house this size," Parker answered. "It's like a doll-house."

"Make that 'Little Dollhouse in the City,' " I said. "For Barbie, of course, and all those dolls from foreign countries that—"

"I bet you could fit your Easy Bake Oven right over there in that corner," Parker told Blair with a nod and a grin.

"We have a real oven, comedy queen," Blair answered.

"I know it's small," Julia said as she squeezed past Lindsey and me. "The thing that's distracting about the size of the house is that the people who live here now have so many things in each room. You have to picture this kitchen without all of the clutter in it."

"And five people in it as well," I added.

"Yes," Blair agreed. "You have to visualize emptiness."

"How about visualizing bigger rooms?" Parker asked.

"Well, that's going to happen," Julia answered as she slapped the palm of her hand against one of the kitchen walls. "We're going to take down this wall between the kitchen and the dining room and then make this little kitchen into a big eat-in kitchen/dining room combo."

"With a long table in it, like a farmer's table," Blair added. "So we can have people over. For potlucks and holidays."

"Well, that's good," Lindsey said. "Because you have to have room for potlucks. That's the only way you'll get lesbians to visit you."

"Except for those lesbians who are cooking challenged, like myself," Parker added.

"And then the dining room—I mean, the new kitchen—will have windows placed on this side," Blair said as she waved a hand in the air and got her fingers entangled in Parker's just-coifed do.

"Watch the hair!" Parker cried out as Blair carefully extracted her hand.

"Big hair doesn't work with the size of this room, P." Lindsey grinned. "You're going to have to get a mullet before your next visit."

"Over my dead body," Parker muttered. "Like I want to look like every other damn lesbian out there."

"We don't have mullets," Julia pointed out.

"We're not like every other damn lesbian," Parker answered. "We've got class. Anyway, who wants to get a haircut that sounds like a food product? Whenever I hear someone say it, I think, *mutton.*"

"Actually, a mullet *is* edible," I said. "It's a fish. There are gray mullets and red mullets and—"

"Even in the mullet community, there's diversity," Lindsey cut in.

"How much hair spray *do* you use?" Blair asked Parker as she wiped her hand on the back of her jeans.

"Did you make a dent in my hair?" Parker answered.

"Shouldn't you ask, 'Did you make a dent in the tent that I've pitched on top of my head today?' " Lindsey giggled.

"I have *a lot* of hair, Linds," Parker snapped.

"I'll say," Lindsey answered. "You could provide shelter for an entire species of birds in there."

Parker placed her middle finger on her nose so Lindsey could see it. Then she removed it and turned to Blair. "Well?"

Blair surveyed Parker's head. "Everything looks fine to me."

Parker smiled. "Then I used the right amount of hair spray."

"Are we finished with the hair discussion?" Julia asked.

"I think so," I answered. "In sum, we don't like mullets, we're not going to get them, Parker has a lot of hair, and she keeps hair spray companies in business. Now, back to the house."

"This will be the first wall that we plan to take down," Julia resumed. "Or have taken down. Blair and I aren't very handy with tools."

"What kind of lesbians are you?" Lindsey challenged her with a grin.

"Girly-girls, remember?" Parker answered.

"Maybe you are, P., but I'm not," Lindsey said.

"I'm kind of midway between girly-girl and butch, wouldn't you say?" I asked Lindsey.

Lindsey peered at me. "I don't see either going on for you."

"Really?" I asked her. "Then who am I?"

"Is it always this hard to carry on conversation with them?" Julia asked Blair.

"This is normal," she answered. "You just have to keep talking. They're listening, even though it seems they're not."

"What did she say?" I asked Lindsey.

"I don't know," Lindsey answered. "I haven't been paying attention. Why are we in this house, Blair?"

Blair rolled her eyes at Lindsey. "Go ahead, Jules."

"Anyway," Julia resumed with a sigh. "We can't do this work ourselves. But I know the woman who hosts the L-TV show, *I. M. Hammered*. She does this type of work all the time. In fact, she drew up a rough blueprint for this house that'll give us a heck of a lot more room. It'll be like a different house when she's done with it."

"It won't be a house at all—it'll be a shopping mall," I joked.

"Next week on *Lesbian Home Improvement*, watch how this six-room house in Arlington is turned into a mansion," Parker quipped. "What started out as a shack in—"

"Hey!" Blair cried out in protest as she clamped a hand on her hip and frowned at Parker. "Listen, Miss I Own an Entire Penthouse in Downtown Boston Because I'm Filthy Rich."

Parker quickly extended a hand to Blair. "I'm pleased to meet you. And you are . . . ?"

"Not everyone has the money that you have," Blair continued, ignoring Parker's hand. "Remember, we're two schoolteachers. We ain't never gonna be rich, sister friend. This is what we can afford." ·

"The couple who lived here before us was retired, and this house suited them just fine," Julia added. "In fact, they said they raised two children here."

"Where?" Parker asked. "In the backyard?"

"Very funny," Blair responded. "But when you've never owned anything this big before—you know what I mean," she immediately corrected herself as Parker started to open her mouth. "*This big* meaning *this expensive*. At least it is to me. To Julia and me. So it's a real thrill. Especially since this is the first big purchase I've ever made with someone else—someone I love."

"So don't rain on our parade," Julia added as she rubbed a hand up and down Blair's back.

"I think this is a nice place," I reassured them. "It's bigger than the apartment Leslie and I are renting. And you have a backyard and trees."

"Tree," Parker corrected me.

"And a one-car garage," I continued. "We don't even have a balcony or a deck."

"I like it," Lindsey said. "Plus, it's an investment. It's better than throwing your money out the window on rent every month."

"So there," Blair told Parker.

Parker shrugged. "Honey, I'm just teasing you. If this is what you want, then I'm all for it."

"This *is* what I want," Blair answered, then smiled at Julia. "It's what *we* want."

"And then you see this little den right through here," Julia said as she directed us out of the kitchen and into the living room.

We formed a single file line and followed behind her.

"This wall will come down, and that'll open up the living room more," she finished.

"Can you move that big hair of yours so we can all get into the living room and see what she's talking about?" Lindsey asked Parker as she stood behind her.

"I know it's small," Blair told us as she stepped next to Julia. Julia placed an arm around Blair's shoulders and smiled down at her. "But you wouldn't believe the price of homes. Especially this close to the city. And the cheaper places are a mess. They would need so much work."

Julia nodded. "This is nothing to knock down a couple of walls."

"So you say," Parker said. "But *you're* not knocking them down. That hammered dyke is."

"We could have a knocking-down-the-walls party," Lindsey suggested.

"Will that be BYOS?" I asked. "Bring Your Own Sledgehammer?"

"Count me out," Parker said. "I have nothing to wear for the occasion. And my sledgehammer is in the shop for repairs."

"Why can't you get a loaner sledgehammer?" Lindsey asked.

"*Anyway*," Julia cut in, then paused and gave us each a hard, determined stare.

"There's that schoolteacher look that Blair sometimes gives us," I whispered to Lindsey. "There's two of them in one house. It's going to be like a superpower standoff if they're ever mad at each other at the same time."

Lindsey nodded. "Judges have that look, too. It's cold enough to freeze you in your tracks."

"Has Judge used it on you?" I asked her.

Lindsey nodded. "A couple of times. It certainly gets my attention."

"I wonder if more than one teacher can give another teacher the look?" Parker asked. "You know, like a gang look. Or can one teacher trump the looks of more than one teacher? Kind of like Jackie Chan taking on a number of enemies." Parker raised her hands in a karate stance and leveled a glare at each of us.

"I didn't know you watched Jackie Chan movies," I told Parker.

Julia expelled a loud sigh and turned to Blair. "No wonder you can never tell me exactly what you talk about when you get together with these women. Being with them is like setting off on a trip, but then taking every exit off of the highway and then forgetting where you were actually heading."

"Is she insulting us, or complimenting us?" Lindsey asked Parker and me.

"Maybe she wants to take a trip with us," Parker suggested.

"*If* we make this house look bigger," Julia cut in, "then if we ever want to move into a fancier home—like that mansion you mentioned, Parker—we'll be able to sell it a lot easier."

"Plus, it's ours," Blair added as she leaned closer to Julia.

"It's something Blair and I are buying together," Julia told us, then she kissed the top of Blair's head. "It solidifies us being a couple."

"You mean more than your constant groping of each other?" Lindsey grinned.

"Well, all I can say is that you two better not have an argument while you're living here solidified as a couple," Parker said. "Because there's nowhere to go in this house when you need space. You're going to be on top of each other all the time."

"That's not so bad." Julia grinned.

"Yeah." Blair nodded. "That doesn't sound bad at all."

I fast-forwarded to present time and again rang the doorbell to Julia and Blair's house. I waited, then rapped my knuckles against the door. I waited again, then rapped again. Seconds ticked by. I knocked on the door one more time, then turned and looked at Lindsey and Parker, who were sitting in the driveway in Parker's Lexus. I held my arms in the air, palms up—sign language for, *Now what do I do?*

"She's gotta be in there," Lindsey called out through the open passenger-side window as Parker killed the engine. "We're only a few minutes late."

"We're *not* late!" I heard Parker shout at Lindsey. "I told you. I'm *never* late. The clock in my car is set ten minutes fast."

"Then maybe we're too early," Lindsey countered.

"Late, early, who gives a crap!" Parker nearly shouted. "It's not as if we were in the neighborhood and just decided to drop by. Blair knows we're supposed to be leaving now." She opened her door and grunted her way out. "Knock harder," she yelled at me. As she walked around the car, she adjusted the three-quarter-length lavender terry cloth robe she was wearing over a one-piece bathing suit that had more flowers pictured on it than an FTD catalog. Her head was crowned with a sombrero-size straw beach hat that was adorned around the rim with plastic fruit slices. ("What are you—the Chiquita banana lady?" Lindsey had asked her earlier when she had slipped into the passenger seat and surveyed her outfit. "I don't know whether to admire your hat or eat it.") Parker's low-heeled white sandals scraped quickly across the driveway, then made their way delicately up the front walk to the house.

I held up my right hand. "I've got bruising," I called out to Lindsey. "I've been banging and banging. You've seen me. Maybe she ran out to the store or something."

"For what?" Parker demanded. "Luggage, so she can pack? I mean, really! This delay is going to set us way off schedule, you know."

"Chill out, would you," Lindsey told her as she unbuckled her seat belt and opened the door. "I've never seen anyone get so stressed out about a few days at the beach. Like the ocean's going to go somewhere between now and when we get there."

"It doesn't matter *where* the ocean goes," Parker answered as she joined me outside the front door. "I want to get to the beach in time to fill my eyes with the sexy lezzies in their skimpy thongs."

"In P-Town?" I asked her. "I don't think I've ever seen a dyke in a thong."

"Is there a song, for a dyke in a thong?" Lindsey asked with a grin as she stepped out of the car. "A dyke in a thong sounds quite wrong."

"Why aren't you the writer?" Parker snapped at her.

"I've seen them in shorts and a sports bra, yes," I continued. "That's standard lesbian beachwear. But in a thong?"

"Just wait till I take you to the secret spot on the beach, honey," Parker said, then bent over to adjust the strap on one of her sandals.

"You stay away from her secret spot, P.," Lindsey told her as she shut the car door.

"Shut up, would you?" Parker told Lindsey, then stood up. "Blair!" she called out.

"Why don't you knock?" I suggested to her.

Parker held up her hands in front of my face. "Nails, Gracy. Just done. Not chipping them."

"Then you're going to be no help to me," I told her. "I need a real lesbian up here with me. Lindsey?"

"Trust me when I tell you that I'll be a help to you later on," Parker said as she turned and carefully descended the steps. "The women on that beach I'm taking you to—as soon as *someone* would answer the damn door" she shouted over her back at the front door of the house—"*are not* dykes. These are the finest-looking lesbians you'll ever see. Sexy. Feminine. And their breasts—mama mia—wow!" Parker exclaimed. "Much better than any set of naked breasts you'll ever see at the popular lesbian section of the beach. The mammaries on those chicks are either microscopically small—those objects *will never* appear larger than they seem in any mirror—or should be harnessed instead of allowed to droop all over the dunes. I mean, why is it that the people who shouldn't be revealing what's underneath their clothing do, and the ones you want to see keep it to themselves?"

"P., not everyone can still do pointy and perky," Lindsey said as she slipped her feet into a pair of loafers. "Unless they're twenty. Or had extensive work done. After decades, gravity *does* create the droop factor, no matter how small you are."

"I've been to P-Town dozens of times, P., and I've never heard about the secret beach," I said.

"You've never been there with me."

"Are there secret lesbians at the secret beach?" Lindsey wondered as she started up the front walk. "Do we need to know a secret handshake to get onto the secret beach?"

"No," Parker replied as she strolled toward Lindsey. "But you do need binoculars. I've brought them, of course. Because there are more than beautiful breasts to see. There are hands and tongues getting a good workout on the beach. It's better than watching a porn movie."

"I think there are a lot of things that are better than watching a porn movie," Lindsey said.

I crinkled my nose. "Why would anyone want to lick a beach?"

Parker rolled her eyes, then adjusted her hat. "Knock on that door again, would you, Gracy? We need to get this show on the road."

"Let me handle this," Lindsey said. "Move over, beach baby," she muttered as she passed Parker and gave her a playful nudge with a hip.

"Fuck you," Parker spit out. "These are *beach* sandals. They know how to walk on sand, not flagstones and grass."

"Perhaps you should've worn your secret flagstone and grass sandals, then," Lindsey told her. "Outta the way," she ordered me as she leaped up the steps. "I'm going to use the secret hand to get a secret response."

"Knock it off, Linds," Parker told her.

I stepped back from the door, and Lindsey pounded against it with her fist. "Blair!" she called out. "Let's go!"

"Besides shouting, which Parker did, how is that any different from what I was doing?" I asked her.

"I'm secretly pounding harder," Lindsey answered.

"Oh, I think not," I countered. "I was—"

"Hey, she's in there," Parker called out as she stood on tiptoe between two rhododendron bushes, peering through a first-floor window. "She's sitting in that damn orange chair."

"Secretly hiding from us," Lindsey muttered.

"Enough with the secret stuff," I told her.

"Secret beach, my ass," Lindsey muttered. "She's only saying that so we'll get going."

Parker rapped her half-dozen arm bracelets against the window. "Yeah, you," she called out. "She's looking at me," Parker told us. "She knows we're here." She rapped on the glass again. "Get up and answer the damn door! Don't shake your head at me, girlfriend. Get out of the damn chair and let us in! What?

What?" Parker shook her head. "She said that it's open," she told us.

Lindsey turned the knob and pushed open the door.

"Then why the hell didn't she say so?" I asked as I followed Lindsey into the dark living room.

Blair was sitting, as Parker had told us, in the orange chair. All of the living room blinds were closed, warping the time of day to dusk rather than just past dawn. She was wearing a pair of wrinkled sweat pants and a bulky sweatshirt. A box of Kleenex was tucked between her legs. On the floor in front of her was a mound of crumpled tissues.

"Blair?" I asked as I took in her puffy eyes and blank stare. "Are you all—"

"What the heck is going on?" Parker shouted as she burst through the front door. "I *said* six A.M., and I *meant* six A.M., Blair. I want to be *in* Provincetown, bags *unpacked* at the place we're staying, *in* a bathing suit—which *I* already am, by the way, and I'm *not* waiting for you gals to get into your suits—and *on* the beach, by eleven *the latest*. That's eleven A.M., Blair. Not P.M. The best sun hours are between ten and two. Ten and two. And I am, as Sheryl Crow sings, gonna soak up some sun. So let's get crackin'."

"I'm not going," Blair answered.

"Oh, for God's sake, *of course* you're going," Parker snapped.

"I'm not going," Blair repeated. She sniffed, then blew her nose.

"You just have a summer cold," Parker told her, then stomped around the living room and started opening up the window blinds. "It's nothing that a little sun, a little surf, a little shellfish, and a little scotch and soda can't cure in an hour or so. We've had this trip planned *for weeks*. Ever since Julia told you that she had a place in P-Town with an available week without renters. *You* invited us all to go down there. We took time off from work, Miss Teacher Who Has the Summers Off. So you can't just decide at the moment we're going to leave that you're not going. Because then that means *we* can't go. And *we're going*. Oh, yes. *We are*. Even if you have pneumonia.

There are hospitals on the Cape. We'll pop in to see you during visiting hours. As long as it doesn't conflict with the best sun time."

"That's pretty harsh," Lindsey commented.

"You guys can go." Blair sniffed again, then rubbed her eyes. "You don't need me to be there. *No one* needs me to be there." She let out a sigh, then dropped her head in her hands and began to sob.

"Oh, come on, Blair—get a grip," Parker huffed.

I glared at Parker. "What is *with* you? Can't you see that she's upset?"

"No, I can't see that she's upset," Parker answered. "I see that she's got a cold or a flu or something. She probably didn't get any sleep last night, so she's tired. And cranky. Which will pass. Especially in the sun." Parker looked at Blair. "I want to *get going*. Have you even packed yet?"

"Remember that little discussion we had some time ago about being selfish, P.?" Lindsey asked. "I think we talked about the fact that there's no *u* in *team*."

"This isn't a team," Parker responded. "We're friends. And while there isn't any *u*, meaning me, in team, there *is* an *i* in *friend*. And *I'm* driving. And *I* want to get on the road." She opened the last set of living room blinds and turned to Blair. "Tell me where your bags are, and I'll throw some of your clothes in them. And then off we'll go. Anything you forget you can get down there. I'll even buy it for you. Just get out of the damn chair. You're holding up the works."

"It's . . . it's not a cold," Blair stammered, then wiped her eyes with a wadded tissue.

"Then it's the damn flu," Parker called out to her. "Or allergies."

"I kind of figured it wasn't a cold," I told her.

"Then what is it?" Lindsey asked as she looked down at Blair.

Blair looked up at Lindsey, started to open her mouth, and then drew her knees up to her chest and lowered her head.

"She's going to be sick," I told Lindsey. "Blair, are you

going to be sick?" I asked as I frantically surveyed the room for a wastepaper basket.

"Julia . . . Julia said . . . she said . . ." Blair's voice trailed off as she sucked in deep breaths of air. She raised her head and looked at us. "Her ex . . . her ex . . ." she began, then stopped and started to sob.

"What are we having here, a breakdown?" Parker asked as she stepped to the side of the chair and started tapping a sandaled foot on the carpet. "Just spit out what's got you in a crying jag, Blair."

"I think sensitivity should be our next topic of discussion," Lindsey snapped at Parker.

"Okay, so I'm not the best person when there are tears involved," Parker confessed to us. "I'm the first to admit it. I learned when I was quite young that the way to handle life's little upsets is by letting them roll off my back. That's all. I guess I just expect other people to do the same."

Blair peered up at Parker through puffy, red eyes. "This isn't some little . . . some little upset, you know," she said. "This isn't an *overreaction* to something that *you* don't think I should get upset about. This is . . . this is *big*. This is something that blindsided me. And I'm still reeling."

"Blindsided you?" Lindsey asked. "Did you lose your job?"

Blair shook her head.

"Did Julia lose her job?" I asked.

"No."

"Did you—" Lindsey began.

"Oh, for crying out loud, Blair, this isn't twenty questions," Parker snapped as she cut Lindsey off. "Just *tell us* what's going on. We can't help you unless we know what's the matter."

"This is obviously hard for her, Parker," I pointed out. "She's upset."

Parker slammed a hand against her chest and gasped. "Really? She's upset? I didn't know that." She paused and flashed a frown at me. "I can *see* that she's upset, Gracy. What I want to find out is what the heck is *making* her upset, *process* it, of course, like a good little lesbian, except in fast-forward, if that's at all possible, and then bring *closure* to whatever it is so we can *get going* on our *damn vacation!*"

"Spoken right from the heart, with caring and concern," Lindsey told Parker.

"Okay, so I'll go out and buy her a Hallmark," she grumbled, then glanced at her watch. "It's *all* of our vacations. She's impacting all of our vacations!"

"I don't think impacting is a word," I said.

"Just . . . just go without me," Blair told us.

I kneeled down in front of the chair and took one of Blair's hands in mine. It met with a wet tissue. "We're not going without you," I said as I slowly removed my hand from Blair's and wiped it against my shorts. "But we need to know what's going on with you. If you don't want to go, fine. But we're not leaving you here in this state."

"No, let's take her to a different state—like Kansas," Parker suggested. "There won't be a beach filled with naked lesbians, but she might be happier there."

I glared at Parker. "Remind me never to go through a tough time around you, Dr. Coldheart."

"I do have a good side, you know," Parker responded.

"Then how about letting Blair see that?" I asked her. "How about letting all of us see that?"

"Okay, okay," Parker answered. She took in a deep breath, then released it. "I'm sorry you're upset, hon. We really don't want to go without you. Honest. I just . . . I just don't know what to do sometimes with someone who's this upset. It makes me very nervous, and when I'm nervous I can spit out really stupid things."

"So basically you've been nervous since New Year's Eve?" Lindsey asked.

Parker threw her arms in the arm and glared at me. "*You see?* You see what I get for trying?"

"Lindsey!" I scolded. "Come on. We don't need a conflict on top of this. Make nice-nice with Parker."

Lindsey flashed Parker a quick smile and tossed an air kiss

in her direction. "Love ya, babes. Now why don't I just get you some water, Blair," she suggested. "Do you want an aspirin?"

"Where's Julia?" Parker asked. "Does she know that you're upset?"

"Ha! Julia!" Blair cried out in a voice loud enough to startle us. "Julia! Julia the liar. Julia the cheat. Julia the—"

"Okay, *now* we're getting somewhere," Parker broke in. "Anger I can handle, much better than tears. So I take it you guys had a quarrel."

Blair clenched a fist and shook it in the air. "A quarrel? A quarrel? Oh, no, I think not. This is not a quarrelable—if that's a word—subject. Not at all. Julia is in P-Town now. She went there two days ago."

"I thought this was just a time for The Girls," I said. "That we weren't bringing our—"

"It *is*," Blair broke in. "It's supposed to be. Just The Girls. Or so I thought. I mean, it *will* be. But last night Julia calls me and says, 'We have everything all set for you and your friends, honey.' And I say 'Great.' Then I ask her, 'What do you mean, *we*?' It turns out that she's down there with her ex!"

"Now?" I asked.

"Now—and before!" Blair exclaimed. "For two days—and two *nights*—she's been in Provincetown—the lesbian capital of the world—with the woman she told me broke her heart into pieces. With the woman who she tells me one time was the love of her life. Like that's supposed to make *me* feel good? That someone *else* was the love of her life? What am I then? The *runner-up* to the love of her life? And now she's been down there, been down there sleeping with her—"

"She's sleeping with her?" Lindsey cut in.

Blair nodded.

"Are you sure?" I asked her.

"What else would she be doing with her ex?" Blair asked.

I shrugged my shoulders. "Getting the place ready for us?"

Blair spit out a burst of air. "Oh, yeah, right, Gracy. I'm sure they haven't gone clubbing. Or dancing. Or had romantic dinners together. Or—"

"Do you sleep with your ex's?" I cut in.

"Of course I don't," Blair snapped. "I'm friends with them. Not lovers."

"My point exactly," I replied. "Julia's down there with *a friend* who happens to be an ex. She's not her lover. *You* are. There's no way Julia would cheat on you. She loves you too much."

"I agree," Parker said. "Why would she call and tell you she was in P-Town with her ex if there was something going on? Think about it. That's just plain dumb. She wouldn't *want* you to know something like that. Right?"

Blair thought for a moment. "Right."

"And Julia's incredibly devoted to you," Parker continued. "She doesn't play games. She doesn't sleep around. Those are things I would do. Not Julia."

Lindsey nodded. "Ex's are ex's. Why would Julia sleep with someone who broke her heart? Who wants to revisit that bad memory? Burn me once, shame on you. Burn me twice, shame on me."

"Ex's are ex's for a reason," I added.

"Then let me backtrack for a minute," Blair answered. "So she said to me that she wanted to go down a couple of days early to P-Town, right? To fix things up, she said, for our visit. The Girls' visit. So I tell her, 'Fine.' Why would I object to that? Last night, when she called, she also told me, 'Neelia has been helping me clean up our place.' *Neelia?* I'm thinking to myself. *Neelia's down there? Why didn't she tell me that?* But just as I'm about to say something about Neelia being with her, I remember what she has just said to me. My heart starts beating faster. So I ask her, 'Did you say *our place*, as in a place that you and I share, or *our place* as in a place that you and Neelia share? And do you know what she told me?"

"Uh-oh," I said.

"Julia's in trouble, Julia's in trouble," Parker chanted.

Lindsey frowned. "She told you that she and Neelia still owned the P-Town place together."

Blair nodded.

"Dum-da-dum-dum," Parker intoned in a low voice.

"You never knew that she owned the house with her ex?" I asked.

"If I had known, do you think I would've bought this house with her?" Blair asked. "I mean, if she had told me that, I would've thought to myself, *Okay, there's some unfinished business here.* It wouldn't have felt right to me."

"I'd feel the same way," Lindsey said.

"Julia did tell me when we were first going out that she had a house in P-Town," Blair admitted. "She said that she rented it out from late spring to early fall, which paid for the mortgage. She told me that during the times when it wasn't rented, she'd take a vacation there. Or arrange for some minor improvements to be made or a top-to-bottom cleaning. I was excited when I heard that she had the house, because that meant we could go to P-Town together on vacations." Blair paused. "But she never once told me that she had bought the house with Neelia or that she and Neelia were still co-owners. I mean, wouldn't you think she would've told me that? I don't go around telling people this is *my* house. I say that it's my house *and* Julia's house—our house. It's like she's had this deep, dark secret she's been keeping from me. And I don't like secrets."

"Unless it's a beach," Lindsey jumped in, then immediately held up a hand. "I know. That was out of line. Just pretend I never said anything."

"I think one of the most difficult things to do in the lesbian community is to create separation between your ex—or ex's—and a lover," I said. "I don't think there's any other population that brings current lovers and past lovers together as much as ours does. It's like we can never get away from the past."

"What I hate," Lindsey began, "is when a relationship has ended and then, sometime down the road, I see my ex with someone new. Except this time around, she's changed all of the things that drove us apart when we were lovers. She's quit drinking. She's lost weight and started working out. She's seeing a therapist. She's gone back to school. Whatever. Suddenly, she has no more issues. *Now* she doesn't. Now that she's no longer with me. And she's happy. Happy, happy, happy." Lindsey sucked air between her front teeth, then looked at us and let out a soft chuckle. "Okay. I guess I have some issues around the whole ex-lover thing. But it galls me, you know. You wish you could just get them out of your life forever. Just be done with them. I mean, I don't need to see all that happiness that I once wanted to share with them being shared with someone else. All those changes that I waited for—begged for—finally happen, but with someone else. But everywhere I go—restaurants, movie theaters, stores—they're there. All over the city. Here an ex, there an ex, everywhere an ex, ex."

Parker let out a quick snort. "Ex and the City."

I smiled. "Carrie wonders, 'Can we ever really let go of our past lovers? Or are we doomed to be forever linked with them?' "

"Is it any wonder that *ex* is part of *sex*?" Lindsey asked. "Once the sex is gone, all that's left is the ex."

"The joys of lesbian ex," I chuckled.

Blair pounded her fists on the arms of her chair. "This isn't funny!" she exclaimed.

"Of course it's not funny," Lindsey agreed. "It's not. But the point I'm trying to make is that we've all gone through what you're going through now. Maybe not with the co-ownership of a home. But the jealousy, the uncertainty, the wondering, *What does this mean, that she's in P-Town right now with her ex?*" You're not the first lesbian to go through this. And you certainly won't be the last. Ex's and lovers don't mix. And yet, in our community, they have to."

"Right," I agreed. "It's just, well, an unfortunate part of lesbian life. I'm certain that from the beginning of time, every lesbian has had problems with ex's that affected their relationships with their current lovers. Every lesbian, of course, except for Parker. Because she's everyone's ex. There are no six degrees of separation between her and every single lesbian in the world. No, ma'am. Now can you imagine the problems *she* creates in the community?"

Blair slowly let a smile emerge. Then she looked down and shook her head. "I hate this fucking chair."

Parker nodded. "It *is* one ugly-ass piece of furniture."

"Too bad Julia didn't leave that with her ex when they split," Lindsey said.

"Maybe that's what broke them apart," I suggested. " 'I love you, but that orange chair—really! Good-bye!' "

"I should just take this fucking chair and toss it out on the sidewalk," Blair said between clenched teeth. "Or maybe I should douse it with lighter fluid and strike a match. Or—"

"You go, girl!" Parker smiled. "I've got the matches."

Blair made a fist and knocked it gently against her forehead. "I'm such a fool. Here I am, buying this house—my first house—and thinking that it was the first house she had ever bought with anyone. And instead . . ."

"Honey, welcome to the wonderful world of lesbian ex-lovers," Parker told her as she sat down on an arm of the chair and patted her leg. "A world in which no one is sacred and most things are secrets. Or, as I like to call the ridiculous phenomenon of former lovers staying friendly with one another even when they have new lovers, The Reason Why Therapists Stay in Business. My philosophy is, when it's over, it's over. Of course, not everyone feels the same way."

"That's because breakups in the lesbian community are never easy, P.," Lindsey said as she lowered herself to the floor in front of Blair and then crossed her legs.

"Of course they're easy," Parker replied. "You just say, 'We're done. We're over. Have a nice life.' But lesbians have to make everything so complicated. They can't distinguish between who's a friend and who's a lover anyway, so ex-lovers fall into that nebulous category of friend-lover. They're frovers."

I laughed and took a seat on the other arm of the chair. "Then I'd like to find some remote island in the Pacific, name it Frover Island, and send my ex-lovers there."

"Why send them to a place that's warm and has an ocean view?" Lindsey asked. "I say give them parachutes, fly them to the Arctic Circle, open the door, and push them out. It's the lesbian version of *The Big Chill*."

"I can't believe how much drama there is in the lesbian community around ex's," Parker said. She placed a hand on her chest and widened her eyes. " 'Oh, no,' someone will say to me in a whiney voice. 'I can't go to *that* party, *that* dance, *that* bar—that *whatever*—because my ex will be there!' I want to ask her, *'Which one?'* Because lesbians can't seem to let anyone go. If lovers were cars, lesbians would have backyards filled with rusting old models. 'Oh, yeah. That's the Chevy Nova I had for three years. Man, she was great. Oh, and there's the Pinto. She was a very dangerous one. I didn't stay with her for long. Ah, and there's the Cutlass Olds. What a beauty. So responsive. Always started up, even on the coldest days. But the mileage— wow! She really drained my pocketbook.' "

Blair giggled.

"I think it's more complicated than just not being able to let go," I suggested. "Sometimes, well, sometimes it's best to remain on good terms with an ex. That keeps things on an even keel whenever you see her. Which, invariably, you will. And then there's the stuff. Like with Julia and Neelia. They own a house together."

"Which they should have sold when they broke up," Parker answered. "Or one of them should've bought the other out."

Lindsey nodded. "Of course that *should* have happened. But maybe it's because you have these love 'em and leave 'em relationships, P., that makes you incapable of understanding how important ex-lovers are in our lives. Don't get me wrong. I don't like my ex's. Not one of them. I mean, why would I? If someone cheats on me or falls in love with someone else or is unhappy with me or doesn't love me anymore, then why would I choose to have that person as a friend? But if every lesbian walked away from her ex-lovers, there would be no one left in her life. Ex's are, unfortunately, a lesbian's link to her social circles. Cut even one ex out of your life, and chances are you'll end up not just losing one person, but a few—or even more."

"An entire softball team, for instance," I added. "That's what happened to a friend of mine—one of my teammates on a rec league team—and her ex, who was on the same team. She and her ex had to sit down and decide who would leave the team. Because they couldn't be around each other anymore without driving the team apart. Particularly since one of them had started seeing the short stop."

"I know a couple who had dogs," Lindsey said. "When they split up, they spent months trying to work out who would get which dog when. And now that lesbians are having children together, well, you wouldn't believe some of the stories other lawyers tell me. As easy as it may be to break up in this community, it's not as easy to walk away from a lover. And the fact of the matter is, lesbians *don't* want to walk away from stuff they've shared with former partners. I'm talking about the material as well as the emotional."

"Oh, *please!*" Parker exclaimed. "Stuff is stuff. Stuff can be bought, sold, traded, discarded, donated, doused with lighter fluid and torched—whatever. Homes. Cars. Furniture. Dishes. CDs. Not that I've ever really bought anything with anyone. But I don't think I'd give a crap who got what during a split. Just get out of my damn life, is what I would say. But with lesbians, it's like ex-lovers are some sort of status symbol. The more you have in your life, the better your prestige."

"I don't know that I'd call it prestige," Lindsey countered. "But, like mosquitoes in the summer, they're everywhere. Name me one social event in the lesbian community where you or your friends won't run into an ex. It's impossible to avoid them."

I nodded. "It's a small community. That's bound to happen. So my point is, why not be friends with them, even if all you're doing is just keeping the peace, so to speak, by being friendly acquaintances? I don't get together with ex's for dinner or the movies. But if I see them somewhere, I'm cordial to them. I'm just not going to go to bed with them."

"Right," Lindsey agreed. "So believe us, Blair, when we tell you that Julia and Neelia are not sleeping together. I'm sure they're just down there doing what she told you they're doing—straightening up the place for us."

Blair sighed. "You know, you guys may be right. I'm friendly with my ex's. And I don't sleep with them. But it's just, well, you'd think Julia would've told me that she still owned a house with Neelia."

"Yeah, but like you said, you probably wouldn't have bought this house with her if you had known that," Lindsey pointed out. "So she was probably too scared to tell you because she thought she'd lose you. She wasn't really lying or keeping a secret. She just wasn't being forthcoming."

"You know, honey," Parker began, "you're probably going to get down to P-Town and meet Neelia and think, 'Oh, I have got it *so over* this woman. This woman's *nothing* compared to me.' "

"Maybe Neelia has a lover now, too," I suggested.

"I hadn't thought of that," Blair said. "I just assumed that Neelia was single and putting the moves on Julia. I got myself all worked up over it."

"Do you know what happens when you assume?" Lindsey asked her.

"Oh, I think she's aware of that," I said.

"Good," Lindsey answered, then placed a hand on Blair's knee, "Julia's living with you. She's in love with you. She sleeps with you. Ex's, well, we just have to accept that they're going to be a part of our partner's life. Sometimes they play a big role, sometimes a tiny role. But they're there, nevertheless."

"What matters most is the here and now, honey," Parker advised. "And in your here and now, it's Julia. Neelia's part of her history. We all have histories with someone. Histories are what we learn from and move on from. But histories are over."

"That was quite well said," I told Parker. "It almost bordered on compassionate and heartfelt."

"Hey, I have a big heart," Parker replied. "I always have a big heart for my wonderful friend Blair."

"You guys . . ." Blair began, then stopped.

"Oh, don't get sucked into her sticky-sweet compliments," Lindsey told Blair. "She just wants to get the hell on the road. I saw her glance at her watch a few minutes ago."

Parker grinned at Blair, then tapped her watch. "Time is fleeting, honey bun. And the quicker we get to P-Town, the sooner Neelia gets the boot. Now let's get those bags packed and hit the road. We're going to get us some fun in the sun!"

The Ex-Files

You once were in love with her, and she was in love with you. You once thought you would spend the rest of your life with her, and she felt the same way. You purchased things together, took trips together, wore each other's clothes, and adapted to each other's lifestyles. You shared all of your memories and dreams with her, and she shared hers with you. She knew your faults and weaknesses as well as you knew hers. The pillow talk you shared was intimate; your lovemaking made you both emotionally and physically vulnerable. You may have exchanged rings, signed mortgage papers, created new wills, adopted children, or had a commitment ceremony in front of your friends and family.

She knows your deepest, darkest secrets.

And now she's out there in the friendship/potential lover circles you share.

She knows your bathroom habits, how you chew your food, how many times a day you pass gas, how you feel about your mutual friends, whether you're a nail biter or a hair twirler or a belly button lint picker. She knows what you feel like inside when you're really turned on, and what you sound like when you come.

And now you're no longer together.

And she's OUT THERE.

She's like a spy who has all of your secrets on file in her head. Can she be trusted not to divulge any of this information, or will she share it with someone who may be interested in you or anyone who cares to listen? Will the pillow talk you once whispered to her become the pillow talk she softly speaks with someone new? Will she take your musical tastes (and your CDs) and call them her own? Will she wear the outfits you once bought for her and tell people she chose them herself?

Worse yet, will she use the recipe books that she took from you when she packed and left, make the dishes you once made for her, bring them to potlucks, and—horrors!—claim that they are hers?

Alas, she's not the only spy who holds your file. Because within most lesbian circles are ex-lovers who share meals with you, attend the same parties you go to, work out at the same gyms, study in the same libraries, hang out at the same bars.

If every lesbian had a single thread that connected her to each of her former partners, we'd all be tripping over one another. Because in the lesbian community, there's no such concept as six degrees of separation. It's barely one degree. We sleep with our ex-lover's best friend and the best friend's best friend; we sleep with our best friend's ex-lover and her ex-lover. We sleep with our coach and some of our teammates, and they do the same, which means, essentially, that we've slept with everyone on the team and the entire coaching staff.

If we were straight men, we'd be writing memoirs that would make us the envy of the male community. That's because we not only sleep with women ("Score!"), but we then choose to keep them around us for the rest of our lives, like some sort of a harem ("She's mine. She's mine, too. She's mine as well. She's mine in addition. She's mine." And so on.)

It's a strange web lesbians weave. All those threads of connection. We keep ex-lovers in our lives like treasured possessions we can't seem to part with. (Why is it that we can throw out every single reminder of her the moment she leaves our lives—viciously slicing pictures with scissors, cramming possessions she's left behind in Goodwill boxes or trash bags— but remain friends with her?)

Newcomers to our circles have to draw up charts similar to family trees in order to see how everyone is linked. But before too long they, too, are included in the lesbian family tree, just another link to another woman who was once linked to another woman, who was . . . well, you get the picture.

Why can't we choose to destroy our ex-files? Why is it that we can't walk away forever from ex's? Why can't we turn our backs on those who have hurt us, who have caused us endless nights of tears, who have slimmed us down through the breakup diet? Why do we continually rub our ex-lover's nose in our current lover or have our nose bent out of shape every time we walk into a room and see our former partner entwined with someone new?

Is it simply that there aren't enough lesbians to go around? Is it that we can't commit for very long before our head is turned to someone new? Do we confuse friendship with intimacy, or intimacy with friendship? Or, because we are women, do we crave peace and harmony in our circles and therefore strive to create and maintain relationships that are conflict-free? Do we hate to hold onto grudges or hate to hate another human being so much that we would rather put ourselves through emotional strife whenever we see an ex with a new gal pal? Do we reason that the pain of the emotional and physical separation from an ex can be less significant than a geographical separation? Or can we never divorce an ex from our lives because we can never release her from our hearts?

Maybe we think of our exes as past investments—things that once made us rich and, like a fool with her money, can't seem to part with them. Maybe the market will rebound, you might think. And then I can compare my new portfolio with my old one to see if I've done better or worse. Or perhaps you're not over an ex-lover, and hope that she isn't as well. So you think, Maybe she'll come back to me, if I continue to make my presence known. Maybe she'll realize that her true happiness was with me.

Or maybe, you think, I should stick around. Just in case she makes her ex-files public and I need to defend myself. That way, she could see that I'm here, too, holding onto her ex-files.

Or maybe being lovers with a woman is a shortcut to a deeper communication than a friendship—to a passionate but impermanent commitment. Because after the sex is over, what lesbians are left with is often a stranger in their bed, an intruder in their lives, a mere acquaintance.

What they are left with is an ex—just another person with whom they've had sex.

10

Beach Blanket Confessions
(I've Had the Breasts of Lesbians
with Sides of Thighs)

"Good Lord, Parker, what *is* that?" Lindsey asked as she watched Parker lift an object out of the trunk of her Lexus and set it down on the parking lot at Herring Cove beach. "Are you reverting back to your kindergarten days?"

"It's my little red beach wagon." Parker beamed proudly as she began to unload the trunk and pile numerous items into the wagon. "See? It's like having my own beach porter. I can fill it with my beverage cooler, my bag of sunscreens and skin lotions, books, snacks, binoculars, towels—whatever—and take it wherever I want to go on the beach. After all, I only have two hands—"

"And a summer's worth of supplies," I finished. "All for a few hours on the beach. We *are* staying for just a few hours, right? My skin hasn't seen the sun since I started working for myself. Even though I've brought the highest number sunscreen I could find, I don't want to be walking up and down Commercial Street tonight looking like a lesbian lobster. So, just to make sure—that cart isn't like a Transformer, is it? It doesn't convert into a camper, right?"

"Haven't I told you before how I feel about camping, Gracy?" Parker answered. "Any activity that doesn't require wearing makeup is not something I either like or want to do."

"Doesn't that wagon have a weight limit?" Lindsey asked as she watched Parker toss a plastic grocery bag on top of the growing pile.

"I've carried more in it," Parker said as she closed the car trunk. "It even has a drain in the middle of it, so I can wash it out at the end of the day." She dug through the small hill of supplies that she had created, cleared a tiny space in the center of the wagon, and beckoned for us to catch a glimpse of the drain.

"Yup. That's a drain all right," Lindsey agreed as she and I looked down at the wagon.

"I ordered this cute little wagon online," Parker told us as she bent over and picked up the handle. "I call her Annette. After the original beach party girl, Ms. Funicello. I was going to go for the classic Red Flyer, but that's made out of metal and quite heavy. This one doesn't weigh more than ten pounds."

"It probably weighs triple that amount now," I commented.

"If I can pull it, that's all that matters," Parker said. "It's actually a kid's wagon that came with plastic beach toys, but I tossed them out."

"Yeah, I think you have enough in there right now to keep you occupied." Lindsey grinned. "Beach toys would just put you over the edge."

"And all these stickers are . . . ?" I prompted Parker as I peered at the numerous stickers that were plastered on each side of the wagon.

"They're from my queer gallery button collection," Parker answered. "I started collecting the buttons in high school and college. Then I went online and found a ton more—all in pristine condition. I bought every one that I liked. Which was most of them. One of my graphic designer friends created stickers out of them for me. Then I donated the entire collection of buttons to the Stonewall Foundation in New York. The foundation displays the buttons at Gay Pride events every year, at various locations around the country."

"These are awesome," Lindsey commented as she propped her sunglasses on top of her head, dropped her beach towel on the hot top of the parking lot, and began to read the stickers out loud. " 'Don't assume I'm straight and I won't assume you're an asshole!' I remember seeing a button one time that went something like, 'I won't assume you're gay if you don't assume I'm straight.' "

"That's on there, too," Parker said.

Lindsey surveyed the wagon for a few seconds. "Oh, yeah. There it is. Now what else do we have here? There's 'Amy and Eve' and 'Adam and Steve.' I've seen those before. 'Nobody knows I fuck women.' *Now* they do, P.! 'Pink sheep of the family.' That's cute."

" 'Girls will do girls,' " I continued as I kneeled down next to Lindsey. " 'Two of a kind beats a straight.' 'Grrrl power!' 'A woman without a man is like a fish without a bicycle.' Ain't that the truth! 'Clit-sucking dyke.' Well, that's clear. 'Cocksucking dyke.' Is that even possible?"

"Anything's possible, Gracy." Parker grinned, then glanced at her watch. "Well, our timing is perfect. We're going to have a few solid hours of great tanning."

"Or burning, as in my case," I added as I picked up my beach bag and tossed a blanket over an arm.

"We made great time driving down here," Lindsey commented as she lifted her backpack and tossed the strap over a shoulder. "Who knew that you could actually *drive* 120 miles per hour? I always thought manufacturers put that number on speedometers as a visual temptation. Sort of like they were saying to car buyers, 'Yeah, you *can* go 120, but if your car disintegrates at that speed, don't sue us.' "

"This way, girls," Parker urged us as she towed Annette across the parking lot.

I watched Parker walk away, wagon in tow, and started to chuckle. I turned to Lindsey. "For the woman who has everything—get her a little red beach wagon."

Lindsey smiled at me, then linked my arm with hers and pulled me along as we caught up with Parker.

"I'm sure glad we didn't have to hang around the house for too long after we arrived," Lindsey said. "It's a nice house and all, and our rooms are great, but—"

"You could slice the air with a knife," I finished. "It was just a *little bit* tense. And talk about a bitch, huh?"

Parker nodded. "Oh, yeah. That Neelia seems like she's got *some stick* up her butt. Big time."

"And that's one *big* butt, I might add," Lindsey commented, and then flashed a smile. "But I'm not a catty lesbian. I meant that in the *nicest* way."

"Oh, sure you did," I answered as I playfully jabbed an elbow into her ribs.

"Quick comparison, girls. Neelia, or Blair?" Lindsey asked.

"Our little Blair," Parker quickly chose. "For the categories of looks as well as personality, sense of humor, charm, and probably talent as well. Can't you just see her onstage, tap dancing, singing, twirling a baton, *and* giving an impassioned speech about wanting world peace? That girl has it all!"

"At least Neelia had the foresight to pack her bags so she was ready for takeoff shortly after we arrived," I pointed out. "Blair doesn't need a bitchy ex hanging around."

Parker nodded. "I just hope Blair and Julia are working things out right now and not fighting."

"Whatever they're doing, Blair made the right decision to bow out of going to the beach with us today," I said. "And, from what I understand, by the time we get back this afternoon, Julia will be gone and it'll be just The Girls."

"Now, don't go jumping down my throat, either one of you," Parker began, "but I don't think I'll be able to stand it if we get back to the house and Blair is crying her eyes out again."

"I don't think you have to worry about that, P.," Lindsey assured her. "Believe me, I didn't hear arguing coming from one of the bedrooms when I made a bathroom stop before we came here."

"Oh, really?" I asked.

Lindsey grinned at me. "And I don't think they were watching a porn movie, either. It sounded to me like a session of good old-fashioned girl-on-girl sex."

"Great!" Parker muttered. "*They* get to have sex, and we have to *abstain* the entire time we're here because *our* gal pals aren't with us. What *will* we do here if we can't have sex?" She let out a sigh. "So many women—and nothing we can do but look and imagine."

Lindsey took a step toward Parker, gently grabbed her, and turned her around. "Who are you, and what did you do with Parker Lowell? I *know* Parker Lowell. And she would never, *ever*, mutter the word abstain, let alone do it."

Parker flashed a fake smile at Lindsey and then resumed walking. "Ha, ha. But my little Cindi-loo wants me to be a good girl while I'm here, and I said that I would be. However, that promise *does not* mean that I'm barred from looking. Just because I can't use my hands or my tongue on any woman I see while we're here doesn't mean that I can't undress her with my eyes and fantasize about ravaging her to my libido's content." She pulled the wagon to a stop as the blacktop gave way to sand, followed by a long wooden ramp that led to the beach. "Are you groovy gay gals ready?"

"Ready!" Lindsey exclaimed. "I've been waiting all day for this, P. Lead on to the secret beach. Gracy and I will follow your wagon's trail."

"Women—ho!" I cried out.

"I'm sorry, P.," Lindsey said as she scanned the beach through Parker's binoculars. "But it's been half an hour and I haven't seen one thong-wearing woman or any of those great lesbian knockouts you told us would be here. What I *do* see are several dykes going topless, with breasts that clearly show how mammary-challenged they are. I'm thinking approximately one apricot per dyke. That equals a half an apricot right and half a one left. Oh, but there *is* a rather large, chest-endowed dyke. And while I wouldn't call her breasts knockouts, I'm certain that, at their size, they're capable of *knocking* someone out."

"Lethal Weapons Two," I quipped with eyes closed, from my prone position on a beach blanket.

"I mean, I've scoped this entire beach twice already," Lindsey continued, her eyes still glued to the binoculars.

I raised my head up from my blanket and lazily rolled from my stomach onto my back. "You *were* just telling us a tall tale about that secret beach, weren't you, P?" I asked.

"More like a *broad* tale," Lindsey muttered.

Parker sucked a noisy slurp of iced tea through her insulated sippie cup straw, then shrugged her shoulders. "Sometimes you get lucky, Gracy. That one time when I was down here, there was a group of a dozen hot-looking women on the beach. Most were one of us, but I think there were a few bi's thrown into the mix. But *all* of them had great figures, and all of them were thonged, topless, and tit-blessed."

"A dozen?" I echoed.

"Why can't we get an eyeful like that?" Lindsey asked, then moaned. "Ugh—there's Betty Big Boobs again. I think I've seen enough of her." She lowered the binoculars. "Okay. There's *nothing* good to look at here today."

"That day, I got much more than an eyeful," Parker told us, then unscrewed the lid from the container of iced tea and re-filled her sippie cup.

"Define *much more*," Lindsey requested.

"Okay. How many deadly sins are there?" Parker asked.

"Seven," I answered.

"Seven?" Parker repeated.

I nodded.

Parker shrugged her shoulders. "Okay. Then how many senses do we have?"

"Five," Lindsey replied.

"Are you sure?" Parker challenged her. "Because I thought there were six. Wasn't there that *Sixth Sense* movie?"

"We have five senses, P.," Lindsey confirmed. "The jury's still out on whether or not there is a sixth sense—a physic sense."

"Oh," Parker responded.

I rolled over, shaded my eyes, and looked at Parker. "Why are you asking us these questions?"

Parker smiled at me. "I was going to define *much more*. I was trying to get you guys to say the number six. Because ·

that's how many of those gorgeous women I—well, why don't I just tell you the story?"

"Oh, boy—a Parker story," Lindsey said excitedly as she placed the binoculars next to her, lay down on her side on a blanket, and propped her head in a hand. "I don't know whether to believe you half the time, P., but you do deliver a great, hot story."

"It doesn't matter whether or not you believe me," Parker answered. "I'm not trying to convince you of anything. I'm just sharing some of my numerous life experiences with you."

"I don't know which I prefer," I told Parker. "Your travel stories or your hot-sex stories. Both of them take me to places I've never been before. I guess that's what makes them so entertaining."

"Is this one x-rated?" Lindsey asked.

"Triple X," Parker answered.

"I don't think you've told us one of those before," I commented.

"Nope," Parker said as she reached into her cooler, extracted two icy bottles of Snapple juice drinks, and handed them to Lindsey and me. "I just want to be sure you two don't get overheated as you listen to my story."

Lindsey unscrewed the lid on the bottle, took a sip, and then looked at Parker. "Okay. I'm ready."

"Gracy?" Parker asked.

"Once upon a time . . ." I prompted her.

Parker took her time pouring tea out of the bottle and into her sippie cup. She recapped the bottle, and then cleared her throat. "Now, I've told you both about a couple of threesomes I've had before. Remember? One happened during the time I was in San Francisco on business, and the other was during the vacation I took, that walking tour of Italy."

I nodded. "I remember."

"Those were great stories," Lindsey added.

"This one, however, is about a *double* threesome," Parker declared as she stared straight ahead at the shoreline. "That makes six—*with* an audience!"

I grinned at Parker. "I didn't know you were a performance artist!"

"It was *an orgy!*" Lindsey exclaimed. "I've always wanted to know what one of those is like. I mean, not that I'd ever do it. It's just one of those fantasies a girl sometimes has."

"It's a good thing Blair isn't here," I said. "Because she wouldn't want to hear this six-sex story, that's for sure."

" 'TMI!' she'd tell you, P." Lindsey chuckled.

Parker grinned. "And I won't have to edit the story either, for her benefit. Sometimes it's hard to convert an R- or an X-rated story into the PG version."

"Then bring on the triple X," Lindsey urged.

Parker pulled the arms up on her beach chair, readjusted the angle of the back of the chair, repositioned herself, and then exhaled a contented sigh. "Picture this. It was about five years ago, I think, during an incredible heat wave. Not just one or two or even three days in a row. This was a week-long span of horrible heat, haze, and humidity. It was excruciating in the city, even with air conditioners on at full blast. I walked into the store on a Monday morning in that hot month of August, took stock of my employees, who looked completely drained and disinterested, and decided that enough was enough. I gave my employees the rest of the week off, with pay, closed the store, packed my bags, and drove here without a reservation."

"I want to work for you, P.," I broke in.

"Once you give up that silly little I'm-going-to-be-a-best-selling-author-one-day dream, Gracy, just say the word," Parker replied with a smile.

"I don't want to *work* for you, P.—I just want to *be* you," Lindsey said. "Sometimes. The times when you have hot sex, for instance."

"Linds, I think the hot sex I'm going to tell you about is a little too hot for you to handle," Parker replied.

"Try me," Lindsey answered.

"Okay," Parker resumed. "So, I arrive in P-Town and decide that what I'm going to do is hit the beach first and worry about where I'm going to sleep later. I set my blanket a little farther down this beach—there were about twenty or so women here at the time—and settled down to read a book. I must've dozed off for a little bit, because when I woke up I looked around me and the beach was much more crowded than when I first arrived. And, several yards away from me, but right in my line of vision, I spot this group of a dozen women. All of them are gorgeous, all of them have thong bottoms on, and all of them are topless."

"Are you sure you weren't dreaming them up?" Lindsey asked.

"Honey, if this was dream, then it was the best dream I've ever had," Parker answered. "Now, to continue. It's illegal to go sans any part of your bathing suit on this beach—there is a nude section, mostly frequented by gay men, that's a bit of a hike in that direction," she told us as she pointed down the beach from where we were sitting. "I thought for sure the women were going to get in trouble, because they weren't making any attempts to be discreet about their partial nudity. Even though the women were causing a bit of a ruckus on the beach—I mean, the lesbians who were set up around them were either openly gawking at them, with their mouths wide open and their tongues hanging out, or they were whispering their disapproval to their beach mates—no one approached them.

"After watching the dozen delightful dykettes for a while, I came to the realization that they were clearly enjoying the show they were putting on as much as most of their audience was. They set up a volleyball net at one point and played a few games. They did play a real game, but spent a lot of time hugging each other after each point was scored. Sometimes these full-body hugs would turn into hands cupping breasts and even mouths sucking on breasts."

"In front of everyone on the beach?" I asked.

Parker nodded. "Oh, yeah. This was not an inhibited group of women."

"Are you sure these weren't porn movie stars?" Lindsey asked.

Parker shook her head. "No, my dear. These were, flat-out, the most beautiful, most sexy group of lesbians I've ever seen." She sighed. "Ah, the glory days. Anyway. After a few games, they put away the volleyball net and decided to make a human pyramid. That was certainly a lot of fun to watch, because as they were kneeling on the women who were kneeling below them, breasts were hanging and swaying in the breeze.

"They followed this activity with refreshments. They took cold cans of soda and handfuls of ice cubes and began rubbing them against each other's bodies. At this point, I remember looking around me and seeing every single lesbian on the beach just staring at these women. It was so quiet I think the waves had stopped to watch them, too. A few lesbians made a big show of being disgusted by the whole thing, stomping off the beach with their things, wrinkling their faces up with expressions of anger and disdain. But the rest of the lesbians had stopped tossing footballs around, put away their softballs and gloves, and were lying on their blankets, watching the free floor show. Or, I should say, sand show."

As Lindsey and I listened to Parker's story, we stared straight ahead of us, trying to picture the scene on that hot summer day.

"Once refreshment time was over," Parker continued, "the girls started to toss a couple of Frisbees around. Their aim was atrocious—as you and Linds would say, Gracy, they threw like girls. Equally bad was their catching ability, so nearly every toss forced a woman to run or to leap or to bend over. If I were a guy, at this point I would've had a towel over my crotch because my Oscar Mayer wiener would've been the size of a deli salami.

"Then, a Frisbee floated in my direction and landed a few feet from my chair. I stared at the disk for a few seconds, considering whether or not I should retrieve it and toss it back. As I'm trying to decide what to do, I see that one of the hot numbers is jogging my way. She comes to a stop near me, smiles at me, turns her beautiful butt toward me, and slowly bends down to pick up the Frisbee. Then she stands up, turns to face me, and strolls over to me. She stops next to my chair and looks down at me. I, of course, look up at her, and enjoy a lovely, close-up view of her gorgeous twin peaks.

" 'Hey,' I say to her breasts.

" 'Hey,' the voice above her breasts answers."

"So," I say. "How goes the Frisbee game?"

" 'Are you liking what you're seeing?' she asks."

" 'Hell, yes,' I tell her. 'It's just too bad you don't need any more playmates.'

" 'Who said we don't need any more?' she asks me. Then she kneels down next to my chair, slowly rubbed her breasts back and forth on my forearm, and says to me, 'If you show me your breasts, pretty lady, the chances are good that you'll get to play with us.' "

"So you obviously—" I began.

"Of course!" Parker exclaimed. "I promptly rolled down the top of my strapless one-piece to my waist and, as she was looking at my breasts, I started to rub my forearm against her hard nipples."

"Oh, my," Lindsey said as she took a long gulp of juice.

Parker smiled at Lindsey. " 'So you'd like to play with us, would you?' she asked me."

" 'Oh, yeah,' I told her. 'I'm a good player—no, a *great* player.'

"The woman then leaned over me as I'm sitting in the chair, dropped the Frisbee between my legs, and then reached down with one of her hands to retrieve it. Naturally she made contact with my crotch as she's doing this, and I knew she could feel how wet I was. I mean, a dip in the ocean wouldn't have made me *that* wet.

" 'We're starting at The Pied tonight,' she told me, 'and we're going to end up at a place you've never been before. The longer you're with us tonight, the more of us you'll get to have.' "

"Holy gamoley," I commented. "Are you sure you're not embellishing this story just a little bit, P.?"

Parker shook her head. "From time to time I may *enhance* a story, make things out to be *a little better* than they really were. But never, ever, will I embellish it. Everything I'm telling you is true." Parker grinned. "Only the names have been changed to protect the innocent. Actually, I don't think I ever learned their names. Or they mine."

I shook my head and sighed. "I just don't know how you do it, P. You've had more sexual encounters than all of my lesbian friends combined."

"More than probably everyone on this beach right now, combined," Lindsey added.

"You *have* to be a player, Gracy," Parker replied. "Remember, except for once in my life, I've never ventured out into the lesbian scene looking for love. Or even companionship. All I've been looking for is sex. When that's the name of your game, you soon discover who the other players are."

"So where did you meet up with the women?" Lindsey asked.

"At The Pied," Parker answered. "I mean, I wanted as many of those women as I could have. As I'm out on the dance floor with a few of them, they tell me they're from New York City. And that they're surprised that a Massachusetts woman would be ready to play. 'I thought you were all repressed Puritans here,' one of them said to me. 'Well, you thought wrong,' I told her. 'At least about me.'

"What I did with them that night turned out to be a once-in-a-lifetime event," Parker concluded. "One I'll remember for the rest of my life."

"Are we getting to the good part now?" Lindsey asked.

"Hell, it's *all* been good to me," I commented. "Much better than all of those lesbian romance novels I read."

Parker nodded. "The good part's coming up, Linds. So we drank and danced a little at The Pied, then made our way to a predominantly male dance club that played really hot music. I don't know if it's still around, but the tunes were awesome and there was a backroom area that had these stalls—obviously for the men to use for sexual encounters. Well, over the course of a few hours, one at a time, six of the women lead me off the dance floor and into this backroom. There, we'd mess around a little bit, but what they were really doing with me was checking out what I was made of, what I'd be up for, whether I'd eventually chicken out.

"After staying at that dance spot until sometime after midnight, we ended up at a private gay and lesbian club that probably isn't in existence anymore. From what I heard, it got wilder and weirder over the months that followed my visit that night. I think I read somewhere that a gay man had been murdered there, and so I imagine that the place is shut down.

"Anyway, the club was in the basement of a large private home. The basement was dimly lit by a few small lamps that had dark-colored bulbs in them. Music was playing, but it wasn't loud enough to drown out the sounds of what was going on in various rooms located in the basement. The point was, of course, for patrons of the club to get turned on by the sounds of other people getting turned on."

Lindsey placed the bottle of juice against her face as she stared at Parker. "Go on," she encouraged her in a husky whisper.

"There were eight rooms in the basement," Parker continued. "Each of them was set up with a couch that folded out into a bed. There were hooks on the walls and ceilings, mirrors on the walls and ceilings, and a few folding chairs near the entrance of the rooms. That meant that people could walk in and out of the rooms, join in if they were invited, or simply watch."

"I don't know if I could do that," I cut in.

"Which?" Parker asked. "Watch, or be watched?"

I thought for a moment. "Be watched, I guess."

Parker took a sip of tea. "When you're into a group encounter, Gracy, you're not really conscious of anything but what's going on with you and the people you're with. You don't even realize that you're being watched. And you're so turned on anyway, you couldn't care less. Anyway, I ended up in one of those rooms with eight of the dozen. Four chose to watch. That left six of the women, plus me, and we had us some fun that night."

Parker paused for a moment in her story.

We listened to the seagulls, the sound of the surf, and the muffled conversations of women coming from nearby blankets.

"Well?" I finally asked, breaking into the silence.

"Well what?" Parker answered.

"What did you do with them?" Lindsey demanded.

"The better question, Linds, would be what *didn't* I do with them—or they with me," Parker answered. "I can't remember every single thing that happened that night in that basement room, but I'll give you the summary form. Everyone was completely naked. There were hands everywhere, on every woman's body. There was oral sex. *A lot of it.* With more than one person at a time. There were dildos and harnesses. There were handcuffs and ropes. Blindfolds. And plenty of taunting and teasing. I experienced things I'd always dreamed about doing and did things I didn't know were possible. It was an education as well as the hottest, most satisfying encounter I've ever had. I don't think I was capable of walking with ease until a few days later."

"Well." I sighed, then drained the juice bottle, dropped it on my blanket, and reached for my water bottle. I pointed it at my face and squeezed out a stream of water. I shook my head. "*That* was quite a story!"

"Maybe you *should* write that titillating novel after all, P.," Lindsey advised. "I'd certainly buy it. Because right now it feels like it's 110 degrees on this beach, and I know it's not. It's just me, having a hot sex–story flash."

"Good story, P.," I said.

"Thanks," Parker replied. "Now what was the wildest sexual encounter each of you has ever had?"

I broke out into laughter. "Oh, yeah, sure, P. Like Linds or I could ever tell you a story that would top yours. That would be like looking at million-dollar homes when all you can afford is a fixer-upper."

"Well, I don't know that I've got a topper to yours, P., or even a story," Lindsey replied. "But I can honestly say that I'm having my hot-sex times now, with Judge. I've done things with her that I've never done with anyone, never even been *asked* to do by anyone. Lately we've been sharing some of our fantasies and then, within reason, acting them out. I nixed having sex with her on a subway during rush hour, and we discovered that you really can't have an orgasm under water. But, anyway. Being with her is a true sexual awakening for me."

We sat in silence for a few moments.

"What about you, Gracy?" Parker asked.

I quickly glanced at Parker and Lindsey, then looked away from them and sighed. "I wish I could say that I've had even *one* wild sexual encounter in my life. But . . . but I haven't. Going to bed with women has always been an enjoyable experience for me, and I hope for them, too. But it's never been wild. Erotic. Hot. Passionate, even." I shook my head. "Ever since I came out, I've been expecting to have sex with wild abandon. But it's never happened. Even with Leslie—well, that's a whole other story. I have pretty good, pretty hot fantasies when I masturbate. I find that gets me more turned on more than being with someone does. That, and using my battery-operated girlfriend. Does that make sense?"

Parker nodded. "It does. You have to have to make the wild abandon happen for real. What about sharing a fantasy with Leslie?"

I shook my head. "That's not going to happen. *Ever.* Believe me, I've considered it, but . . ." I took in a deep breath, then released it. "Les is, well, she's not very passionate in bed. Or creative. Or even really interested, it seems. Sometimes I think she could take sex or leave it. And that's . . . that's something that's been bothering me for the past month or so. I thought that when we got back together, things would be different. But this time is just like the last time. We started out being really focused on sex. And now, well, I can't even remember the last time we made love. Maybe it was the night when Blair used her sex toys."

Lindsey raised her eyebrows. "*That* long ago?"

I thought for a moment, then nodded. "But not for lack of trying, on my part. I mean, I don't want to be a stick in the mud here. After all, we've already processed one emotional outpouring this morning. But I don't think I'm very happy with Leslie. I don't feel like she's the right one for me, the one who I want for a long-term partner. Maybe I expect too much, need too much, from her. From anyone. But what I want is to be with someone and have a strong, deep, *passion* for her. Passion not just in the bedroom, but passion for her life. It seems as if Leslie and I do the things we each want to do, and we're supportive of our doing them, but we don't really embrace what's important to each of us. I want that. I want someone who feels as passionate about me being a writer as I do about writing. I want to feel passionate about the things someone I'm with is passionate about. Am I making sense?"

"Perfect sense," Lindsey replied.

I looked at Parker. "What do you think, P.?"

Parker met my eyes. "I think you've put into words something I've been thinking about for a while now. You both know that Cindi and I are very different from one another. But her profession, what she likes and dislikes—even that damn voodoo booth she's set up in my place—have come to mean an awful lot to me. I realize now, after listening to you, Gracy, that it's *passion* that I have for her." Parker gave us a lopsided grin, then shrugged her shoulders. "It's funny, but sometimes I'll find myself thinking about her when we're apart and wondering, *What's she doing right now? Is she enjoying herself? Laughing? Holding her own in a dangerous situation? Chewing out her partner? Grabbing a bite to eat at her favorite lunch counter?* It's like my life and her life"—Parker paused, held up her hands, and laced her fingers together—"are intertwined. Meshed together." She looked at me and smiled. "So, yeah, Gracy. I *do* know what you mean. It must not feel good to have that feeling missing from a relationship."

I shook my head. "It's not."

"Have you told Leslie how you feel?" Lindsey asked.

"No," I answered. "The more I think about it, the more I realize that even if I talked to her about it, it wouldn't change things. I think Leslie and I have done the best we can together, for ourselves and for each other. But there's something missing. Something big. And I'm pretty sure she's not the one who's going to give that to me."

"So what are you going to do?" Parker asked.

"I don't know," I answered, then smiled. "But one thing I do know is that I'm going to remember your dirty dozen story for quite some time. You're something else, P. You've done so much in your life. I mean, you're really *living* your life. Everywhere you go, everything you do, seems to be one adventure after another. I must admit—I'm jealous."

"Don't be jealous," Parker said as she reached over and took my hand in hers. "Enjoy your own adventures, Gracy. They're out there, hon. You just have to be willing to look for them, to experience them. Because once you are, life *can* be one grand adventure."

We joined Blair back at the house for a late lunch, after Parker had given Lindsey and me the cue for our departure from the beach shortly after the stroke of two. Julia had left, but Blair was beaming from ear to ear, so we knew that they had been able to patch things up to Blair's satisfaction.

After lunch, we all headed out for an afternoon of shopping in the stores that lined Commercial Street. We decided to stick together as we went from store to store and then do our own browsing and shopping later on in the week.

We let Blair tow us around to a few art galleries, then followed Lindsey into the army and navy store.

"You be the army grunt, and I'll be the medic." Parker grinned at me as she tucked a nurse's cap on top of her big hair and wiggled her eyebrows at me. "Tell me, soldier, where does it hurt?"

I laughed.

"In the navy," Lindsey sang as she held up a pair of sailor's pants in front of her legs.

"Do these things actually work?" Blair asked as she pulled a grenade out of a box.

"My God, Blair, put that thing down!" I yelled at her. "Are you trying to get us all killed?"

Blair gently placed the grenade in the box and backed away from it.

Lindsey laughed and shook her head at me.

"That makes no sense," Blair said as she stared at the box. "I mean, someone could just come in here, grab a few of those, and then heave them out into the street. It would be chaos."

"Not if I have this," Parker replied as she used both arms to hoist up the housing for a rocket launcher, then immediately dropped it back onto the shelf. "Why women want to go into the military is beyond me. It's way too much work. All those push-ups and crawling in the mud and—"

"Those aren't *live* grenades, Blair," Lindsey cut in as she walked to the box of grenades. "See?" she asked as she pulled out a grenade and waved it above her head.

"Lindsey, don't do that!" Blair cautioned her.

"Here—catch!" Lindsey said as she lobbed the grenade at Blair.

Blair squealed and ran away from it.

The grenade landed on the concrete floor with a thud, then rolled on the floor for a few feet.

I bent over, picked up the grenade, then tossed it back in the box. "Well, I know one person who won't be asked to play softball."

Blair walked back to us. "I *could've* caught it if I really wanted to. I've played on a softball team before. I can catch *and* hit."

"Hit the dirt, maybe!" Lindsey laughed. "You should've seen your face when I threw that grenade at you."

Blair stuck her tongue out at Lindsey. "Now Parker gets to choose which stores we go to."

"Come on, ladies, it's jewelry-shopping time, followed by clothing, of course," Parker informed us as she took off the nurse's cap. "I'm on a twenty-four-hour pass, so let's get hopping."

A few hours later, The Girls waited while I paid for a stack of books at a women's bookstore—my choice of where I wanted to shop.

"This is as close as I get to my fantasies," I told Parker as I showed her the books I had stacked on the counter. "Girl meets girl. Girl has sex with girl. Girl loses girl over some stupid thing. Girl gets girl back and has sex with her again."

"Those two look like mysteries," Parker said as she surveyed the titles of the books I was buying.

I nodded. "Those books are written a little bit differently. Girl has lost girl through a tragic accident. Girl grieves. Girl then finds a dead body. Girl pines over lost girl and over corpse. Girl meets new girl. Girl has sex with new girl. Girl solves the mystery."

Parker rolled her eyes. "Sounds like girl will be reading girl books."

I nodded, then handed my credit card to the clerk after she had rung up the total.

She swiped the card through the machine, then stared at the card. "You're Gracy Maynard? *The* Gracy Maynard? The one who writes the column in the *Boston Globe*?"

"Neat, Gracy—a fan." Blair smiled as she clapped her hands.

I felt my face redden as I took the card back from the clerk. "Yeah. That's me."

"I *love* your column!" the woman gushed. "See?" she said as she turned and waved an arm at a bulletin board that was posted on the wall next to the cash register. "That's your latest column up there. I post each week's column on the board. I *can't wait* for Thursday's paper to come out. I go to your column first. I've told all my friends to read your column. Now they're hooked. They've been faxing copies of your articles to all of *their friends* who live around the country. But I keep telling them, 'I saw Gracy first.'"

Lindsey raised an eyebrow in my direction and mouthed to me, *I saw Gracy first.*

Shut up, I mouthed back to her.

"Now you can have her autograph," Parker said as she watched the woman place the credit slip on the counter. "Have you been practicing your I'm-famous signature, Gracy?"

I shook my head. "I think I'll sign this the same way I always have." I scratched my signature on the slip, then handed it back to the woman.

"I'm so thrilled to have met you, Gracy," she gushed as she

handed me a yellow copy of the slip. "I wonder, um, well, here's my card." She held a business card out to me. "Maybe you could do a reading of some of your columns here during the women's weekend that's held in October? I'm sure I could get quite a crowd in here to listen to you. There's a big meeting room behind the building that the landlord lets me use for open mike night, book signings, and other events. You could call me or—" The woman paused, then glanced up as a trio of women walked through the door.

I took the card, then pocketed it and lifted the bag of books from the counter. "Thanks," I told her. "I'll, uh, think about it, okay?"

"Okay," she answered. "Be sure to call me. You have my number." Then she turned her attention to the new customers. "Is there anything I can help you ladies find?"

Lindsey turned to share what I knew would be a teasing comment, but I gave her a playful push against her back, and she headed for the door.

As Lindsey and Blair stepped outside the shop, Parker put her hand on my arm and stopped me. "Life's an adventure, Gracy," she said. "But only when you're ready to find that out for yourself."

The bar was crowded, and the dance floor even more so, but somehow all of us had been able to create a space that allowed us first to chat at the bar, and then gyrate together on the dance floor.

"I'm done," Parker puffed out several minutes later as she stopped moving and patted her face with a lacy handkerchief.

"Me, too," Blair called out above the music and stopped dancing as well.

"I'm with you two," Lindsey agreed as she stood still, took a few deep breaths, and then wiped her brow with the sleeve of her shirt.

"Oh, *come on*, you guys," I complained as I kept my body moving with the music. "We haven't been dancing that long.

Ten minutes more." I did a quick spin turn, and then tap-danced my feet on the floor. "Look at me! I'm still rarin' to go!"

Lindsey raised a hand in the air and waved good-bye to me.

"Linds!" I called out. "Five minutes! Just five more minutes!"

Lindsey waved again and then headed off the dance floor, working her way through the crush of bodies.

"But I don't want to go!" I pouted at Blair and Parker.

"Just stay out here then," Parker yelled over the music. "It's so crowded, no one will notice that you're dancing alone."

I shook my head. "It's too weird, dancing alone."

Blair touched my arm. "I'd stay with you, Gracy, but I just don't have it in me. Between crying this morning and then making up with Julia this afternoon, I feel like I'm a zombie. I'm going home and going to bed. Tomorrow night, maybe, okay?"

I watched as Blair disappeared into the crowd.

Parker put her arm around my waist, then lowered her face to my ear. "There's no harm in asking someone to dance, Gracy. Have a good time while you're here, hon. Dance your little feet off. I'm sure you can find at least one willing woman in this crowd."

I shook my head. "I don't know, P. I don't think I could—"

"I'll dance with you, Gracy," a voice cut in.

"Why, it's your number-one fan." Parker grinned as she looked at the woman who was standing in front of us on the dance floor. "I guess if you buy enough books, you get a dancing partner. A dancing partner named—?"

"Vickie," the woman replied. She flashed me a tentative smile. "The hair was up when you saw me, Gracy. Now it's down," she explained as she touched her blond, shoulder-length hair with her fingers. "I was wearing jeans and a T-shirt, and now . . ." She paused as she held her arms out from her sides. "Evening wear by Silk by Design, one of the clothing stores here. *Tres* expensive, but I've been paying for it on lay-away since last summer. So this style is exactly one year old."

"But *tres* chic, nonetheless, girl." Parker smiled approvingly as she surveyed the teal-colored silk jumpsuit. "You have that perfect slim but tall figure that's absolutely necessary for a one-piece."

I nodded at the woman. "Nice," I muttered, then looked up at Parker. "Well, I guess we should call it a night. It was nice meet—"

Parker jabbed a quick elbow into my ribs. "You're not going anywhere, sister friend. You *said* you wanted to *keep dancing*. Here's someone who *wants* to dance. Vickie, meet Gracy. Gracy, meet Vickie. Now enjoy yourself, chicklettes. Mama hen is heading back to the roost."

Parker squeezed one of my hands, then released it and was quickly swallowed up by the crowd.

I watched Parker disappear from sight.

"I'm not following you around, Gracy," Vickie assured me. "I mean, after you left the store I thought about how I must've sounded to you. I think I was a bit much. But I was planning to go out tonight. To this bar. And it seems like your friends have abandoned you, but you still want to dance. I *love* to dance. But I can never find anyone who really wants to. Everyone is usually with someone. And the ones who aren't . . ." She paused and shrugged her shoulders. "Okay. I'll shut up. I'm Vickie. I'll be your dancing partner tonight, if you would do me the honor."

I stared at her, struggling hard to formulate a reply.

Vickie met my eyes for a few seconds, then nodded. "Okay, I understand. You want to see *exactly* what you're getting into. Here goes." She suddenly launched into a silly, spastic dance for a few seconds, then stopped. "See what a good dancer I am? Wouldn't you be proud to be seen on the dance floor with me?"

I smiled.

"Just don't write about me in your column, Gracy Maynard," Vickie pleaded as she started to move her body to the beat of the music. "A shop owner down here can't handle both the crowds *and* the fame."

"I won't," I assured her.

"So, Gracy," she said as she moved closer to me. "Can you dance as well as you write?"

I hesitated outside the front door to the house, then sucked in a deep breath.

I reached for the knob, then turned it and pushed open the door.

"Just in time for breakfast, girlfriend," Parker greeted me as I stepped into the kitchen. She waved a piece of bacon in the air. "We opted for the cholesterol-laden breakfast. We also have sausages, scrambled eggs, bagels, and cream cheese."

Lindsey met my eyes and started to open her mouth.

"*What* is going on, Gracy?" Blair cried out as she slammed her napkin on the table. "Do you know what time it is? It's *eight* A.M. I know your bed *wasn't* slept in, because I checked. I've been *worried sick*. Now, *where were you*?"

"Calm down, Mom," Parker urged Blair. "Your daughter's all grown up now, you know? She's old enough to vote, smoke, and drink."

"But Gracy—I mean, *really!*" Blair exclaimed. "*Cheating?* Didn't you see what I went through yesterday, thinking that Julia was cheating on me?"

"I haven't cheated on anyone," I answered as I slipped into a chair at the kitchen table. I reached for the carton of orange juice and poured a glass. "After you guys bagged out on me, I danced with Vickie. The woman from the bookstore. Actually, she owns the bookstore. We danced for a while, and then we went for a walk on the beach. The one at the East End of town. It was a beautiful night. All we did was talk. For hours. Under the stars. I must've closed my eyes at some point and fallen asleep, because when I opened them, it was light. I walked Vickie home, and then walked here. That's it. No cheating, Blair. And I *do* know what it feels like. Remember? Leslie cheated on me—*for real*."

Blair quickly nodded. "I'm sorry, Gracy. I didn't mean to jump all over you."

"Now that would be a sight." Parker grinned.

"What did you and Vickie talk about all night?" Lindsey asked.

I swallowed some orange juice, then grabbed a bagel and sliced it in half with a knife.

"Do you want me to toast that for you, Gracy?" Blair offered.

"She has make-up sex with Julia," Parker began as she looked at me, "and then makes up with you by toasting your bagel."

"Lucky me," I answered as I handed the bagel to Blair, then leaned back in my chair. "I talked to Vickie about a lot of things. Writing. Working for myself. My great American novel ideas. Wanting a house in the country. Relationships in the past. My relationship with Leslie. Stuff. I shared. She shared. It was—" I paused and thought for a few moments. "It was the most intimate conversation I've ever had with a stranger. I felt like I just opened myself up to her and poured my life out into her hands. And I realized, well, I realized that that's another thing that's missing in my relationship with Leslie." I quickly glanced at Blair, who was standing by the toaster oven.

She met my eyes and nodded. "I know. Linds and P. told me this morning how you were feeling about Leslie."

"I hope you don't mind, Gracy," Lindsey said.

"Mind?" I echoed. "Why would I mind? You're my best friends. I would tell you anything, and I hope that you'd do the same. Sure, I talked with Vickie for hours last night. But she's not my friend. She was just a listening ear at a time when I needed to talk. You guys are much more than that to me. We can laugh together, cry together, have fun together, help each other out, get mad at each other. Everything we do together, everything we talk about, brings us closer together. I can't tell you how much your friendships mean to me."

Blair opened the toaster oven, pinched the hot halves of the bagel between her fingers, and raced them over to me.

"Hot!" she shouted as she tossed them at me.

"Figured," I called back as I deftly snagged them out of the air and dropped them on my plate.

Blair put her fingers in her mouth, then sat down at the table.

Lindsey pushed the container of cream cheese in my direction. "What I like the most about our friendship is that you guys don't judge me," she said. "I mean, you sometimes do, especially about Judge, but I know you do that because you don't want me to get hurt."

"What I like the best about our friendship is that I haven't wanted to sleep with any one of you," Parker added as she picked up a breakfast sausage with her fingers. "Now that we're friends, I realize that I never really had people in my life who I could call *true friends*. I like the way you guys sometimes ride me for the way I am. Sometimes it's tough to hear, and even tougher to accept, but it shows me that who I am matters to you. Will I ever change my ways? I don't know. I'm pretty happy the way I am. But you've gotten me to see that the way I am can sometimes be hurtful to other people. So I'm trying. Sometimes I succeed. Sometimes I don't. But no matter what I do, you guys are always there."

Blair removed the fingers from her mouth. "I know that things aren't the way you want them to be with Leslie, Gracy. That makes me sad, that it might not work out. But what makes me even sadder is knowing that you're unhappy. You can talk to me—you can talk to *us*—anytime, about any thing. All we want is the best for each other, right? It doesn't matter how you feel or what you say. Those things stay right here, between us girlfriends." Blair slowly reached a hand out, made it into a fist, and held it above the tabletop. "Come on, ladies," she urged us as she glanced down at her hand.

Lindsey, Parker, and I stared at Blair's hand.

"Are you hiding the last sausage?" Parker asked as she grabbed Blair's fist and started to move it around.

Blair pulled her hand out of Parker's grasp, and then placed her fist in the center of the table again. "I want us all to touch hands," Blair instructed.

"Why?" Lindsey asked.

Blair rolled her eyes at Lindsey. "Because I think the situation calls for a kind of, you know, rallying thing for us girls to do."

"I'm not touching Gracy's hand," Lindsey sniffed. "She's been out all night, and hasn't even washed up yet."

Parker stared at Blair's hand, then shook her head. "I'm not doing any of that Three Musketeers, all-for-one-and-one-for-all bullshit. We're friends. We know it. Let's move on."

"You guys are such assholes," Blair snapped as she pulled her hand back.

Lindsey exploded into laughter.

Parker and I joined in with her.

Blair glared at us. "What? What?"

"You're just too damn predictable." Parker grinned as she licked her fingers, then held out her hand.

Lindsey and I immediately slapped our hands on top of hers.

"Oh, fuck you guys," Blair huffed as she placed her hand on top of ours, then quickly removed it. "You know, that wonderful emotional moment is long gone."

"But their friendship still endured," I added.

"And I am *not* predictable," Blair argued. "I can be very spontaneous, you know. In fact, today I hope you're taking me to the secret beach. Because I'm going to go topless. *Yes, I am.* Linds said everyone at the beach was topless yesterday. She said that you guys went topless, too. So if you can, I can. I'm not even bringing my top to the beach. See?" Blair lifted her T-shirt, jiggled her breasts at us, and then covered them up.

Parker wagged a finger at Lindsey. "How *could* you, girl?"

"Blair, we didn't go topless," I told her. "But they're wonderful breasts, and I thank you for showing them to me."

Blair slowly turned in her chair to face Lindsey. She glared at her, then slapped her on the arm. "Lindsey Tompkins—I'm going to get you for that!"

Lindsey sprang up from her chair and raced into the living room, with Blair following in hot pursuit.

Parker and I sat at the kitchen table, listening to the thumping sounds coming from the floor above us.

Parker glanced down at her watch. "I hope they get this resolved pretty soon, because I want to get to the beach for the best sun time."

I nodded. "Let's give them another fifteen minutes. And I'm taking those last two sausages, P."

"Over my dead body," Parker answered as she jabbed her fork into the dish in front of her and then held the sausages up in front of me.

"Are you going to *give* me those sausages, P.?" I asked. "Or am I going to have to *take* them from you?"

Parker slowly stood up from the table, clutching the fork in her right hand. "You have to give me at least a thirty-second head start, Gracy."

"Fifteen," I offered.

"Fair enough," she replied.

"Starting when?" I asked.

Parker picked up a glass of water from the table and put it to her mouth.

I watched her for a few seconds, then tipped my head to one side. "Oh, P. I can't believe you're even thinking about dumping that water on me."

Parker shrugged her shoulders, then slowly placed the glass on the table.

"That's a good girl," I told her.

Parker met my eyes, then gave the glass a quick slap with the back of her hand. The glass tipped over. "Oops," she said as she watched the water flow across the tabletop and onto my lap. "Bye now," she added, then quickly trotted out of the room.

I sat in my chair, watching water continue to drip onto my pants.

When I heard Parker thumping up the stairs, I slowly stood up.

I took the empty glass to the kitchen sink, then filled it from the tap.

"Come on, Gracy!" I heard Parker yell from upstairs. "I still have the sausages!"

I walked out of the kitchen, wearing slacks that were soaked and a big smile on my face.

Where "The Girls" Are

From time to time readers will write to me and ask, "So what's up with The Girls, Gracy?" It's been a while since my last update, so here's what's happenin' with the chicks.

Blair and Julia are still, as Parker says, "Sticky-sweet in love." And they are always happy.

"They love their jobs. They love their house. They love their two cats. They love their goldfish. They love each other. They love everything!" Lindsey grumbled one evening before Blair joined us for after-work cocktails and dinner. "Doesn't a gray cloud ever come into their lives?"

Lindsey made partner in her firm last year and bought a house on the South Shore, with a great ocean view. The Girls finally met Judge, and she turned out to be nothing like any of us had pictured. She's short, quiet, shy—certainly not the type you'd expect to forcefully grope a woman in the backseat of her BMW or keep a dildo in her office desk.

But, as Parker said one night, "It's always the quiet ones."

Judge has finally left her partner, but after her long, drawn-out stint with Brenda, she's not ready yet to cohabitate with Lindsey. She bought a house on the South Shore near Linds and they spend a lot of time together.

"Someday," Lindsey says.

OLA resides in Lindsey's home. She hasn't yet worked up the courage to ask Judge, "What the fuck is this?" She's positioned OLA near a picture window that looks out over the ocean. "Because," Lindsey told Blair one evening while The Girls were out to dinner, "I guess OLA's my Wilson, and Wilson lives by the ocean." (Later on that night, Blair confessed to me in the ladies' room that she didn't have the heart to tell Lindsey that Wilson was lost at sea. I reminded her once again that Wilson was a soccer ball, and that neither soccer balls—nor OLAs—really care much where they live.)

Parker and Cindi, the group's oddest couple—the femmy-femme woman who believes that making money and fashion, in that order, are the most important things in life, and the down-to-earth cop who thinks the most important things in life are keeping the city's streets crime-free and working out at the gym, in that order, have lasted. Despite Parker's incessant grumbling about the monotony of monogamy, we all know that she's secretly enjoying being in a committed relationship.

That's because one night, over cocktails, she took a small velvet box out of her purse and held it open for us to see. "These are the rings I bought for Ana Maria and me," she told us. "I don't know. Maybe I'll make Cindi my señorita." But before anyone could respond, Parker had snapped the box shut and then wagged a finger in the air at us.

"I don't want to hear one word," she cautioned us. "Maybe you'll see us wearing them. Maybe you won't. And don't ask me what it means, because I don't know. We're not having a commitment ceremony and we're not going to have a baby." She paused and smiled at us. "But she's good for me, you know? And she's good to me. I have the bigger bank balance and more of everything, but she's rich in love. She has a heart of gold, and I don't think I'm ever going to find someone like her."

I'm hoping to find someone who's rich in love for myself. Things never really got better between Leslie and me after I returned from P-Town. It's not that we didn't love each other—and still do. But I don't think we loved each other enough to want to be a committed couple. Perhaps we fell into the category of "flovers" rather than lovers; perhaps we were once in love but the second time around couldn't help us recover that love.

A few months ago, we looked around for apartments and went our separate ways. While we know that this is for the best, the ending has made us very sad. Sometime in the future, we may end up being good friends. But, for now, we're taking our separate space and, as my therapist tells me, "regrouping."

On New Year's Eve, The Girls will celebrate their first anniversary as friends. We're still arguing about what we'll do for the evening. But I'm sure that we'll eventually find common ground.

We always do.